When the Stars Align

When the Stars Align

Alexis Harris

Map Illustrated by Kirsten Stiles

RESOURCE *Publications* · Eugene, Oregon

WHEN THE STARS ALIGN

Resource Publications
An Imprint of Wipf and Stock Publishers
199 W. 8th Ave., Suite 3
Eugene, OR 97401

www.wipfandstock.com

PAPERBACK ISBN: 978-1-7252-5288-2
HARDCOVER ISBN: 978-1-7252-5289-9
EBOOK ISBN: 978-1-7252-5290-5

Manufactured in the U.S.A.   02/26/20

Dedicated to my first readers.
Your motivation, criticism, and fandom pushed me to finish.
Thank you! Vondre Green, Kirsten Stiles, and Lauren Breed

Contents

And as the wind whipped through her hair and the trees became a blur, all she could think was that she was finally free. No more rules; no more boundaries. The time was finally here to discover the true wonders of life for herself. She could almost taste it. Even with the sound of her pursuers' steeds pounding along behind her . . .

Princess Celestia

1

"Come on, milady. We must get you up and ready. Your mother is waiting for you," Garrita said. She was the lady-in-waiting to the princess; a thin, pretty, young woman, not so different from the princess herself, with light brown hair and a fair complexion.

Princess Celestia groaned. "Five more minutes," she said, burying her face in her pillow. She hated mornings. Her mother always insisted on starting the day early, but she'd rather clean the stables than get out of bed in the morning.

"You've already had over an hour," she said, shaking her. Her white bonnet bobbed up and down against her head.

Celestia turned over, groaning again. She stretched out on the giant bed, her light blue nightgown ruffling up. Garrita helped her up and took her over to the tub she'd filled for her bath. She slipped out of her nightgown, revealing her pale skin, and climbed into the tub. Garrita helped her wash and then dried her off.

"Is everything ready?" Celestia asked as Garrita helped her slip her undergarments on.

She silently lifted her blue ballgown around her and started lacing the corset before she answered, "Yes, milady." She pulled the laces tight, adding, "But, are you sure you want to do this?"

"Today's the day, Garrita," she said confidently, "I can feel it."

Her lady-in-waiting helped her slip her shoes on, and then returned to her place behind her as Celestia sat before the mirror. She started brushing her long, blonde hair, saying, "If you say so, milady."

Just then, another servant burst in, saying, "What's taking so long? The queen is waiting!"

"She'll be along momentarily, Jameson," Garrita said, brushing faster.

"The queen doesn't like to be kept waiting," he said, slamming the door. He was a short middle-aged man with brown hair and an attitude problem. He never was very friendly and was always stressing over keeping the queen happy and keeping everyone on task. Or, as some would see it, sucking up to the queen and bossing everyone around.

The princess looked in the mirror at Garrita behind her. A few strands of hair were falling in her face as she hurriedly styled Celestia's. She wore a common brown dress with a white apron, like many other members of the staff. She was Celestia's best friend more so than servant. They'd grown up together. If there was anyone the princess was close with, it was Garrita. In her eyes, they were basically sisters. But, their stations in life forced them into different roles. In spite of that, they managed to maintain their friendship past the play dates of their childhood.

Celestia's room was huge, with walls and floor of stone. Tapestries were hung up to decorate, and there wasn't much furniture in the spacious chamber; only her bed, her vanity, her tub, and a large wardrobe of cherry wood. Her pale blue sheets were all in disarray, but soon her chambermaid would arrive and have the room clean again in no time.

Garrita finished up her hair and makeup and assisted with her jewelry. As Celestia looked in the mirror at her own reflection, she thought, *Today's the day.*

"There you are, finally," Queen Eva said as Princess Celestia entered the throne room, "So glad you were able to make it out of bed only an hour and a half late." She was tall and beautiful, with light brown skin and caramel-colored hair. She had brown eyes and a lavender ballgown. Celestia was the lighter version of her mother.

Celestia didn't say anything, knowing it was futile. She stood straight and tried to look lady-like.

Queen Eva sighed, "You know the drill. When you're late, you make up for every five minutes with an extra song. Get to it." She pointed to the piano in the corner. The throne room was probably the largest room in the castle, consisting of a spacious floor for balls and other occasions, with two thrones at the back up a short flight of stairs, and the piano across the way.

Princess Celestia sighed and reluctantly walked over to the piano, starting to play. She knew she would have to play nineteen songs—one for every five minutes she was late, plus the one she would've had to play anyway. She was so sick of training to become queen. She didn't even *want* to be queen. But, she was an only child, and therefore, sole heir to the throne of Ivétoiless. Her parents had both been heirs to their thrones, and so their marriage had merged the two kingdoms, formerly known as Tristétoiless and Ivonneveille.

As she played the piano, her mother paced, answering questions and giving orders as the servants came and went. It was the same thing every day. She'd play piano, walk with a book on her head, learn about a lot of boring kingdom history, astronomy, and arithmetic, have lunch, be quizzed on what to do in different scenarios as queen, and have the rest of the day until dinner time to do what she pleased, so long as it was appropriate for royalty. She lived for her free time, which was soon to be taken from her when she became queen. She'd stroll in the garden, practice her archery, and ride her horse.

"Celestia," her mother was saying, "that's enough. It's time to work on your dancing."

"Mother," Celestia said, as their plates were cleared away at lunch, "Might I ask you something?"

"Certainly," Queen Eva said, looking at her with a mixture of suspicion and concern. They sat in the dining hall—a large stone room with a long mahogany table in the center surrounded by tall, ivory-cushioned chairs. The queen's eyes were close to the color of the table, and her skin almost matched the chocolate mousse they had for dessert.

Celestia twisted her spoon around in the mousse. "Do you think you . . . I mean, could you . . . Would you tell me about my father?" she said finally.

Eva sat back in her chair. The look on her face was one Celestia had seen many times before. She was clamming up and getting ready to refuse.

"Just one thing?" she said, "Please, I don't know anything about him."

"He was a great man," Eva said, taking a drink of wine from her gold goblet, "There's your one thing. That's all you need to know."

"Tell me something else," she begged, "You always say that."

"I think that's quite enough," Queen Eva said, "We're done with this conversation."

"But, you never tell me anything about him!" Celestia said, "It's been 20 years! What's wrong with talking about it?"

"I said enough!" her mother snapped, "And that's the end of it."

Princess Celestia couldn't take it anymore. She rushed from the room and to her chamber, slamming the door behind her. She'd been ready to give royal life one last shot, but if her mother refused to tell her anything about her father, she couldn't stay. All she knew of him was that he died during a war with another kingdom when she was an infant. She'd spent her whole life trying to figure out the other half of who she was, and wondering why she felt so out of place as a royal. Her mother refused to talk with her about such things, and she was a mere four months away from her twenty-first birthday, and her coronation as queen. She knew her mother would leave it alone until dinner, and then try to make up like she always did, so she called for Garrita.

"Yes, what is it, milady?" she asked, rushing into the room.

"It's time," she said, kicking off her shoes.

"Now?" Garrita asked, sounding panicked.

"Now," Celestia said with authority, "Help me unlace."

Garrita began unlacing her corset, "Are you sure about this?"

Celestia remained silent as she slipped out of her ballgown and into a peasant's dress. She took her hair out of its clips and washed off her makeup, taking her jewelry off as well. Finally, she set her tiara down meaningfully, saying goodbye to who she was, and the life she'd always known. She looked in the mirror. She hardly recognized herself; she looked like a peasant. Her white-blonde hair went down to her waist. She had a blousy white off-the-shoulder shirt under a dark brown front-lace corset. A light brown skirt flowed down to her brown shoes—shoes made for comfort and functionality rather than appearance. Her blue eyes shone. Though it was hard for her to let go, she couldn't bear to stay.

She took a breath, mustering her courage, "Goodbye, Garrita," she said, hugging her lady-in-waiting.

Garrita couldn't respond, except to nod, tearing up.

Celestia hurried out of her chamber and to the stables. Her horse, Razel, was waiting for her, ready to go. She'd had Garrita, and a stable-boy named Matthew, get everything ready for her escape. Razel—a beautiful brown mare she'd had since she was a girl—already had her saddle and reins, and saddlebags filled with food and supplies for the road. She leaped upon her back, kicking her sides to get her going. She rode hard, headed for the nearby forest. It was now or never.

She heard the alarm sound, and she knew what that meant: they knew she was running away. The guards would be after her in a matter of seconds. And as the wind whipped through her hair and the trees became a blur, all she could think was that she was finally free. No more rules; no more boundaries. The time was finally here to discover the true wonders of life for herself. She could almost taste it. Even with the sound of her pursuers' steeds pounding along behind her . . .

Bridgot

2

She made it to the forest, and the trees gave her some cover as she rode. All she had to do was make it to the other side of the river, and the hounds wouldn't be able to follow her scent. She steered Razel toward the water, and waded quickly through it, climbing up to the other side and taking off again. The thunder of hooves hitting the earth faded as she got farther and farther away.

Celestia guided Razel to a walk once she could no longer hear them behind her. *I actually did it,* she thought, *I got away.* She was free. Royal life had always felt like a prison. She had to look a certain way, act a certain way, speak a certain way. For being at the top of the food chain, someone was always telling her what to do. She never got to think or make decisions for herself. That was the true reason she'd run away; her mother not wanting to talk about her father was only a small part of it. It was the factor that had finally pushed her over the edge.

She rode along, thinking to herself, feeling happy she'd left, and wondering what she was going to do now. As it started growing dark, she decided to stop for the night. She pulled Razel up next to a large tree and made a small fire. She'd learned survival skills as part of her princess training, in case she was ever captured, so she could get away and survive long enough to either get back home, or be rescued. She knew those skills would be useful now. She took some bread and cold stew out of the saddlebags. She had a pot as well, and she heated up the stew for herself. In the meantime, she pulled out an apple for Razel, and let her graze on the grass and get a drink from the river.

She washed her pot in the river when she was done, and as she was putting it away, she heard a rustling noise. "Who's there?" she said, sticking close to Razel and looking around. As she turned to pull her sword from its scabbard, a group of men sprang out from the brush. Two of them grabbed her, and another three grabbed her horse. Their leader shouted for them to follow, and started treading across the river. They were pulling and pushing Razel, and dragging Celestia along as she kicked and flailed and tried to fight.

Just then, a man on a horse came riding up and saw what was happening. He leaped off his horse and drew his sword. "Let her go," he said.

The leader sneered, nodding to his followers.

The men that were holding Razel, along with one of the ones holding Celestia, drew their swords and surrounded him. The other man holding Celestia gripped both of her arms behind her back, holding her firmly in place. The leader grabbed Razel's reins and snickered.

The mysterious stranger smiled and swung his sword, engaging the men who'd surrounded him. He fought them off with ease, killing one of them. The rest ran away, leaving the leader and the man holding Celestia.

He walked up to the one holding her and pointed his sword at his throat, "I said, let her go."

The man dropped Celestia and ran, with the leader chasing after them and calling them a bunch of worthless cowards.

The mysterious stranger was tall and lean, with curly brown hair, blank, gray eyes, and unevenly tanned skin. He wore a brown peasant's shirt with dark brown pants and brown boots. A belt with a scabbard hung around his waist. He sheathed his sword in it and offered his hand, "Are you alright?"

"I'm fine," Celestia said, getting up on her own, "I didn't need your help. I had everything under control."

"Yes, I could see that," he said, "I suppose getting dragged through the river was all part of your plan."

She got ahold of Razel's reins and led her ashore.

"What on earth would possess you to travel alone?" he asked, leading his own brown stallion ashore.

"Do you always make it your business to know the travel plans of strangers, or am I just lucky?" she asked, putting Razel's saddle back on.

"It's dangerous," he said. "Look, why don't I accompany you? At least for a while."

"You want to accompany me?" she looked at him in disbelief.

"No one should travel alone. Not even a brat like you," he said.

"Excuse me? A *brat*? Who do you think you are?" she demanded.

"My name's Bridgot," he said, extending his hand and smiling smugly.

She stared at it a moment, then mounted her horse. "Thanks, but no thanks," she said, turning to ride away.

"How can you be so conceited?" he asked, "Is this the thanks I get for saving your life?"

Celestia paused, realizing how rude she was being. She sighed, turning back toward him. "Thank you," she said.

He shifted, giving her a slight nod, "You're welcome."

"But, you're traveling in the opposite direction," she said, gesturing back the way she'd just come.

"Look, I just have some business to conduct in the next town over, and then I'll be on my way back this way. It won't take long."

"I'm not going an *inch* back that way. So, this isn't going to work," she said.

"Alright, how about this?" he said, "I saw an abandoned farmhouse a couple miles back. It looks like it's been uninhabited for a while, so looters and slave traders won't bother you. You'll be safe there for a couple of days while I complete my business, and then we can set out the way you were headed."

She paused, considering. Realizing she couldn't continue traveling alone, she agreed. He hopped back on his horse, and they headed toward the farmhouse.

"So, you never told me your name," he said.

"It's . . . Margarita," she said, "And this is my horse, Razel."

"Margarita," he said, smiling, "Nice. As I said, my name's Bridgot, and this is Samson."

She nodded, "Nice to meet you, Samson."

His horse snorted, turning his head her direction in greeting.

"So, why are *you* traveling alone?" she asked.

"Well," he said, "I know these woods. I've traveled all through them selling things at market. I know what areas are safe, and which ones to avoid. My village sent me to fetch some things this time, and so I am." He paused, "So, what's your story?"

"Well, if you must know, I ran away from home, and I am *not* going back."

"That bad?" he asked.

"It's a long story," Celestia said.

"We've got time," Bridgot said.

Celestia remained silent, not wanting to tell anyone too much. If someone found out she was a princess, it would draw too much attention, and risk her being discovered and "rescued."

"Alright," he said, "Fine. I get it. We just met; I'm a stranger. You don't want to tell me your business."

She nodded in affirmation, and they continued silently until they saw the farmhouse. They dismounted and began walking toward it cautiously. Bridgot drew his sword and went ahead, with Celestia and the horses following behind.

As they neared it, Bridgot said, "Okay. You wait here with the horses. I'll go in first to check it out, and make sure it's safe."

"No way," she whispered, "I'm not waiting anywhere. I'm going with you."

Bridgot turned toward her, annoyed, and quickly jumped backward as an axe came down right where he'd been standing. Celestia screamed, and Bridgot lunged forward with his sword, ready to fight the old man who'd swung the axe.

"Get off of my land!" he yelled, swinging his axe up to meet Bridgot's sword, "Thieves! Trespassers!"

"No!" Celestia yelled, "Stop!" She rushed forward and got in between them as they were starting to lunge at each other again. They both stopped, and she faced the old farmer. "Please," she said, "We're only looking for a place to stay. We thought this house was abandoned."

The old man, who had gray hair and a gray beard, and was wearing a plaid shirt and overalls, stopped and lowered his axe.

"Come on, Margarita," Bridgot said from behind her, "Let's get out of here."

"We didn't mean to trespass," she continued, "But, it's not safe on the road. We only need a place to stay for a couple of days."

He looked from her to Bridgot, and then over to the horses. After a pause, he said, "Very well. You can stay here for a couple of days. Come on; I'll show you to the stable for your horses."

Celestia led Razel and followed the old man. Bridgot led Samson and reluctantly followed, annoyed and wary. They put Samson and Razel in the stable, taking off their saddles and reins. Then, they followed the old man into the house. He led them upstairs to a spare bedroom.

"Blankets and pillows are in the wardrobe," he said, "Don't try any funny business. I sleep with my axe." With that, he headed down the hall to his own room.

Bridgot sighed, "I'll take the floor." He crossed the small room to the wardrobe, and pulled out a couple of blankets and a pillow for himself, spreading out a blanket to lie on, and keeping his sword next to him.

"You're sleeping with your sword?"

"Yes," he snapped, "Because I don't like this; I don't trust that guy. You got us into this, and I'm only trying to be prepared."

"*I* got us into this?" she said, sarcastically adding, "'Oh, yes, I saw an abandoned farmhouse. You'll be safe there.'"

"Well, it's not abandoned," he said, "*I* said we should go. But, *you* talked him into letting us stay here."

"And where do you propose we go?" she asked.

"Well, it doesn't matter now," he said.

"Men," Celestia said, crossing to the wardrobe to pull out a pillow and blanket for herself. The room had only the wardrobe, a small table, and a twin bed. She couldn't see much of it, since it was dark, the only light being from the moonlight streaming in through the window. She went to the bed and sat down, unlacing her corset and removing it and her shoes. She then loosened her skirt to make it more comfortable to sleep in and lied down, closing her eyes and drifting off.

When she awoke, the floor was empty. Sunlight was pouring in through the window, and there was no sign of Bridgot anywhere. She got up quickly, tightening her skirt and putting her shoes and corset back on. She headed down the stairs and found the old farmer cooking breakfast.

"Good morning," he said, "Sleep well?"

She got a better look around the house now that it was daylight. It was wooden and old. The outside was in obvious disrepair, but the inside looked nice enough. The staircase creaked, but it was intact. The downstairs was simply a living area with a gray couch and chairs, an oak coffee table, a fireplace, and some bookshelves, as well as a kitchen and dining area. The kitchen had a fridge, a stove, and a sink, with white-painted wood cabinets over gray counter-tops. The dining area was a large, square table with four matching wooden chairs.

"Have you seen the man I was with?" she asked.

"He left, early this morning. He didn't abandon you, did he?" he asked. She could see him better as well. He had tan, ruddy skin, and his hair and beard were cropped short. He looked lean and muscled for an old farmer.

"No," she said, remembering that he had said he had business to conduct in the next town over before they departed, "I just didn't expect him to set out so early."

"You like eggs?" he asked, lifting the pan he was stirring off of the stove.

"I've never had them," she said.

"Never had eggs?" he asked, surprised.

She shrugged, "My mother liked to have me eat healthy. She said eggs were full of fat."

"Well, have a seat, my dear," he said, "Because you're gonna try them today."

Celestia pulled out a chair and sat down.

The old man served up a plate of eggs, toast, bacon, and some form of potatoes. He caught a glimpse of her face, looking at it questioningly. "It's hash browns," he said.

She looked at him blankly.

"You've never had any of this before, have you?"

She shook her head, "Only the toast."

He set a glass of orange juice in front of her plate, "Well, you're in for a treat today."

He got his own plate and sat across from her, "Dear Lord, we thank you for this day, for our life and good health, and for this bounty before us. Please bless this meal we are about to receive. In your name, Amen."

He began eating as she continued to stare at her plate, unsure. Finally, she picked up her fork and tried the eggs. To her surprise and delight, they were delicious. She continued eating, and cleared her plate, washing it down with the orange juice.

The old farmer took her plate and began doing the dishes. "Well," he said, "How was it?"

"It was delicious," Celestia smiled, "Where'd you learn to cook like that?"

"From my wife," he said, scrubbing slowly.

"Oh," she said, "What happened to her?"

"She died," he said, drying a plate, "Pneumonia."

"I'm sorry," she responded sympathetically.

They were silent for a moment. "Well, since then, I've just been trying to keep this place up on the inside. I let it look abandoned from the outside, so no one would bother me. I have my own garden, hidden by some shrubs, and I go hunting for meat. The only time I go to town is if I need something, and I just trade my kill for it."

"Sounds lonely," she said.

"What did you say your name was?" he asked, turning toward her.

"Margarita," she said, "What's yours?"

"Wells," he said, "Farmer Wells." He turned back to the sink, "So, what's your husband's name?"

"My husband?" she asked, momentarily confused, "I don't have a . . ." She trailed off, realizing he thought she and Bridgot were married. "Oh, it's, uh, Bridgot," she said.

"You don't sound too sure about that," he said.

"Sorry," she said, "we're newlyweds, and it's still strange calling him 'husband.'"

"I see," he said, draining the sink. "Well, shall we go tend to your horse?"

"Yes, of course, that would be wonderful," she replied, getting up.

Farmer Wells led Celestia out to the stable, and they brought Razel out of her stall. He pulled out a couple of brushes and handed one to Celestia. They began brushing Razel's brown coat. It was relaxing, just tending to Razel as she often did at home. The soft, repetitive movements kept her hands busy and allowed her mind to wander. *What am I going to do now?* she thought. The question had been nagging at the back of her mind since she'd run away. She still didn't have the answer. She wanted an exciting life of adventure, rather than the life she'd come from, full of rules, expectations, duty. But, traveling alone was out of the question. She'd never realized the dangers of the road. How could she? She'd never been outside of the palace grounds, except for royal balls and parties in neighboring kingdoms.

Once Razel had been groomed, they put her back in her stall, and Farmer Wells gave her some hay and fresh water. "Well," he said, "now that she's taken care of, I suppose I should tend to my garden. You're welcome to join me."

"Sure," she said, not having anything else to occupy her. He led her over to some overgrown shrubs near the back of the farmhouse. The house was a faded blue color, which she could now see in the daylight. The paint was chipped and peeling, and the doors and windows looked as though they were rotting. When they reached the shrubs, she looked within the oval of untrimmed branches and weeds and saw a beautiful little garden, full of tomatoes, peas, carrots, peppers, and potatoes. "Wow," she said.

"Thank you," he said, "I may not have a field of crops, but I do like to think I have a green thumb." He put on a pair of faded yellow work gloves and handed her a white pair with a faded pink floral print. "If you wouldn't mind," he said, "we just need to pull the weeds, and water them."

"Oh, sure," she said, putting on the gloves, not at all sure what she was doing. She watched how he located the weeds and pulled them up, tossing them into the shrubbery. She copied him, amazed at how easy it was to pull the weeds from the ground, and at the intricate little system of roots they had at the bottoms.

He grabbed a couple of watering cans he had pre-filled, and they watered all the plants. It was more work than Celestia had done in her life, and she was tired when they were done.

"Thanks for the help, Margarita," Farmer Wells said, "Why don't I show you where you can wash up while I make lunch?" She nodded, and he led her upstairs, and down the hall to a bathroom. It was small, with limited space to move between the toilet, sink, and tub. "Wait right here," he said.

She watched him go down the hall to his own room, and she noticed a picture on the wall of a younger him outside the farmhouse with a woman. She was lovely, a simple beauty with curly brown hair peeking out of her bonnet. As he came back up the hall, she asked, "Is this your wife?"

"Yes," he said, "Her name was Elizabeth."

She noticed he was carrying a bundle of clothing, "Those were hers, weren't they?"

He nodded. "You're about the same size, I think. I figured it would give you fresh clothes to wear, so that I can wash yours for you."

"Thank you," she said.

"I'll show you how to work the tub," he said.

While she was washing, which was her first time washing herself, Farmer Wells was preparing lunch downstairs. She took her time, trying to figure out how to reach her back, and how to wash her hair properly. Once she was clean, she carefully dressed in his wife's clothes. It was a blue striped peasant's dress, with sleeves that puffed out at the shoulders, and a ruffled collar. She gathered up her own garments and headed down the stairs.

"I've just made a light lunch since breakfast and dinner are heavier meals. I hope you don't . . ." he trailed off when he saw her, " . . . mind."

"What's wrong?" she asked.

"Nothing," he said, "It's just . . . well, it's nice to see someone wear that dress again."

Celestia smiled, nodding.

"Shall we eat?" Farmer Wells asked, shaking his head.

She set her clothes on the vacant chair next to her and took a seat.

He set her plate in front of her, and they ate a quick meal of deer jerky and mixed vegetables.

After lunch, Celestia helped him with the dishes—another first for her, and they did laundry together. Being a simple farmer on the outskirts of town, he didn't have the amenities they had in the castle, like a dishwasher or a washer and dryer for clothes. Although, Celestia had hardly seen those either, except when she was being watched by the servants as a child. Farmer Wells merely had a sink for the dishes, and outside he had a washtub and a clothesline. Both were located where it would be nearly impossible to see them from the woods. It was behind the house, so you wouldn't see it in front, but it was in front of the barn, so you wouldn't see it from behind.

He led her over, and she watched in amazement as he scrubbed the clothes against the washboard. He'd hand them to her when he was done, and she'd hang them on the line to dry. It was strange to her, but she figured out the clothes pins fairly quickly. It took her a moment, fumbling, as she stared at the pins and the line. But, she realized the only thing that made sense to do and got them strung up. Her white peasant's blouse flapped in the breeze, and she struggled to hang her corset, trying to get the pins around the thicker material.

Once the chores were done, they went inside, and she noticed a small door under the staircase. "What's in there, if you don't mind my asking?"

He opened the door, revealing a tiny room that housed only a piano. "Do you play?" he asked.

"Yes, quite often," she answered softly.

He gestured at the keys, "By all means."

Celestia sighed, feeling as though she'd never truly escape from her training. She slid onto the bench and began to play. Her countless hours of extra songs, training every day, poured out through her fingers. She lost herself in the music, as she often did when she played. It was natural for her, and, for a moment, she felt as though she were back home in the throne room, waiting for her mother to tell her she was done for the day.

"Beautiful," Farmer Wells said, snapping her back to reality, "Where'd you learn to play like that?"

She got up, brushing her hair behind her ear nervously, "My mother."

He nodded, staring at her suspiciously, "Where did you say you were from?"

"I didn't," she said.

He raised an eyebrow.

"I, uh . . . don't really have a home. I'm from all over," she said, covering.

He remained silent, staring at her.

"I'd better go check on Razel," she said, shuffling past him and out the door. *Hurry back, Bridgot*, she thought, panicking. She couldn't just set out on her own again, but if Farmer Wells figured out who she was, he could turn her in, and her life of adventure would end before it began.

Farmer Wells

3

She went into the stable and refilled Razel's troughs with hay and water. "Hey there, girl," she said, "I hope you're ready to set out in a
hurry again."

Razel snorted at her, drinking.

Celestia pulled up a stool and sat beside her horse, stroking her mane.
She looked around the barn. It was old but well-maintained. There were
several stalls, even though he had no animals. There was plenty of fresh
hay, and supplies, such as brushes, buckets, saddles, and reins. A lever was
positioned by each water trough, which, when pulled, filled the trough with
water from the plumbing lines. She wondered why he kept the hay fresh
when he had no animals to eat it or lie in it.

She took her time hanging out in the stable with her horse. When it
started to get dark, she headed back to the house. Farmer Wells was cooking dinner. It looked like he had washed up, and he'd changed clothes. His
plaid shirt was now blue instead of green.

"I was wondering when you'd be back, or *if* you'd be back," he said,
"Have a seat. It's almost ready."

She sat at the table cautiously, still wary.

Farmer Wells turned and gave her a plate of deer steak, potatoes, and
carrots. "What do you like to drink?" he asked. "I have water, apple juice,
pear juice, or cranberry juice. Squeeze it fresh myself."

"Whatever you're having is fine," she said.

He poured two glasses of apple juice and sat across from her with his plate.

Celestia twisted a few strands of her white-blonde hair around her fingers nervously.

He took a bite of his steak and looked up at her, chewing. He set down his fork and swallowed, taking a drink of juice. "Look," he said, "I know who you are."

She looked up at him in surprise, eyes widening.

"You're Princess Celestia of Ivétoiless."

Her already pale face grew paler, and she was frozen with fear, "H-how do you know who I am?"

"It doesn't take a genius to see you're royalty," he said, "And besides, you have your father's eyes."

"You knew my father?" she asked, releasing her hair. She wanted to run out of there as fast as she could, but that fact glued her to her seat.

He smiled, seeing the conflict in her face, "Don't worry. Your secret's safe with me. I have no intention of turning you in."

She breathed out a sigh of relief. After a moment, she asked, "Why not?"

"It's not my place. I think your father would've wanted you to be happy, and to choose your life for yourself. Who am I to tell you what to do?"

"How did you know him?" she asked.

"I fought beside him in the war. I was his right-hand man."

She sat there, breathless, not daring to move. Here was someone who could finally tell her about her father.

He looked at her carefully, "You want to know more about my time with your father." It wasn't a question.

"Yes," she answered anyway, barely blinking.

"I was already well past my youth at the time," he said, his dark eyes looking off in the distance as if he could see the memory in front of him somewhere. "Your father was a young man—just barely assumed the throne, just barely married, just barely a father. I had never seen a wiser, braver, more honorable man in all my years. To see that kind of character in someone his age . . . it astounded me." He paused, stroking the thick gray hair on his chin, and smiling to himself in fresh amazement.

"If you don't mind my asking, what did he look like?" Celestia said. He shot her a puzzled look, which made her start messing with her hair again. "It's just . . . my mother never really liked to talk about him. I guess, well . . . I don't really know much about him. You're the first person I've met who knew him, and who would actually tell me anything about him. I've never even seen a picture."

"Well, he had tanned skin from years of hunting and horseback riding, but it wasn't too tanned just yet. He was too young and privileged to have a truly deep tan. He had brown hair, clipped short on his head. He had a brown beard, trimmed short and well-kept, like mine. He had bright blue eyes, exactly like yours. You even have the same twinkle in them when you smile. During the war, we'd always smile at each other before a battle charge. It helped us not to take our situation so grimly, I think. He had your ears, too, small and round."

She sat there for a moment, taking in what he'd just told her. She could picture him. She could picture him with her mother. She could picture the way her family should have been. She felt closer to him, finally knowing at least what he looked like. She thought that maybe someday she'd be able to accept the loss of what she never had. But, for now, this was enough. "Thank you," Celestia said.

Farmer Wells smiled, tears forming in his eyes. He blinked them back, coughing, "He was a good man. You deserved to know that." He went back to his plate and cut off another bite of steak.

Celestia nodded. She was too happy and relieved to eat, but she forced her food down anyway. Now she knew why he was so muscular for an old farmer. He was a retired warrior who had fought beside her father! After helping him with the dishes again, she borrowed a book from one of the bookshelves and headed upstairs. She read until she heard Farmer Wells come up and walk past to his room. Then, she turned off the lamp and went to sleep.

Celestia awoke to the smell of bacon cooking. She got up and headed down the stairs. After breakfast, she and Farmer Wells headed out to the stable to feed Razel.

As they were departing the stable, Farmer Wells said, "How's your skill with a blade?"

"Uh, um, I mean . . . I haven't really—"

"That's what I thought," he said, "The road is a dangerous place. It's full of robbers and slave traders. You need to know how to protect yourself."

"I know the basics," she said.

"The basics aren't good enough," he said, "Come on." He led her to the field between the house and the barn and picked up two sticks, handing her one, "Let's see what you've got."

She stared at him in surprise as he took a fighting stance, holding up his stick. She took her stance and waited for him to thrust. He did, and she swung her stick to block. It only took a couple of swings for him to knock the stick from her hand.

"Yes, the basics aren't nearly good enough," he said, "You have the generic stance, and you somewhat know how to block. It's good that you wait for your opponent to make the first move, but it's not *always* necessary; it depends on the fight." He sighed, "We have a lot of work to do."

Celestia looked at him, wondering how he intended to teach her sword fighting in two days.

"Again!" he shouted, taking his stance.

She picked up her stick and took her stance.

"Now, you try attacking first."

She lunged forward, swinging her stick. He merely stepped out of the way, and her blow landed on nothing but air. He waited for her to turn, and they engaged for another couple of swings before he knocked the stick from her hand again.

"Plant your feet firmly," he said, "You must have a strong stance, so you don't fall backward. Be aware of your surroundings at all times. Watch my steps and mirror my movements."

They did some drills, and he showed her how to stand properly, and how to move.

"Alright," he said, "Why don't you give Razel a workout, and I'll go make lunch."

She went back into the stable, and led her horse out of her stall to the field, letting her trot in circles. It made Celestia happy, seeing her horse able to run around again. Razel snorted in pleasure, feeling the grass beneath her hooves as she trotted along. The fresh air filled her nostrils, and she whinnied happily.

After a little while, Farmer Wells called out to let her know lunch was ready. She put Razel back in the stable again and went inside to eat. It was a quick lunch, just a plate of salad. Then, they went out to the stable for the third time that day and took Razel out again. It felt like a lot of back-and-forth, but it got her horse taken care of. They led her to the side of the barn where there was a hose. Farmer Wells filled up a bucket, and added some soap, wetting a couple of sponges and handing one to Celestia. They started giving Razel a bath, and she felt the way she had when brushing her—relaxed. The soap foamed up on her horse's side, and she could see the dirt from the road coming off. They got her all clean and hosed her down. Farmer Wells pulled out a couple of towels, and they dried her off. Then, they led her back into the stable, giving her more hay and water. He also had brought out a couple of apples, to treat her.

They spent the rest of the afternoon working on her stance again, until Farmer Wells thought she had it down. He went inside to make dinner, and she went upstairs to wash. Her clothes were waiting in the guest room; she still had on his wife's dress. He must've finished the laundry the day before when she'd been out in the stable with Razel for so long.

They had a dinner of fried fish and veggies. Afterward, she went back up to the guest room and continued reading the book she'd borrowed. She could hear as Farmer Wells washed up, and went downstairs. Then, she could hear when he came back up and walked past to his room to go to sleep.

She thought she could get used to this lifestyle. For her, it was exciting, simply because it was new and different. She enjoyed spending time with Farmer Wells. He was a kind old man, and he'd known her father. He could teach her how to defend herself, he was a good cook, and he helped her understand the value of hard work. As she drifted off to sleep, she thought, *Maybe I should just stay here, help him out, keep him company. He's getting old, and he's all alone. This could still be a new life for me . . .*

Skill with a Blade

4

The next day after breakfast, they watered the garden, tended to Razel, and did the chores. They were developing a sort of routine. After lunch, they went out to the field to work on her sword fighting again.

"Okay," Farmer Wells said, "We'll have to keep working on your footwork, but today, we'll work on blocking."

Celestia nodded, taking her stance. It was another quick round as he disarmed her on the first thrust.

"Make sure you keep your grip," he said, demonstrating, "Hold your sword tightly. Otherwise, it's too easy to disarm you."

She nodded again, picking up her stick. Again, he knocked it from her hand.

"Like this," he said, gripping her hand against the stick to show her, "Hold it tight. Try to keep your arm straight, and only bend at the elbow. Your wrist will bend as you swing, but don't let it bend too much, or your opponent will knock it from your hand. Bring your sword up to meet the blow. If you don't, they may not aim only to disarm you. Your counter swing isn't just offense—you're protecting yourself. Your momentum will help counter the force, and as long as you hold on tight, you won't lose it."

"Okay," she said, holding her stick up.

They practiced the rest of the afternoon, and she got better, lasting longer each round. But, she still had a lot of work to do. Even at her best, she was disarmed after only six swings. He told her what she could do to improve her grip strength: squeezing a clamp together. He gave her one to keep, and she figured she could do that while reading at night, to help build it up over time.

She washed up while he made dinner, furthering their new routine. She had brought in her changes of clothes from her saddlebags, so she was able to still wear her own things. She bathed quickly, ready to enjoy some nice food and conversation. She was hoping to ask him more about her father, since he seemed willing to talk about him, and she wanted to know everything she could. She came down the stairs and sat at the table as Farmer Wells served up some deer steak and veggies. She eyed it hungrily, ready to enjoy his cooking more.

"Tomorrow I'll make stew," he said, "It needs to slow cook all day over the fire."

"That sounds good," Celestia said, taking a bite of vegetables.

"You can help if you like," he said, pouring a couple of glasses, "I mean, I can teach you how to make it."

"That would be lovely," she said, "I've never cooked before."

"I thought as much," he chuckled, sitting, "It's not exactly something a royal would do."

"Well, I've done things that might surprise you," she said.

"Oh?" he said, starting to eat, "Like what?"

"Well, I spent a lot of time with the servants for one."

"That's supposed to surprise me?" he said, "You were a child. Someone had to take care of you, and it sure wasn't going to be your mother."

"What do you know about my mother?" she asked defensively.

"I didn't mean anything by it," he began, "Only that she's a quee—"

Just then, the door opened, cutting him off.

"Bridgot," Celestia said, recognizing his curly brown locks and scrawny build.

He closed the door behind him and looked from Celestia to Farmer Wells, and down to their plates.

Farmer Wells finally closed his mouth, which had been hanging open in surprise, and swallowed his half-chewed bite of food. "By all means, join us," he said, standing, "Let me get you a plate." He quickly assembled another plate of food, and set it in front of the empty chair closest to the door, pouring a glass of juice to go with it.

Bridgot sat down and began eating. They all continued to eat in silence; no one quite sure what to say. Afterward, Farmer Wells cleared their plates, and Celestia got up to help him with the dishes.

"No, Margarita," he said, "That's alright; I've got this. Why don't you two go ahead and go upstairs? I'm sure you have lots of catching up to do."

"That's a good idea," Bridgot said, getting up and heading up the stairs.

Celestia wavered, "Are you sure? Really, it's no trouble."

"No, no," Farmer Wells said, "I insist. Go on." He waved his hands, shooing her.

She headed upstairs reluctantly. When she got to the guest room, she saw that Bridgot had made his bed on the floor.

"Oh good," he said, turning to look at her as she entered, "Now you can get some sleep. We leave at dawn."

"No," she said.

"Excuse me? No?" he said, getting up.

"I'm not leaving," she said. "It was nice of you to offer to accompany me, but I'm happy here. Farmer Wells is all alone in this house since his wife died, and it's been so nice the last few days. I can't leave him."

"Are you crazy? Do you hear yourself right now? You want to stay here, in this decrepit farmhouse, and live with an old man?"

"You may not understand it," she said, crossing over to the bed and sitting down, "but I'm happy. This place feels like home."

"What about your travels?" he said, "Your great adventure?"

She shrugged, "I'm needed here."

"You're needed? By who? Thi-this old guy?" he practically yelled, "He was taking care of himself just fine before you got here, and he can take care of himself just fine after you leave."

"I'm not leaving," she said with finality. She took her shoes off, lying down, and facing away.

"Well, that's just great!" he said, angrily turning off the light and lying down on the floor. He punched his pillow into place and flung his sword next to him with a *thud*.

Celestia undid her corset and pulled it off quietly, setting it by her shoes. She loosened her skirt to sleep and got comfortable. As she thought about it, she wondered why it bothered him so much. *Who cares if I changed my mind and decided not to go with him anymore? How does that affect his plans?* She didn't understand him at all.

Celestia expected Bridgot to be gone when she woke up, headed back home on his return journey. But, there he was, on the floor, sound asleep. She got up quietly, tightening her skirt, and putting her corset and shoes on. She headed downstairs, and Farmer Wells was leaning against the counter, drinking a cup of coffee. He hadn't yet started to make breakfast.

"Good morning," he said, "You're up early."

"Yeah," she said, rubbing her neck, "I'm usually never up this early."

"So, how are things with the husband?" he asked.

She squinted at him questioningly, wondering how he could still believe they were married when he knew who she was.

He noticed her look and said, "I know you're not really married, but that's gonna be your best cover for the road. May as well start practicing now. I'm sure you don't want to tell him, so just play along. If he thinks I'm in the dark, he won't get suspicious. You're welcome."

"Well, I don't think I'm gonna need to worry about a cover for the road," she said.

It was his turn to look at her questioningly.

"I was . . . well, I was thinking of . . . maybe . . . staying here," she said.

He smiled in happy surprise for a moment, his dark eyes lighting up. But then, he turned sad, "No," he said, "I won't have you waste your life away. You ran away seeking adventure, not the life of a commoner. I'm honored, truly, but you should go."

She looked at him in disappointment.

"It's not the life your father would have wanted for you," he said, "Don't worry about me. I'll be fine. I know how to take care of myself. I chose this life. You don't have to, and you shouldn't."

She looked down, a feeling of deep sadness coming over her. It was overwhelming for a moment, but she composed herself. It was the way she'd felt when she left home. It was bittersweet, saying goodbye to people and places she loved, in order to truly find herself and experience life. She never imagined she'd have to go through that twice.

"I'm sorry," he said, "I'd love to have you stay. Really, I would. But, you deserve to find what you left home for. And, you're never gonna find it here."

She nodded, unable to speak.

"Look," he said, "Why don't you stay until we complete your training, and *then* you leave?"

Celestia looked up with a half-smile, her blue eyes glistening with almost-tears, "That might be a while."

Farmer Wells chuckled, "You might be right about that. But, once I teach you what you need to know, the rest is up to you to keep practicing and perfecting." He drank the last of his coffee from his mug, "Come on, I'll have you help me with the cooking today."

They prepared the stew first, him showing her how to chop vegetables, make a broth, and season it. She was fascinated with the whole process, watching the chunks of meat and vegetables spinning in the pot. Then, they prepared breakfast. The most interesting part for her was the eggs. She marveled at the different ways to cook them. Today, they were scrambling them. They transformed before her eyes from a runny, yolky, mess to lumpy, fluffy, cheesy food.

As they served up the plates, Bridgot came downstairs.

"Good morning," Farmer Wells said, "Sleep well?"

"As well as one can," he said, eyeing Celestia.

"Wonderful," he said, "Shall we eat?"

The three of them sat at the table and enjoyed another silent meal. Bridgot kept shooting angry sideways glances at Celestia through the meal, and she wished he'd just leave.

After breakfast, Celestia and Farmer Wells began their routine of doing the dishes, doing the laundry, tending to Razel, and tending to the garden. Bridgot followed them around, not offering to help, but watching with an annoyed look on his face.

When they got to tending Razel, Farmer Wells said, "Are you going to tend to your horse, or just stand there, useless?"

Bridgot grumbled, but grabbed a brush and pulled Samson from his stall, grooming him.

Farmer Wells shot a quick smile at Celestia, and she smirked, shaking her head as she groomed Razel. They fed and watered the horses, and as the two of them headed to the garden, Bridgot stayed behind in the stable. Celestia was relieved to be rid of him, and get to spend her time with Farmer Wells again. They had a quick lunch, and he took a plate out to Bridgot, who was sitting with his horse, talking to him. Once he'd gotten him his food, he came out to the field to do more training with Celestia.

"Well, there's plenty still to teach you about blocking, but I think the best way is to put everything together, so today, we'll work on your offense."

"Sounds good," she said, taking her stance.

"Okay," he said, "You have the basic moves down already. So, I'll show you a few more advanced moves, and you'll work on countering them. Then, you'll copy my moves."

She nodded, and he began swinging, jabbing, and thrusting. She countered as best she could, still not sure of herself. Then, it was her turn to mirror his moves. She began swinging, imitating what he'd shown her.

Bridgot came out of the stable on hearing the sound of their sticks clashing together. When he saw what they were doing, he laughed.

"Something amusing, Bridgot?" Farmer Wells asked.

"Oh, nothing," he said, still chuckling.

"Please," he said, "Do share."

He stopped for a moment, still smirking, "It's just that *you* are teaching *her* how to joust?"

"Why is that funny?" he asked.

"Well, obviously," he said, "You're an old farmer. What do you know about it? And you're teaching a *lady*?"

"Why don't we take a break, Margarita," Farmer Wells said.

She nodded, dropping the stick and heading for the house, glaring at Bridgot.

He turned to walk away.

"Bridgot," Farmer Wells called.

He turned back around, "Yes?"

"How about a duel?"

Celestia turned back toward them, grinning, ready to watch this.

Bridgot laughed again, "I don't have time for this."

"What's the matter?" he said, "Afraid of getting beaten by an old farmer?"

Bridgot stopped laughing, sizing the old man up. He walked over, picking up the stick she had been using.

They took their stances, and Celestia stood by, crossing her arms, waiting.

Bridgot lunged forward, and they engaged. To her, it looked like a dance. They were swinging and circling. Their footwork was incredible, mirroring each other so quickly, she could hardly keep up. *How am I ever going to master this?* she thought. Farmer Wells landed a couple of blows to Bridgot's arms, which she could tell surprised and infuriated him. He swung back angrily, and Farmer Wells merely stepped out of the way. The duel lasted for a few minutes, and Bridgot never landed a single blow. Finally, Farmer Wells knocked his stick from his hand, and held the end of his own stick against his neck, saying, "Touché."

Celestia applauded, cheering.

"Touché," Bridgot said, not sounding so arrogant now.

Farmer Wells lowered his stick. "You fight well," he said, "But, you still have much to learn."

"Where does a farmer learn to fight like that?" Bridgot asked.

He chuckled, "I've only been a farmer since I retired."

He paused, "What were you before?"

"Rule #1: Never underestimate your opponent," was all he said. Then he added, "I shall need to go hunting tomorrow. Care to accompany me?"

"Sure," Bridgot said, "But, what about her?"

"She can handle herself for a day; she knows where everything is. So, how's about we work on *your* jousting today?"

"I'll tend to the stew," Celestia said, heading inside.

As she stirred the large pot over the fireplace, she could hear sticks clashing, and Farmer Wells shouting encouragement and instruction, as well as a few taunts. She thought she might get her wish to stay after all, as long as it would take to teach *both* of them. She headed upstairs after a while to wash up, and came back down just in time for the three of them to eat dinner.

Afterward, she helped Farmer Wells with the dishes, and Bridgot went upstairs to wash. When she headed up, he was already done and going to sleep. She lied down to read her book and shook her head.

When she awoke, Bridgot was gone. She went downstairs, and there was no sign of Farmer Wells. She remembered that they had said they were going hunting. When she opened the fridge, she saw that Farmer Wells had left her a plate of breakfast. She breathed a sigh of relief, not sure if she could cook a meal totally by herself. There was also plenty of leftover stew for lunch and dinner. She ate quickly and washed up—her first time doing dishes on her own.

After breakfast, she headed to the stable, and fed and watered the horses. It was her first time in her life being truly alone for a day. She wasn't entirely sure what to do with herself. She sat in the stable until it looked like the horses were finished eating, at least for now. Then, she took Samson out of his stall and led him to the side of the barn to give him a bath. He was much dirtier than Razel had been, and she was sure he'd feel a lot better when he was clean.

Once she'd finished bathing Samson, she let him and Razel trot around to get their exercise in. She put them back in the barn and went inside the house. After lunch, she spent a while finishing her book and then started another. She went to check on the horses again and then heated some more stew for dinner.

As she was heating it up, she heard voices outside. Upon peering through the window, she saw that Bridgot and Farmer Wells were returning, dragging a large deer behind them. Bridgot also had a few rabbits slung over his shoulder. She quickly added more stew to the pot, so there would be enough for all of them. She smiled to herself as she stirred, truly happy for the first time.

A New Home

5

The next day, and for the next few days, they continued in their new routine. She and Bridgot helped Farmer Wells maintain his house, they took care of the horses and practiced their sword fighting. Bridgot even helped him with a few home improvement projects, and Celestia learned how to cook. Each day, their sword fighting improved. It didn't take long for Bridgot to be able to hold his own against Farmer Wells; he even beat him a few times. Celestia improved greatly, but she was still far from an expert. Her grip strength increased, and it became tougher for Farmer Wells to knock the stick from her hand.

The three of them even took a fishing trip one day, heading into the forest, to a spot by the river where Farmer Wells said he always had good luck. It was relaxing, just sitting by the river, feeling the grass beneath her fingers. She'd never been fishing before, but Farmer Wells said you had to be quiet so as not to spook the fish. She got lost in her thoughts, enjoying the fresh air and the calm breeze. She even tried fishing, and caught a fish!

She was sitting there, holding the fishing pole, and she felt a tug. She got excited, turning to Farmer Wells for help. He showed her how to reel it in, and the two men helped her pull in a large trout.

"You did it!" Farmer Wells said.

"Not bad," Bridgot said.

Celestia beamed with pride at her catch. That night, they cleaned it, deboned it, filleted it up, and fried it. She felt a sense of satisfaction in her work, looking at the meal they'd prepared, and knowing it was all due to her, catching and cooking the trout.

One day, after lunch, they went out to the field to work on her sword training.

"Bridgot," Farmer Wells said, "I think you've got your jousting down. Why don't you show us what you've got on your archery today?"

"How?" he said, "We have no targets."

"Wait right here," Farmer Wells said, running into the barn. He came back carrying a large target. "Well, don't just stand there. Come and help!"

Together, the two men carried out five large targets and put them in a row outside the barn. He handed Bridgot a bow and quiver of arrows. Farmer Wells and Celestia stood back by the house and watched as Bridgot fired arrows at each of the targets. He hit two out of the five. One hit the edge of the target, and the other hit the fourth ring.

Farmer Wells sighed, "It seems your archery isn't as masterful as your skill with a blade."

Bridgot shrugged, "Well, if I'm skilled with a sword, why do I need to also be skilled with a bow?"

"Because, if you have multiple opponents coming at you from a distance, it's very useful to be able to decrease their numbers before they reach you. Fire your arrows at them as they approach, and when the remainder get close enough, pull out your sword, and you'll have fewer opponents to face at once."

"How many opponents do you imagine I'll face?" he asked, sounding perturbed.

"I'm sure I don't know, but it's always better to be prepared," he said, "Alright, let me show you how it's done." He walked over, taking the bow and quiver from Bridgot, and firing at each of the targets. He hit three bullseyes, and two in the second rings.

Bridgot stared at him in surprise, "You know, you never told me what it is you did before you retired."

"I was a knight," he said.

"I knew it!" he said excitedly.

"Alright, alright," he said, "Now, focus. Let's see your stance."

Bridgot took his stance, and Farmer Wells showed him how to adjust it, "Feet closer together. With a stance that wide, you're more likely to fall

over than hit something. Rest your mouth against the bow. Close one eye
when you fire. And, get your elbow down."

He fired, and the arrow hit the second ring.

"Good," Farmer Wells said, "Now, keep practicing. Margarita, let's go
work on your jousting."

Celestia nodded. She wondered how much longer they would stay.
Farmer Wells spent less and less time teaching them, and more and more
time helping them practice. He had only little critiques, and he mostly just
kept dueling her so she could work on the things he'd already told her.

As Farmer Wells prepared dinner that night, she helped Bridgot put
everything away in the barn.

"You know, I never told you, but you did well on the fishing trip," he
said, "It was . . . impressive that you caught that trout."

"Thank you," she said, surprised. In all the time they'd spent there,
they'd barely spoken. The most they'd talked was when they'd argued about
her staying there, and then a couple of nights later when she'd told him she
was only staying until she completed her training. Other than that, they'd
only given each other acknowledgment and spoken when necessary.

"You're not the average lady, are you?" he asked.

She smiled, "No, I'm not."

He nodded, "Well, I think that's a very good thing. Most women I
know are content to live a life behind the scenes, running their household
and caring for the children. They certainly never travel alone, and they
don't have any sort of combat training."

She smirked, "Why do you think I ran away?"

He paused, contemplating her comment.

"So, you respect me now, is that it?" she asked.

He smiled, "Yes, I think I do."

As she looked at him, she realized she hadn't been paying attention.
Over the couple of weeks they'd been at Farmer Wells', he'd grown. He wasn't
the skinny, scrawny boy he was when they'd met. He had muscle now, and
he looked like a warrior. All the training, all the hauling, all the heavy lifting
had transformed him. "Good," she said, "But, you should learn to respect
all women, regardless. They hold an important place in our society. Not all
women are the same, just like not all men are the same."

He looked down.

"You were raised by a woman, were you not?"

He cleared his throat, "Yes, I was."

"Do you not respect your own mother?"

"You're right," he said.

She paused, taken aback, "I'm right?"

"Yes. My mother and sisters do deserve respect. I never really thought about the fact that they bring to society what most women do. How can I respect them, and not the others?"

She looked at him in surprise, and then her expression softened, "Well, I'm glad to see you've had a change of heart."

Just then, Farmer Wells called for them to come in for dinner.

"Where's Bridgot?" Celestia asked as she came downstairs for breakfast.

"He had an early start this morning," Farmer Wells said, "He's out practicing his archery."

Her blue eyes widened in surprise.

"I know," he said, "I was surprised, too. Our friend has become very dedicated to his training of late."

"Yes, he has," she said, looking out the window at him.

"He's gotten stronger, too; turned from a scrawny little peasant into knight material."

Celestia nodded, twisting a few strands of white-blonde hair between her fingers as she watched Bridgot shoot his arrows. It took her a moment to notice that Farmer Wells was watching her carefully. She turned toward him, "What?"

His dark eyes surveyed her face. He scratched his short, gray hair, and his recently-trimmed beard. After a moment, he said, "You've developed feelings for him, haven't you?"

"No," she said, "Of course not. I'm a princess; he's a commoner. All that's happened is I've grown to care for him as a friend and to respect him. When we met, I despised him."

Farmer Wells nodded, "Very well. I believe you. But, you may come to find with more time that you do care, as more than a friend."

She paused, thinking. She hadn't considered anything of the sort before. Was what she was feeling truly just friendship? Or was Farmer Wells right? She looked back out the window, lost in her thoughts as he served up the breakfast.

Once the chores were done, and they'd eaten lunch, it was time for practice again. Celestia picked up her stick and prepared herself, as Bridgot began firing with the bow and arrow. He was improving, slowly. Very slowly.

"Bridgot!" Farmer Wells called as he came out to the field.

He stopped and set down his bow and quiver, jogging over, "Yes?"

"I want to try something new today," he said.

"New?" Celestia asked.

"What's that?" Bridgot asked.

"I want you two to duel," he said.

"What?" she said, shocked.

"Are you serious?" Bridgot asked.

"Look, I've been doing all the training so far. Bridgot, you know as much as I do at this point, save for my own personal tricks that I will teach to no one. And, it's better if you're trained by more than one person. Margarita's been dueling me for over a fortnight, and I think she would learn more by dueling someone else for a change."

They looked at each other, and Bridgot sighed, picking up the stick.

Celestia took a breath, unsure how this was going to go. She took her stance as he took his, and they watched each other closely, circling, mirroring each other's movements. He swung first, and she brought her stick up to meet his blow. They engaged for a few minutes, and she was surprised at how well she was able to keep up with him. She didn't land any blows, of course, and he eventually knocked the stick from her hand, but she was proud of her performance.

"Well done!" Farmer Wells clapped from beside the house, heading back over.

"I'm impressed, truly," Bridgot said, bowing his head to her, "You did very well."

She smiled, "Thank you."

As Farmer Wells reached them, he said, "I think we've reached the point where that's all I can teach you. Now, it's up to you to practice on your own. So, on to your archery. I'm sure you'll have plenty to work on in that aspect as well; let's see what we're working with."

Bridgot and Farmer Wells walked toward the house, giving her space. She went into the barn and pulled Razel out of her stall, saddling her. When she came out of the barn, the two men were looking at her questioningly.

"What are you doing with Razel?" Farmer Wells shouted, "You're supposed to be showing us your archery!"

Celestia didn't answer but picked up the bow and quiver Bridgot had dropped on the ground. She climbed onto Razel's back and had her trot away from the targets. Once she was far enough, she turned, giving a thumbs up to the two of them, who were looking at each other in sheer confusion. "Yah!" she yelled, kicking Razel's sides to get her going. She galloped forward, toward the targets. As she rode past, she fired five arrows at them, hitting all bullseyes. Then, she grabbed the branch of a tree that was in the yard, just on the outskirts of the field, pulling herself up onto it. She whistled, and Razel turned around, running back toward the targets. Celestia jumped from the tree, landing on her horse's back, and shot off a final arrow before guiding Razel to a stop. The last arrow she fired split one of her first arrows in half.

The two men's jaws dropped. It took them a moment before either one could say anything. "Where did you learn that?" Bridgot finally exclaimed as the two of them came over.

"I . . . uh . . . took archery lessons from some friends back home," she said, "I mean, I've been studying my whole life."

"Obviously," he said, "That was amazing!"

"Indeed," Farmer Wells said, finally finding his voice, "It appears I was wrong—you don't have plenty to work on in this aspect."

Celestia smiled. She knew her years of practicing archery would be useful someday, even though her mother disagreed.

After a few more days of Bridgot practicing his archery in the morning, and helping Celestia with her sword fighting in the afternoon, they were starting to feel ready to set out. One evening, as Celestia was reading, Bridgot came upstairs.

"Hey," he said, "Mind if I come in?"

She lowered her book, sitting up, "Not at all."

"Listen," he began, "I've been thinking. I know you said you wanted to stay here until you completed your training, but—"

"Stop," she said, "I know what you're going to say. But, you don't need to. I know that training can take years. As Farmer Wells said, he's taught us all he can. The rest is up to us to practice." She paused, "I'm ready to set out, too. The time for adventure has finally arrived in my life. I confess I was ill-prepared for the dangers that would bring when I ran away. But, I feel confident enough to face them now."

He stood there a moment, running his hand through his curly, brown locks, "Well . . . great. We can set out the day after tomorrow, then."

"Perfect," she said.

The Prophecy

6

They spent one final day with Farmer Wells. As Bridgot got in some last-minute archery practice before they went to bed, Celestia was helping him clean up the house.

"We're leaving in the morning," she said.

"I know," Farmer Wells said.

She looked at him questioningly.

"I figured that had to be why Bridgot decided to practice again tonight—it must be his last chance." He paused, dusting the bookshelves, "We all know you've completed your training. So, I knew it would be soon."

She looked at him sadly.

"I'll miss you, too," he said, "You've made me feel alive again—the both of you. These last few weeks have been the greatest of my life since my wife passed."

She looked down at her brown peasant shoes, "Before I go, do you think you could . . . possibly . . . tell me more about my father?"

He sighed, "What is it you want to know so badly?"

"Anything really. Just details to get to know him by; things to help paint a clear picture of who he was."

He sat down on the couch, "I'm afraid all I knew of him was who he was during the war. Men become who they have to be to survive in times like that. It may not be who he truly was."

"That's okay. Any side of him's better than none at all," she joined him, fiddling with her brown peasant skirt in her lap.

"Very well," he said, "He may not be one the war did change, anyway. He had the strongest, noblest character I've seen, even to this day. He put his men first. Despite being a king, he didn't act like one. He dined around the fire with the rest of us. He spoke to us as friends and fellow warriors, rather than subjects, or soldiers under his command. To me, he was my best friend more than my king. We had each other's backs. I'd saved his life, and he'd saved mine. He listened to me talk about my Elizabeth, about how I wanted to go home to her, and how we wanted to build a farm on the outskirts of the kingdom, to live out our lives in peace. He rarely spoke of his own life, however, preferring to listen to the stories of others. We, of course, knew who he was already, as our king. We knew he was married to our beloved Queen Eva, and that their marriage had merged two kingdoms. We knew that they had just had a daughter—heir to the throne—Princess Celestia. I was at the presentation of your birth."

She looked up for a moment. She hadn't realized he'd been there for any part of her life. It was strangely comforting, knowing he was there.

"Though he never spoke of you, I knew he loved you both very much. He had a locket, presumably from the queen, that he never took off. It was hidden under his armor. But, when we were in our tents, I often saw him open it and stare inside. One day, I asked him what was in it, and he showed me. It had a picture of your mother on the left, smiling. And on the right, a picture of the three of you. It wasn't a king and queen holding their heir. It was a mother and father holding their daughter."

Celestia looked at him, tears in her eyes turning them bluer.

"He would've been a wonderful father," he said, "If only he'd had the chance."

She nodded, letting a few tears spill over her cheeks.

"I was there the day he died," he said.

She looked up at him in wonder.

"He got hit by an arrow. We're not sure who fired it—it could've been anyone. He didn't die right away. I hurried to him on the battlefield, and, with the help of another knight, took him to the castle. The doctors came, but there was nothing they could do—he was dying. Your mother rushed to his bedside, and he asked us all to leave. He spoke his last words to her before he died. No one but she knows what he said. But, before he spoke to her, his final request was to see you one last time. He kissed your head, told you he loved you, and you were taken by your nanny back to your room.

And, that's all I can tell you," he said, finishing his tale with sorrow in his eyes and in his voice.

Celestia's face was soaked now, tears flowing freely.

"I'm sorry you didn't have the chance to know him," he said, "But, it does no good to dwell on the past. His time has come and gone. Your time is now. For his sake, don't waste it." He reached out to hug her then.

She leaned into it, letting her tears stream down.

"It's alright," he said, stroking her hair, "You're so much more like him than you know."

After a few moments, the door opened, and Bridgot came inside. Upon seeing Celestia's tears, he asked, "What's going on?"

"Nothing," she said quickly, wiping her eyes, "I just . . . was telling Farmer Wells how much we've enjoyed our stay with him, and that I'm going to miss him. This is goodbye, after all."

"I'll miss you both, too," Farmer Wells said, patting her back, "It's been a privilege, truly."

"Oh," Bridgot said, "Yes, I'll certainly miss this place as well. I feel I've learned so much, and, honestly, it's begun to feel like home."

"Thank you, Bridgot," he said, "Thank you both." After a moment, he added, "Well, you two better get some sleep if you're setting out at dawn."

They nodded, and the two of them headed upstairs.

As the sunlight started to light the room, Celestia awoke to Bridgot shaking her gently. She blinked, trying to clear the sleep from her eyes.

"Come on," he whispered, "It's time to go."

She nodded, stretching and rubbing her eyes.

"I'll meet you in the stable," he said. He was already dressed in his brown peasant's pants and boots, and his light brown peasant's shirt. He picked up his scabbard and secured it around his waist, heading down the stairs.

She sat up. She still most certainly hated mornings. But, when traveling, it was safest to move in the daylight and camp when it got dark, so they had to make the most of the daylight hours. She yawned, tightening her brown peasant's skirt around her loose, white, off-the-shoulder peasant's shirt. She got up slowly, tiredly, and put on her shoes and her dark brown front-lace corset.

Celestia folded up the blankets and stacked them next to the pillows at the foot of the bed for washing. She looked around the room at the wooden floors, faded wallpaper, and the simple furniture, realizing this was the last time she'd set foot in this house. But, she had no time to dwell on it, for it was time to go. She headed out to the stable, and Bridgot was there waiting with the horses. Razel already had her saddle and reins on, and her saddle-bags were attached.

As she approached, Bridgot leaped onto Samson's back. Celestia reached Razel and climbed into her saddle. They looked at each other, and she could tell he was feeling the same as her in saying goodbye to this place.

They headed off into the forest, the ground worn and trodden beneath their horses' hooves. The crisp, morning air was fresh with dew, and the birds were whistling through the trees. Celestia looked back at Farmer Wells' house, with its peeling blue paint and cracked window frames, and let one final tear cascade down her soft, pale cheek.

They rode through the morning hours and watched as the forest was awakened all around them. The small woodland creatures darted through the trees and bushes, the air around them grew warmer, and the sunlight grew stronger, streaming in through the treetops.

Bridgot pulled a few apples out of his saddlebags, and they ate breakfast as they rode. When lunch rolled around, they stopped and pulled out some sandwich supplies, courtesy of Farmer Wells. They let their horses graze and get a drink from the river.

"So," Celestia said, "I never asked, but, did you find what you were looking for when you went into town that day?"

Bridgot paused with his mouth full of sandwich. He quickly chewed it and swallowed before answering, "No, it wasn't there. This whole journey turned out to be for nothing."

"Oh, I'm sorry," she said, "What was it you were looking for, anyway?"

He let out a humorless laugh, "Well, my people are supposedly the village said to be where a warrior from an ancient prophecy will be from."

She looked at him curiously.

"He is supposed to be the one who can solve the 'unsolvable riddle.' Anyway, I solved it, and they pronounced me to be the warrior of the prophecy. So, they sent me to find the one whom, according to the prophecy, I am destined to protect, and to bring her back to the village."

"And who are you destined to protect?" she asked.

He looked at her, "The princess of Ivétoiless."

She swallowed, barely breathing.

"But, when I got there, she was nowhere to be found. Apparently, she went missing *two days* before I got there. *Two days!* Maybe I'm not the warrior of the prophecy after all," he looked down, shaking his head, his curls bobbing against it.

"Or, maybe she's not the princess," she said.

He looked up, "She has to be."

"Why? What does this prophecy say?"

"It says that a princess from a great merged kingdom, born at the turn of the century, will be the one to save the land from a terrible evil, with the help of a great warrior, solver of the unsolvable riddle, born in the village of Chance."

She looked at the grass beneath her, pondering.

"Well, the *only* princess born at the turn of the century in a merged kingdom is Princess Celestia of Ivétoiless. So, it *has* to be her. Anyway, people assumed it was our village, since its name, Kataran, means 'chance.' But, maybe it wasn't supposed to be our village."

"Maybe . . ." she said, staring at the river.

"Anyway, Margarita, we'd better go," he said, "We're wasting precious daylight." He extended his hand, helping her up.

They rode the rest of the day until it started to grow dark.

"We'd better find somewhere safe to make camp," he said.

She nodded in agreement.

He led her into a small clearing through the trees, "This is a good spot. It provides us with some cover from the road. We'll have to sleep in shifts, so one of us can always be awake to watch for danger. Let's eat and get some rest."

They let their horses graze and get a drink first, and then led them into the clearing and tied them to the backside of the trees. They sat and ate some deer jerky and berries, and then lied down against a large tree to get as comfortable as they could.

"I'll take the first watch," Bridgot said, "Go ahead and get some sleep."

Celestia curled up under one of the blankets she'd brought from the castle and drifted off.

Too soon, Bridgot was waking her to tell her it was her shift. She let herself wake up, and Bridgot laid back to get some sleep. She looked up at the stars, watching them sparkle against the night sky. It didn't look just black, but she saw shades of deep blues and violets. It made her wonder how big this world truly was, and how she could ever hope to see even half of it.

She wasn't sure how long her shift was supposed to be, but, when she felt she could no longer keep her eyes open, she woke him, and drifted back to sleep. It was a difficult night for her, not only because she had to keep waking up, but because this was her first time sleeping on the ground instead of in a bed. It was acutely uncomfortable; it was hard, and the bark of the tree kept scratching her, but leaning against it was more comfortable than placing her head directly on the ground, and she kept getting poked by sticks and rocks.

As the soft glow of the rising sun peeked in through the trees, they set out again. Celestia was exhausted. Her hair was a mess, and she couldn't stop yawning. She had no idea what adventure meant in terms of sleep and hygiene, but she felt tired and dirty.

They continued like that for a few days until they reached a small village one evening.

"Why don't we stop here for tonight?" Bridgot asked, "I think we could use a hot meal, a bath, and a good night's sleep, don't you?"

Celestia perked up, "Yes, I think we could."

They rode into town and found an inn. The village was so small that they could see all four sides of it from any point. It had dirt roads and little wooden buildings. Its people were bustling about, trying to squeeze use out of every ounce of daylight.

Bridgot called upon the innkeeper, "We require accommodations if you please."

The innkeeper, an old woman, with wrinkly, liver-spotted skin, and a worn, old peasant's dress, looked from them to their horses, "Nigel!"

An old man, presumably her husband, came out, "Yes, what is it?"

"Take their horses to the stable, dear," she said, "Come along, you two, your horses are well-tended."

They followed her inside, and she led them upstairs, down a long hallway, and to a room. "Here we are, dears," she said, "A lovely little room for a lovely couple."

"Oh, we're not—" Bridgot began.

Celestia elbowed him, "Thank you. It's perfect."

"Now, what did you say your names were, dears? I have to keep a record of all my guests."

"I'm Margarita, and this is Bridgot," she said.

"Lovely, and your last name?"

"Brown," Bridgot said.

"Bath's just down the hall, last door on your left. Don't be afraid to call if you need anything," she said, "I'm Mrs. Norton."

"Thank you," they said, ducking into the room. It was small, and the walls and floor were made of a dark wood. It had a full-sized bed and a small closet, as well as two bedside tables.

"Mind telling me what that was about?" Bridgot asked.

"I think it would be best if people thought we were a couple, for our own safety. It would look suspicious if we were two strangers traveling alone together. So, we just need to keep that as a cover for the road."

He nodded, "Okay, whatever. Why don't you go wash up, and I'll see about getting us some food."

She gathered up her change of clothes and headed down the hall to the washroom. It was pretty standard, with a tub, sink, and toilet. She closed the door and tried to figure out the tub. It was different from Farmer Wells', and it confused her for a moment. Finally, she figured out that you pull the knobs instead of turning them.

It felt wonderful to bathe after spending a few days on the road. She was covered in dirt, and her white-blonde hair looked more like it was a grayish auburn. Once she was clean, she looked in the mirror as she brushed her hair. She hardly recognized herself; she'd changed during their stay at Farmer Wells' as well. She was toned and muscly, and her face looked so different without makeup. Her pale skin had even developed a bit of a tan. As she heard people waiting in the hallway, she cleaned her teeth quickly and headed back to the room.

Bridgot brought up some fresh stew and biscuits for their dinner. They hungrily devoured it, and Bridgot headed down the hall to wash. While she was waiting, Celestia searched for somewhere to wash their clothes. The innkeeper told her she'd wash their things for them, so Celestia gave her her dirty clothes, and let her know that Bridgot was washing up.

When they got back to the room, they realized there was not enough space for Bridgot to sleep on the floor. They looked at each other.

"We'll just place some pillows between us," he said.

She sighed, "It's alright, Bridgot. I've spent enough time with you to know you're a gentleman. We need to get some real sleep. Even if you were a hoodlum, I'm sure you would be too tired to try anything tonight."

He nodded, yawning, "I suppose you're right."

With that, the two of them collapsed into the bed, falling asleep almost instantly.

A Journey Begins

7

When she awoke, she felt refreshed, well-rested, and ready to continue on. Bridgot was still asleep, and she realized his arm was around her. She quickly clambered out of the bed, almost falling. Her sudden movement woke him, and when he opened his sleepy eyes, he smiled at her. She'd never seen him look that way before. In his most vulnerable state, he was actually kind of adorable. His gray eyes, which, at first, she'd thought were blank and unfeeling, had a twinkle in them, and they seemed more like a soft fog than harsh concrete.

"Good morning," he said.

"Good morning," she responded.

"What time is it?" he yawned and stretched, sitting up.

"I'm not sure," she straightened up, realizing her corset had shifted around in the night, and quickly adjusted it.

"I hope we didn't oversleep," he said, coming to full consciousness and sliding out of the bed. He tucked his shirt in and put his scabbard and shoes on.

Celestia slipped on her own shoes, and they grabbed the saddlebag they'd brought inside, heading down the stairs. The bottom level of the inn was a bar/diner, and there they found the innkeeper. She saw them coming and intercepted them with a pile of clean, folded clothes.

"Headed off, are we, dears?" she asked.

"Yes, I'm afraid we must be leaving," Bridgot said, "Do you have the time?"

44

"It's almost noon," she said, "Why don't you have some lunch before you go?"

"Noon?" he said, sounding panicked, "I'm afraid we really must be off."

"Bridgot, why don't we at least eat first?" Celestia said, "We don't get many hot meals on the road."

"Very well," he grumbled, "But, we must be quick about it."

"Excellent," Mrs. Norton said, "I'll fix you something. Here are your clothes, all washed and ready."

"Thank you," Celestia said, "We really appreciate it." She put the clothes in the bag, and they sat at one of the tables to wait for the food.

Mrs. Norton was quick. It only took a couple of minutes for her to bring them a couple plates of turkey legs, green beans, potatoes, and rolls. They cleaned their plates in less than five minutes, and she had Nigel fetch their horses from the stable.

They set out again, with half the day already wasted. Although she had to admit, it wasn't much of a waste getting a proper night's sleep. Besides, there was really no reason to hurry. She felt a lot better being clean, fed, and well-rested.

They made camp in another clearing when it grew dark, and settled down for the night. It was easier taking shifts after only a half day. They continued for another few days and stopped in another village. After about a week of traveling, Celestia was becoming all too familiar with the routine of the road. The little villages blurred together. She and Bridgot had their story down pat.

Over the short amount of time they'd spent on the road so far, she began to feel something different toward him. She couldn't explain it, but there was something there, something more than friendship. It was strange and new, and she didn't know why. She just kept thinking to herself, *Maybe Farmer Wells was right . . .*

"Is there an inn in this village that *has* a stable?" Bridgot asked. The innkeeper there was an old man who was hard of hearing.

He shook his head, not in negation, but in indication that he didn't know.

"We need somewhere with a stable for our horses," he said.

"Horses?" the old man's voice was raspy and strained, "Horses stay in the corral."

"No," Bridgot said, "We don't want a corral; we want a stable."

"Bridgot," Celestia said, "Don't waste your time; he doesn't know. Let's just try the next one." More loudly, she added, "Thank you, sir."

They headed to the next inn, and there was a stable available.

"Newlyweds? Oh, how sweet. James! Come quick, we have newlyweds!" the innkeeper's wife was a middle-aged woman with dark hair and dark eyes.

"How exciting!" the innkeeper said, rushing over. He was a middle-aged man with tawny brown skin and black hair, "We haven't had newlyweds in a while. Come, I'll show you to your room while our stable-boy tends to your horses."

They headed up to the room and took turns washing up. When they went downstairs for dinner, the waitress—a young, blonde woman—came to take their order.

"What can I get you?" she asked.

"I'll have the ham and potatoes," Celestia said.

"And . . . you?" she asked flirtatiously.

"Uh . . . I'll have the steak and eggs," Bridgot said.

"Good choice. How do you like your steak?" she asked, almost seductively, leaning against the table and displaying her cleavage.

"Medium, please," he said, laying his menu down, and looking at her questioningly.

"Anything else?" she batted her eyelashes, sitting on the table, and leaning toward him.

"That's alright," he said.

She got up, disappointed, and headed to the kitchen to give them the order.

Celestia scoffed, rolling her eyes.

"What?" Bridgot asked.

"Seriously?" she said, "That waitress was hitting on you."

He laughed, "No, she wasn't."

"Are you kidding me? She practically threw herself at you."

"Really?" he said.

Celestia nodded.

"Hmm," he said, scratching his chin.

She backhanded his chest, "You're not considering it, are you?"

"Why?" he asked, "What does it matter?"

"It doesn't," she said quickly, picking her menu back up, "I just don't want to blow our cover, that's all."

He eyed her suspiciously but didn't say anything. After dinner, they headed upstairs to get some sleep. They climbed into the bed and got comfortable, nestling in for the night.

As she was closing her eyes, Bridgot said, "Margarita?"

"Yes?" she whispered.

"I hope this doesn't sound strange, but I've really enjoyed traveling with you."

"I've enjoyed traveling with you, too," she said, a bit confused.

"Goodnight," he said, "See you in the morning."

"Sweet dreams," she said, feeling a twinge in her stomach.

They set out again at dawn. It was long and repetitive, and she was beginning to see why people preferred to stay in one place, rather than live on the road.

"How far is it to your village?" she asked.

"Another fortnight," he said.

She sighed, *Two more weeks on the road.*

"What will you do once we arrive?" he asked.

"I'm not sure yet," she said. The truth was, she hadn't thought about what exactly she was doing, or what her plans were. From the moment she'd run away, she'd just wanted a life of adventure. However, the open road was proving a lot more boring than expected.

During their shifts at night, they'd begun practicing the skills Farmer Wells had taught them. Bridgot worked on his archery, shooting the trees and shrubs, and an occasional animal that happened across them. Celestia squeezed her clamp to maintain her grip strength and practiced swinging her sword, stepping, blocking, and thrusting with imaginary opponents.

Occasionally, they'd duel during their lunch stop, using sticks they found on the ground. Bridgot would offer her critiques to keep improving, and she'd give him advice on his shooting, showing him the proper way to hold his bow and aim.

Another week went by, and it felt like it would take an eternity to reach his village. Early on in the week, Bridgot was acting sweet and awkward, and she'd often catch him looking at her. It gave her butterflies each time, and he'd try to hide it, but then they'd smile at each other and laugh.

But, recently, he'd been acting strange, pushing her away, and it seemed like something was bothering him. He wasn't as talkative, and his answers were cold and clipped. He hardly looked at her anymore, and she wondered why.

Finally, when they stopped for lunch one day, she asked, "Is everything alright?"

"Fine," Bridgot said, pulling food out of the saddlebags.

"Are you sure?" she asked, letting Razel drink from the river.

He gave her a slight nod, and sat down, eating an apple.

She let Razel begin grazing near Samson and sat beside Bridgot on the riverbank. "You know," she said, "You've been acting weird lately. Did I do something wrong?"

He sighed, lowering his apple and looking away, "No. You haven't done anything. It's me."

She looked at him, confused, "What do you mean?"

"I've done something, and I've been feeling incredibly guilty about it," he looked at her, "I've grown fond of you, and I can't do this anymore."

"Do what?"

"I know who you are," he said.

Her eyes widened, "Wh-what do you mean?"

"You're Princess Celestia of Ivétoiless," he said.

"How did you—"

"I've known for a while," he said, "When I went into town and found out the princess had run away two days before I got there, I headed back to Farmer Wells'. I was frustrated, but it didn't take me long to put two and two together. You'd told me you ran away. I'd met you two days prior. It didn't take a genius to figure it out."

"Why didn't you say anything before?" she asked.

"I was bringing you back to my village. You're the princess of the prophecy, remember? I thought it'd be easier to get you there if I didn't tell you I knew it was you."

She stared at him, not quite sure what she was feeling. It was a mixture of shock, hurt, betrayal, and anger.

"I can't go on lying to you—not now. I have to tell you because I . . . I have . . . feelings for you."

"You have *feelings* for me?" she scoffed, jumping up, "First, you tell me you've been lying to me and luring me to your village, and then you say you have *feelings* for me? If you did, you wouldn't do that to me."

"That's what I'm saying," he said, rising, "That's why I'm telling you now. I can't do that to you."

"You're unbelievable," she said, storming off toward her horse.

"Wait," he said, following her, "Please. I shouldn't have lied, but I didn't know how to tell you."

She placed her hands on Razel's saddle, readying herself to mount her and ride away when Bridgot grabbed her arm. "Let go," she said, yanking it away. As she turned to tell him off, she saw a group of men coming up behind them. Before she could react, one of them knocked Bridgot unconscious. She quickly turned to grab her sword, but before she could pull it from its scabbard, she felt a hard knock to the back of her head, and the world went dark.

Slave Traders

8

Celestia felt like she was moving. The back of her head throbbed with pain. She opened her eyes slowly and saw unfamiliar faces staring back at her. She sat up, looking around. She was in the back of a covered wagon, surrounded by women and young girls. Their faces had one thing in common: fear. They were all afraid, huddled together in clusters. Some were weeping, some were shaking, and the rest were sitting in quiet resignation.

She looked at the woman sitting closest to her. She had to be in her forties, brown hair, brown eyes. "Where are they taking us?" she asked her.

The woman looked at her for a moment, then said, "They are taking us to be sold at the slave market."

Celestia's eyes widened, and she looked around again. "Where are the men?" she asked, trying to figure out where Bridgot was.

"They're in a separate wagon," she said.

"What about the horses?"

"They're guiding them along behind us. Where are you from that you know nothing of the slave trade?"

"I'm a traveler, from far away. I've never encountered such atrocities as this. What about all of you? Where are you from that you know so much about it?"

The woman looked from her to the little girl in her arms, "We're from a nearby village. The slave traders raid us from time to time, capturing our people to sell them. Most of our men were killed during a feud with another village some years ago. So, we have no one to protect us."

"You should learn to protect yourselves, then," she said.

The woman scoffed, "Is that how you got captured?"

Celestia looked toward the entrance of the wagon, seeing the bright sunlight streaming in through the opening. She could think of only one thing: escape. *How am I going to get out of here? And how will I find Bridgot and the horses?*

The wagon slowed to a stop, and they waited, breathless, for what would happen next. They heard voices outside, too muffled to understand. After a minute, the entrance was opened, and a group of brawny men started yanking everyone out.

Celestia jumped up and ran at them, kicking one in the face. She leaped out of the wagon and started running. As soon as she took off, she felt the pain of a blow to the back of her head, in the same spot she was hit before. Everything went black again.

When she awoke, her head was killing her. She'd never known a pain like this before. She found it hard to focus, and her vision was blurry. She was sitting in a corral with the other women and girls, and her hands and feet were shackled.

After a few minutes, the slave traders started lining everyone up and shackling them together. One of them—a burly, bearded man—picked her up off the ground and unshackled her from the fence, roughly putting the new shackles on, and adding her to the line.

They posted guards every few feet along the sides of the line, with one at the rear, and two leading them forward. As they moved toward the market, she frantically searched for the line of men, and for the horses. She caught a glimpse of two horse corrals nearby, and she tried to focus her vision long enough to see into them. In one of them, she saw Razel! But, Samson wasn't in the same one. She searched the second one, and thought she saw him, but couldn't be sure. The line of men was nowhere to be found.

They were forced to line up near a platform, and there was a large group of people seated in front of it. An auctioneer was standing on it, and, to Celestia's horror, he began auctioning off a young girl to the crowd. Her search became even more frantic, but she couldn't see where Bridgot might be. The line started moving as each of them was being sold. Finally, she realized that the men and boys had already been sold. She searched through the crowd and spotted Bridgot, shackled in a small group of men, standing next to a man in gold-threaded clothes, with a fancy hat and cape.

As she reached the front of the line, she was dragged onto the platform. She made eye contact with Bridgot, pleading with her eyes for him to have a plan. He looked desperate, but unable to do anything as they began auctioning her off.

"Let's start the bidding at 10 shillings!" the auctioneer yelled. The people in the crowd responded, someone taking the offer right away.

"I bid 15! I bid 20! 25!" they shouted. Finally, it seemed as if all the offers had been shouted out.

"35 going once, twice," the auctioneer said.

"I bid 50 shillings!" someone yelled suddenly.

"50 going once, twice, sold!" he responded.

She was dragged off the platform, and over to an old man who had a couple of men shackled behind him already. As she went past, she desperately looked over at Bridgot. He tried to run toward her, but his shackles held him back. One of the guards to the man who'd bought him punched him in the gut for trying. He doubled over in pain, attempting to catch his breath. She tried to shake the slave traders off and go over to him, but they shoved her down and hooked her shackles to the other slaves the old man had bought.

"Careful with this one," they said to the old man, "She's a runner."

They finished selling off the women and girls and brought the horses up from the corral. When they led Samson onto the platform, she straightened up, watching carefully. After he was sold, she heard the old man tell his assistant, "What a pity. That horse was a fine specimen. Those meat packers always get the good ones."

Her eyes widened, and she tried to wiggle out of her shackles. No matter what she tried, she was stuck. The old man bought one of the horses, and he seemed to be interested in a workhorse. When they brought Razel up, she lunged forward, getting pulled back. She watched helplessly as the bidding commenced.

"15 going once," the auctioneer was saying. She realized it was the meat packer who'd bought Samson.

"No!" she yelled.

The old man turned in surprise, looking from her to Razel.

"Twice," the auctioneer said.

"I bid 30 shillings!" the old man shouted.

"30 going once, twice, sold!"

They brought Razel over, and Celestia was overjoyed and relieved. Razel whinnied as she was led past her and hooked up with the other horse he'd bought.

After all the horses were auctioned off, the crowd dispersed, leading their slaves and horses to their respective houses. Celestia was put in another wagon with the two men, and Razel was led behind with the other horse. They were silent the whole way there, and when they arrived, the old man led them to a small, stone building next to the huge manor. Inside, it had several rooms. There were already a few slaves living there, and the old man gave them each a room. "Servants' washroom is the door closest to the entrance," he said, "I hope you like it here."

He left, and she noticed there were guards posted at the entrance. Her room was tiny—smaller than any she'd been in. It just barely fit a twin bed, a small table, and a tiny closet. The closet had a few servants' dresses in it. She closed the door and sat on the edge of the bed. It felt like she was sitting in a tomb. There were no windows, and the only way in or out was past the guards. But, worse than that, Samson had been bought by meat packers. She kicked the table in frustration, not sure what to do. Finally, she broke down in tears, throwing herself on the bed and crying herself to sleep.

Life of a Slave

9

Celestia was awakened by horns blaring as the guards came down the hallway, pounding on their doors.

When she walked into the hall, two of the guards nodded to each other, and one of them pushed her back into the room. "You are needed in the manor. Change into your uniform," he said. He closed the door, and she could hear him standing outside, waiting, his breath loud and heavy.

She stared at the closet and realized the servants' dresses were for her. Although she didn't want to, she didn't see much choice at the moment. So, she changed clothes, tucking her own ensemble under the bed. She opened the door again, and the guard looked her over. The servant's dress had blousy sleeves and an apron covering the front.

"Bonnet, too," he said. She glared, but turned and put her hair up—another first for her. She put the bonnet on and turned back around. He nodded in approval and led her outside.

The grounds covered almost as much space as the palace grounds back home. The majority of it was a large field of crops, where she could see the male slaves working, along with a few of the strong females. The horses were being used to load and plow, and, among them, she could see Razel. It infuriated her, seeing the pride of the royal stables used as a workhorse. And for 30 shillings!

When they got inside the house, she saw the tall, spiral staircases in the entryway, and the long corridors both upstairs and down. There were large paintings and massive chandeliers.

"This way," the guard said, heading down the corridor to the left, "No dawdling."

She followed him down the hallway, looking at all the paintings along the way. Through the windows, she could see out to the field. She wanted to run out, hop on Razel's back, and get out of there. But, she wasn't sure how to find Bridgot, and her last escape attempt hadn't gone so well.

He led her to a door near the end of the hall and knocked. "Come in," a voice from inside said. The guard opened the door and pulled her inside. It was an office, decorated in red, black, and cherry wood. The old man was standing there, dressed in a blue suit, with his gold pocket watch chain dangling along his waist. He had thin, wispy hair, with a large bald spot on top of his head. He had a pointy, gray beard that reached his chest, and his eyes were dark and beady.

"Thank you, Frederick," he said, nodding to the guard. He nodded in return, and backed out of the room, closing the door.

She stared at the old man, not sure what he wanted with her.

"Welcome," he said, "I hope you've found your accommodations adequate."

"They'd be better if I were free," she said.

He paused, "I'm told you're a runner. Am I going to have problems with you?"

"Not if you let me and my horse go," she said.

"*Your* horse?" he smirked, "Ah, I see. That's why you cared for her fate. She belonged to you."

"*Belongs*," she said, growing angry.

"You know, I don't appreciate your tone after I rescued both you and your horse yesterday."

"*Rescued?*" she said, ready to lose it.

"That's right. It may interest you to know that the man who almost bought you is well-known for buying sex slaves."

She froze, eyes widening.

"And he almost bought *you* for 35 shillings," he said, walking over to his desk and sitting down, "Not to mention, you already know what I rescued 'your' horse from."

She paused, "Why did you do it?"

He began writing something, seemingly no longer interested in their conversation, "I thought you were a beautiful young lady. You reminded me of my late wife, and I didn't want to see *him* buy you. As for your horse, well, I saw what she meant to you, and I couldn't let the meat packers get their hands on *every* fine specimen."

She looked down, not sure how she should be feeling toward this man. On the one hand, he had bought both her and her horse and forced Razel into hard labor. But, on the other hand, he had saved them both from a worse fate. "Thank you," she said.

He gave her a slight nod, focused on whatever he was writing. She stood there, looking at the reddish, wooden floors, wondering what she was supposed to be doing. After a few moments, she began looking around the office at the bookshelves that lined the walls.

"I didn't buy you to stand there and look pretty," he said finally.

It shook her out of her reverie. She looked at him.

"Frederick will show you around. You'll be under Moira, the head maid. Your job will be keeping the manor clean. Go on," he said.

She turned and headed out of the office. The guard was waiting outside, and he led her back up the hall, and down the one to the right of the entrance. He pounded on one of the doors, "Moira! Moira!"

The door opened, and a middle-aged woman with wrinkles too deep for her age stepped out. She had curly, red hair popping out from beneath her bonnet, and it was already graying. "What? What is it?" she asked, annoyed.

"Your new charge," he said, pulling Celestia in front of him.

She looked her up and down, and said, "She does look a bit like the mistress, doesn't she?"

The guard shrugged, walking away.

"Come on," she said, "I'll show you around."

Celestia followed the woman down the corridor.

"This corridor is the servants' corridor. All of the rooms we need are here. There are three supply rooms," she tapped the doors to show her as they went up the hallway, "Each one has different cleaning supplies, depending on the room you need to clean. This one's for bathrooms, this one's for the kitchen, and this one's for the other rooms. We also have our break room, our own bathroom, as slaves aren't allowed to use the same bathrooms, and our own small dining room and staff kitchen."

Celestia followed her in utter horror and dismay, feeling as though she were watching all this happen through someone else's eyes. She needed to get out of there, but she had to come up with a plan. *How am I going to get past the guards?* she thought.

"The other corridor has all of the master's public rooms. There's the library, his lounge, the main bathroom, his study, and his office. Straight ahead, past the staircases, you have the living room on your left, the dining room on your right, and just past the dining room is the main kitchen. With me so far?"

She felt herself nodding, not sure if she was actually processing everything enough to remember it. It felt more like a bad dream than anything else.

"Great. Upstairs, you have three bathrooms and several bedrooms. You also have the master's personal library and the mistress' studio. That's the room down the right-hand corridor, very last door. You must never go in there. The master hasn't touched it since she passed."

She stared at the grand double-staircase and looked up at the red carpeting and the sparkling chandeliers. For a moment, she expected to see her mother coming down one of the staircases, telling her to start playing the piano for being late.

"She was a great lady. You look a fair bit like her," she paused, "There are four of us now, including you, who are responsible for keeping this whole place clean. We've separated the work into the four corridors of the house. As head maid, I'm in charge of the servants' corridor. Irene is in charge of the main hallway, and Colleen is in charge of the right-hand upstairs corridor, to ensure you don't go snooping into things you shouldn't. You'll be in charge of the left-hand upstairs corridor. We work together on the three main areas, so you'll be expected to help with those as well. Any questions?"

She shook her head.

"Good," she said, "What's your name, so I can keep track of you?"

"Margarita," she said, "And yours is . . . Moira, right?"

"You keep up nicely. Now, get to work."

Celestia headed to the supply rooms, not at all sure what she needed to grab. She'd never done real housework before. She looked out the window and wondered if she could sneak past the guards. *Not without Razel*, she thought. She shook her head, turning toward the first door. She opened it, looking inside. She'd never cleaned a bathroom in her life. There was toilet paper, towels, scrub brushes, and various cleaning supplies. She wanted to just grab one of everything to be safe, but there was too much for her to carry.

"For goodness' sake," Moira said, popping back out of the room she'd just gone into. "I said this corridor has everything you need. There are carts in the break room. Honestly," she walked away, muttering to herself.

Celestia went into the break room. It was decorated similarly to the old man's office, but it had sofas to lounge on, a couple of tables, a few bookshelves, and a row of wheeled carts. She seized one, and pushed it back to the supply room, grabbing one of everything. She went to the third supply room as well, snatching up the miscellaneous supplies it held.

She wheeled the cart toward the staircases, wondering how she was going to get it up the stairs. As she reached the bottom, a woman in a servant's dress came up to her. She had blonde curls peeking out of her bonnet. Her face was plain and freckled.

"Here, let me help you with that," she said, "I'm Colleen. You must be the new girl."

"Margarita," she said.

"What a lovely name," Colleen said, grabbing one side of the cart. Celestia grabbed the other side, and they lifted it up the stairs together.

It was a bit of a struggle, but they tugged it along.

"Thanks," Celestia said when they'd reached the top.

"Sure, no problem," Colleen said, catching her breath, "You're new at this, aren't you?"

"How could you tell?"

"You grabbed every supply closet item there is," she chuckled, "You won't need all of that."

"Better to be safe than sorry."

"I suppose you're right. Anyway, I hope we can be friends, seeing as we're both assigned the upstairs cleaning. It'll be nice to have a partner up here."

"I'm certain we can," Celestia said.

Colleen smiled, "Well, we'd better get to work."

She nodded, "Thanks again."

Celestia spent the morning trying to figure out how to clean. She made beds, not entirely sure if they looked right, and dusted furniture, trying to emulate the way her servants had always dusted things. The hard part came when she got to the bathroom. She had absolutely no idea how to clean a tub, or a toilet, or a sink. All the cleaning supplies on her cart were pretty much foreign to her. She soaped up a sponge and used it on the tub and sink, hoping it was good enough. She found a scrub brush with a long handle, and used that on the toilet so she wouldn't have to touch anything.

After the first couple bedrooms and the bathroom, Colleen found her and let her know it was time for lunch. They went down the stairs and into the servant dining room. The cook served up some stew, and they all sat and ate. The dining room was small—much smaller than any she'd been in before. It was just big enough to fit the rectangular table and chairs. It seated eight; she was used to tables that seated twenty people.

After lunch, it was back to cleaning. She got the other bedrooms done and finished with the library. It was a good size for a personal library. It had plenty of bookshelves lining the walls, and a large desk in the middle, much like his office downstairs. There was a large window overlooking the street behind the house. A couple of soft, comfortable-looking chairs sat in the corner. She dusted the bookshelves and the desk. Then, she swept the floor.

When she was done, she looked out the window, trying to find an escape route. There was nowhere she knew she could go. Everything was unfamiliar. She had no idea where she was, or where she needed to go. She turned toward the desk in despair. He had a few papers on it. She nosed through them, and saw various auction ads, papers from a company called Agri-Grow—which she assumed was the operation he was running, selling the crops they were harvesting outside—and a rejected purchase agreement from Townstin Meat Packers.

Her eyes widened when she saw the name. She slid the paper toward herself and looked at it more closely. It had an address on it. She grabbed a piece of paper and a pen and wrote it down, folding it up and tucking it in her apron. She tried to put everything back where she found it, and then she headed down the hall.

Colleen met up with her along the way, "Hey there. I see you've finished for the day."

She nodded.

"What's wrong? Aren't you glad to be done?"

"Yes, but I never should've had to begin," she said, shoving the broom that was sliding off back onto the cart.

"I can't afford to think that way. Everything happens for a reason. We're all here, and our job is to clean. Come on. I'll help you take the cart downstairs. It's time for dinner," Colleen said.

They each grabbed a side of the cart and lugged it down.

"Would you mind?" she asked, gesturing back up the stairs to her own cart that was waiting.

"Not at all," Celestia said, going back up with her and helping her lug the cart down.

They wheeled their carts into the break room and headed into the dining room for dinner. It was stew, again. After, Moira led them into the main kitchen to start clean-up. She had Celestia and Colleen team up to do the dishes, and she and Irene got to work on the rest of the kitchen. Irene had long, black hair that was falling out of her bonnet. She had the best skin, after Celestia, and she looked like she might've been someone of importance as well. She and Moira wiped down the counters, took out the trash, and put everything away.

Once they'd cleaned the kitchen, dining room, and living room, they were off-duty for the day, and they got to return to the servants' lodge or their corridor of the house, and do as they pleased. Celestia wandered the grounds, trying to find a way out. It was completely fenced in behind the house, too tall and slick to climb. The front was where all of the guards were, watching their every move. There was no clean exit. She would have to sneak past the guards and take Razel with her somehow.

As she went to sleep that night, she visualized the ways she could escape. She'd have to figure out the time of day with the least security. Maybe during the night . . .

The next day, she went through her new routine, watching everyone's moves. The old man seemed to stick to the downstairs corridor most of the day, the other maids stuck to the areas they were assigned to clean, and the guards were posted at the doors, as well as throughout the field where the other slaves were working.

That night, she tiptoed out of her room. The wood floor had creaky spots, and she did her best to avoid them. When she got to the door, the guard was sitting outside, fully awake and aware. She had been hoping to catch him asleep, as it was the middle of the night. She guessed that the guards took shifts through the night, so she was never going to catch them unawares. She snuck back to her room, and went to sleep, feeling disheartened.

As Celestia and Colleen joined their coworkers for lunch, they overheard Irene talking to Moira, "Did you hear? There's talk of an uprising at the Conant's plantation," she paused, "It's beginning."

"I don't want to hear anything about such talk," Moira said, helping the cook serve the stew.

"What's beginning?" Celestia asked as she took a seat.

"Some slaves are fighting back," the cook said. She was an older woman, with pruning skin and thin, wispy hair.

"Rumor is that a young man got a group together, and they're recruiting others to join them," Irene said.

"Bridgot," Celestia whispered.

"What?" Irene asked.

"Oh, I was saying . . . we should join them," Celestia said.

"That's enough," Moira said, "Now, the master's been good to all of us, and I don't think we're doing him or our late mistress a lot of good by talk of an uprising."

"It's not about how he's treated us," Celestia said, "We were captured against our will, sold, and forced into manual labor for no pay. It's time we fought back."

"Yeah," Irene said.

"I agree," the cook said.

"Absolutely not," Moira said.

"But, how would we join them?" Colleen asked, "We have no way to communicate."

"They're sending coded messages to all the plantations, and only slaves are able to decipher them," Irene said, "I think the boys got something this morning."

"Well, we need to find out," Celestia said, "If there's an uprising, I want in. And you all should, too." She shot a pointed look at Moira, who glared in return.

"I think I can get the message," the cook said.

"Great," Celestia said, "Let us know tonight at dinner."

Celestia scurried about, quickly completing her chores for the day. Her excitement was building as dinner-time approached. All she could think of was getting out of there. Two days of slave labor were more than enough for her. She didn't understand how others could resign themselves to such a fate.

When Colleen came to get her, they hurried to the servants' dining room and took their seats. As the cook served dinner, Celestia eagerly asked, "Did you get the message?"

"I did," the cook said quietly, ladling the stew.

"And?" she said, prompting her.

She looked around, and quickly slipped her a note, going back to serving. As Moira came in, the cook said, "There will be no more talk of an uprising. They shut the whole thing down. Sorry, ladies."

"Aww," Colleen groaned.

"What?" Irene said in disbelief.

"Good," Moira said, "Now, we can all go back to normal. Eat your supper, girls."

Celestia ate her meal quickly, eager to look at the note. They all finished, and cleaned the main rooms together, concluding their work for the day. As soon as they were done, she hurried to her room and unfolded the note. It had already been decoded, and at the bottom, it said, *We move at dawn in two days. Everyone who's with us, be ready to fight.*

That's it? she thought, *What are we supposed to do? Where are we supposed to go?* Just then, she heard muffled voices in one of the other servant's rooms. She peered out of her door, and she could hear men's voices two doors down. She tiptoed closer and pressed her ear to the door, "We need to be ready for anything. Whoever sent that note has a plan of attack."

"Do they?" another voice said, "Because that note didn't exactly lay out a detailed summary."

"How much do you expect them to fit on a little note?" yet another voice asked.

"They told us what we needed to know. The rest is up to us," the first voice said.

"So, we're basically forming our own uprising, then," the second voice said.

The floorboard she was standing on creaked as she shifted, and they all stopped talking. The door opened, and she saw five men sitting inside, staring at her. The one who'd opened the door held a pitchfork.

After a short, awkward silence, she said, "Sorry for eavesdropping." She held up the note, "But, I want in."

The Resistance

10

The next day, she snuck down the right-hand upstairs corridor and found Colleen. "Psst," she said, peeking into the bedroom she was cleaning.

"Margarita!" Colleen said with relief, holding her hand over her heart.

"Sorry," she said, "I didn't mean to scare you. I just need to talk to you for a minute."

"Talk to me?" she said, "About what?"

"About this," she said, holding up the note.

Colleen shot her a confused look.

Celestia came all the way into the room and closed the door, crossing to where Colleen was standing, and handing her the note.

She unfolded it and stared at it for a moment, furrowing her brow. Then, her eyes widened, and she looked up at Celestia, "Is this for real?"

She nodded, "But, we have to keep it quiet. Some of the slaves are on the master's side."

"Like Moira?" Colleen asked.

"Yes, exactly like Moira," she said, "If she finds out, she could blow the whole thing. I talked to the men yesterday. They're planning on arming themselves and fighting the guards. They caught wind from a nearby plantation that that's what they're going to do, and they've decided to join forces afterward. I don't know about you, but I'm planning on doing the same."

Her eyes widened again, and she stared at the paper.

"Are you in?"

She nodded, still staring at it.

"Good. We need to talk to Irene, but I'm not sure how we can without unwanted ears. The only times we see her, Moira's there, and she works in the main hallway."

She grabbed a pen from the nightstand and started scribbling on the back of the note, "Why don't we just write it to her? And we can slip her the note at lunch."

She moved closer and looked over her shoulder to see what she was writing. *The plan is a go. Don't tell Moira. We're going to arm ourselves and join the men. They plan on taking down the guards and joining the neighboring plantation tomorrow. In or out?*

At lunch, Colleen slipped the note to Irene, signaling her to be quiet. Irene tucked it into her apron pocket, and they could only hope she was in, and that she'd have a chance to read it. They ate lunch nervously, exchanging sideways glances with each other.

Once everyone had gone back to their corridors to clean, Celestia decided to try to figure out how to save Samson. She snuck past Colleen and ducked into the room at the end of the hall. If the master hadn't entered it since his wife passed, and the servants weren't allowed inside, it was the only room she knew she wouldn't get caught in.

It was a quaint little studio, resembling his office of cherry wood. It seemed she had been a painter, as there were beautiful portraits all over the room, and containers of dried-up paint and brushes. On the wall hung a particularly large painting of a woman with blonde hair and blue eyes. *That must be the mistress,* she thought. She was wearing a yellow dress with a white collar and holding a paintbrush. Celestia could see a slight resemblance to herself. It was strange that another person could look so much like her. *No wonder I remind him so much of her,* she thought.

She shook her head, focusing. There was stationary on the desk, as she'd been hoping. She grabbed a pen and a piece of parchment and began writing a letter, addressing it to Townstin Meat Packers. It stated that the owner of Agri-Grow was very interested in purchasing a certain brown stallion from them immediately, which they had purchased in the recent auction.

She wrote another letter as well, to a made-up address, and quickly snuck back out of the room, returning to her corridor to clean. Once she finished, she slipped down the stairs, flashing the made-up letter to the guard, and saying she just wanted to let her family know she was alive. He nodded, and she slipped the other letter into the mailbox, tucking the fake back into her apron pocket.

After sending out the letter, she returned to the upstairs corridor, and met up with Colleen, taking the carts back down the stairs, and meeting in the servants' dining room for dinner. As they headed to clean the main areas after eating, Irene slipped the note back to Colleen. Once the cleaning was done, Celestia met Colleen in the servants' quarters, and they looked at the note. Irene had written a response to Colleen's message on the back. All it said was, *I'm in.*

Celestia was hardly able to sleep that night. She laid awake, staring at the ceiling. All she could think of was getting out of there, and finding Bridgot. She only hoped that it wasn't too late for Samson. The last thing she thought of before she faded out of consciousness was seeing Bridgot's face again.

She awoke to footsteps outside her door. She got up, quickly dressing in her own clothes. As she peeked out into the hall, she saw the men tiptoeing out, weapons in hand. She grabbed the broom she'd brought with her—it was the only thing she could find. Then, she joined them in the hallway. Through the windows at the end, she could see the sun just peeking over the horizon. The guard was sitting outside the door. One of the men lifted his finger to his lips, telling everyone to be quiet. He slowly turned the knob and swung it open.

The men charged out, trampling the guard. Celestia caught a glimpse of Colleen with a candlestick, and Irene with a mop, stampeding with the rest of them. When they got outside, she could see the pink and purple hues of the sunrise, and the silhouettes of the men fighting the guards. She gestured for the women to follow her, and headed for the stables.

When they got there, she shouted, "Let's get the horses! It'll make for a faster escape!" Irene helped her open the stable doors, and the women rushed inside, pulling the horses out and saddling them. Celestia ran straight to Razel and got her ready to go. She took some weapons as well, since she no longer had any, and leaped on her back. The women with her each climbed onto a horse as well, and they rode out of the stable.

She rode to the aid of the men, firing arrows at the guards. She leaped off Razel's back, swinging her sword, and cutting them down. "Grab a horse and some weapons!" she shouted. The men ran to the stable, getting the remaining horses, and arming themselves properly. As the men were pulling the horses from the stable, it became more challenging for her to fight the guards. She used the moves she'd learned from Farmer Wells. This was the time to test her skills with real opponents. It was easier than she'd expected, but, with so many of them, she still struggled.

As the men rejoined her, she launched herself back up onto Razel's back, and they fought their way off the plantation. They charged down the dirt road, kicking up dust behind them. Celestia didn't look back, but she heard Moira shouting after them as they put distance between them and the plantation.

They rode to the neighboring plantation and saw the slaves there still fighting their guards. Celestia and the men leaped from their horses and hurried to their aid. She noticed she was the only woman fighting. She couldn't believe what cowards they all were. Or, perhaps, it was because no one had trained them. At least they had tried at their own plantation.

As they cut down the last of the guards, one of the slaves they were helping shouted, "Follow us! Everyone's meeting in the town square!"

Their combined group numbered around thirty. They headed to the town square, and Celestia saw many more slaves riding in on their horses. Their number grew to around two hundred. She searched for Bridgot but didn't see him. The massive crowd cheered and waved their swords in the air, celebrating their victory and their freedom.

They rode out of town, passing many of the townspeople, who were standing outside staring, or peering out of their windows in shock. As they reached the edge of town, they rode faster, still cheering, and feeling the wind on their faces. Another large group of slaves rode up, joining them, and increasing their numbers further. She guessed they were around five hundred.

"That's the last of them!" A voice shouted.

"Are you sure?" asked a familiar voice. She turned around quickly, spotting Bridgot. He was leading the group that had just come up, riding upon Samson's back. He looked worried, searching through the crowd of slaves. She realized he was looking for her.

"Bridgot!" she yelled, overjoyed to see him.

His head snapped in her direction, eyes wide. When he saw her, he smiled, showing all his teeth. She could see that over the course of their time on the road, and his time as a slave, his hair had grown. It was long and messy, nearly covering his eyes, and he had grown a ragged beard. His expression went from worried to surprised to overjoyed to relieved, and finally, back to worried again. He rode over to her, looking unsure.

"I'm so sorry," he said, "Truly. I never should have lied to you. We wouldn't be in this mess if it weren't for me."

"It's alright, Bridgot," she said. "I was upset, but I forgive you. Honestly, I'm just so happy to see you right now."

"Really?" he smiled, looking relieved again, and also giddy.

She nodded, smiling coyly.

"Come on, you two!" someone shouted.

"You guys go on," Bridgot said, "We're gonna hit the road."

"Not without a proper send-off!" a woman yelled. Celestia recognized her as the woman who'd been sitting next to her in the wagon when she'd first been captured.

"Yes, you must come with us!" Colleen said.

"Alright," Bridgot said. The two of them caught up to the group, and they journeyed through the forest to a neighboring village. It took a few hours to get through, but when they got there, the villagers started running out of their houses, jumping for joy, and reuniting with their loved ones.

She saw Colleen hop off her horse and get enveloped by hugs from presumably her mother, as well as some children she guessed were siblings. The woman from the wagon, along with the small girl she'd been holding, embraced with another woman and a small boy. She assumed they were sisters, as they looked alike, and he was either her nephew or her son. Celestia remembered how she'd said most of their men had been killed off. She noticed that the majority of the villagers were women and children.

Bridgot and Celestia, along with the other slaves not native to the village, were invited to stay in several of the villagers' homes. She noticed that Irene was among those who didn't live there. She and Bridgot were welcomed by an old widow, who put their horses in her stable, and led them inside her small cottage. It was quaint and cozy, a single level. She had only one extra room, and she offered it to them. It was small, but bigger than the one she'd had at the plantation. It had a full-sized bed, two end tables, and a small closet. It had light, wooden floors, faded yellow wallpaper, and grayish-blue bedding.

"Thank you," Celestia said.

"No, thank *you*," the old woman said. "You, sir, are the reason we're free, and you, miss, I heard were very brave. You fought alongside the men and led several of the women. I am honored to host two such heroes in my home."

"We're humbled by your praise," Bridgot said.

"I'll fix you some dinner," she said, "Tomorrow, there'll be feasting to celebrate."

"That's very kind of you. We'll probably head out in the morning, though," he said.

"Nonsense," she said, "You're our guests of honor. You must stay for the feasting."

As Bridgot tried to object, she waved her hand to cut him off, "I won't have it. Not another word of this. You two wash up and settle in for the night. The bathroom's just to your left if you leave this room." With that, she headed to the kitchen to prepare the meal.

"I guess there's no arguing with her," Bridgot said, turning toward Celestia.

"I suppose not," she said, smiling and looking away.

"Why don't you wash up first," he said.

She nodded, "I don't have any other clothes to change into, though."

"I'm sure the slave traders took all of our stuff," he said, "I'll go see if she has any you can borrow." He went out of the room and crossed the space to the kitchen, where the old widow was cooking dinner. She could see them speaking for a moment, the old woman pointing and gesturing, and then he went into the woman's room and came out with a bundle of clothes. "Here you are," he said, separating a dress from some men's clothing.

"Were those her husband's?" she asked.

He nodded, "Hopefully they fit."

She headed into the bathroom and washed up, changing into the dress. It smelled like mothballs and old people. It was big on her, and she had to tie the waistband tightly to avoid it falling off. It resembled the servant's dress she'd had to wear at the plantation.

As she came out of the bathroom and headed back to the guest room, Bridgot gathered up the clothes and went to wash up. On his way past, their arms brushed against each other, and she shivered. They locked eyes for a moment, and he opened his mouth, as if to say something, but changed his mind, and ducked into the bathroom. She turned back toward the room, and the old woman turned around, saying, "Just set your clothes on the mantle, dear, and I'll get them washed for you."

"Thank you," Celestia said, "That's very kind of you."

"Oh, nothing to it, dear." She began serving up the stew and bringing it over. "I apologize, but all I have is stew. It's the only thing still good, since it was in the freezer. This place hasn't been touched in quite a while . . ." she trailed off, looking away.

"It's alright," she said, sitting, "This is more than enough."

"Honestly, I'm surprised no one else claimed this place in my absence. I'm sure they didn't think I'd be back," she looked down.

Celestia reached over and grabbed her hand, patting it.

The old woman went back to get drinks, filling two glasses with cold water, and bringing them to the table, taking a seat. "I'll wait and serve his up fresh," she said, nodding toward the bathroom, "Shall we eat?"

She nodded, and they ate their stew. When Bridgot came out of the bathroom, she could see that he had shaved his face, and it was smooth and clean, as it had been when they'd met. She could also see that the clothes were far too tight, pulling across his chest, and squeezing his arms.

"Oh dear," the old widow said, "I'm afraid my late husband was a scrawny fellow."

"It'll be alright for a short while," Bridgot said.

Celestia chuckled.

"Let me get you some stew," the woman said, "Just place your clothes on the mantle and take a seat."

Bridgot set down his clothes, and Celestia could see all of his muscles as he moved. He could barely sit, and she thought his pants would rip the moment he bent. As he ate, the woman took their clothes to start the washing.

"What was your name?" Celestia asked, "So we can properly thank our host."

"Mary," she said, "Mary Calvert."

"Ms. Calvert," she nodded respectfully, "I'm Margarita, and this is Bridgot."

"Pleasure making your acquaintances. I'll have these clean in no time," she said. With that, she headed out to clean their things.

"She's very proper," Celestia said.

Bridgot nodded, shoveling stew into his mouth.

She shook her head.

Once he was finished, they headed back to the room. "How'd you do it?" she asked.

He shot her a confused look, "Do what?"

"How'd you get the slaves to fight? How'd you save Samson? How'd you do it?"

"Oh," he said, "That."

"Yeah," she said, shaking her head and smiling, "That."

"Well, it was pretty easy getting the men to fight," he said, "They wanted to be free; they just needed a little push."

"So, you gave them one," she said, sitting on the bed.

"So I gave them one," he agreed, sitting opposite her, "Anyway, once I got the guys at our plantation on board, it was easy to fight off the guards and get out of there. After we were free, we hid out in the forest nearby and tried to figure out how to help the rest of the slaves escape. Some of them bailed once we were free, but I had several brave ones with me. We just had to figure out a way to communicate with the other plantations without getting caught. So, one of them suggested a coded message that only a slave could figure out. It was a riddle about the slave trade that a slave owner wouldn't understand. We snuck through in the night, sticking to the shadows, and distributed the notes. We were all supposed to join forces, fight off the guards, and get the hell out of there. We could only hope that everyone would be able to decipher the message."

She nodded, "That's pretty much what happened."

"I, of course, also had to find you and the horses," he said, "And I had no idea how to do that. But, I asked some of the others about the men I'd seen buy you all, and they told me the ones who'd bought Samson were meat packers. So, he was my first priority. I knew I had to move fast, or it would be too late. A few of the men sympathized with me, and they volunteered to help me rescue him. That same night, after distributing the messages, we broke into the meat packing plant, and there he was, in one of the corrals, waiting to be slaughtered."

She gasped, raising her hand to her mouth. She'd known where he was, but hearing it made it all the more real.

"I freed them all. The men who came with me took horses for themselves as well. The next day, as we lied in wait, we watched as the meat packers searched the town, yelling and screaming, and trying to find the horses. They didn't, of course, and the following day, at dawn, we rode into town and joined the first plantation's fight. We helped several of them on our way through town. I was trying to find you at each one. I knew you and Razel had been bought by the same man, but the other slaves didn't really know who he was. So, I didn't know where to find you. When he told me that was everyone, I panicked, because I hadn't seen you. Then, there you were," he smiled, his gray eyes twinkling. The look in his eyes was one she'd never seen before. He looked as though there was nowhere else he'd rather be. She didn't know how else to explain it. He seemed almost captivated.

"You saved the whole town," she said, looking at him in awe.

The twinkle in his eyes turned foggy, and he grew serious, "So, what happened to you?"

"Nothing interesting," she said, "I had to clean, and Razel was put to work in the field. As soon as I heard talk of an uprising, I knew it was you." She looked at him, "And, I wanted to get out of there as soon as possible. So, I got the other ladies involved, and I worked out the plan with the men. When the day came, I fought with a broomstick."

They both chuckled at that. "I'm sure that was quite the sight," he said, his twinkle returning.

"I'm sure it was," she agreed. "Anyway, I led the women to the stable, and we freed the horses and stole some *real* weapons. Then, the men did the same, and we rode to the next plantation to join forces."

He nodded, "It seems you fought bravely."

"So I'm told," she said, twisting a strand of hair between her fingers, "But really, I was just trying to get out of there and find you." She paused, looking up and meeting his eyes, "Farmer Wells' training did the rest."

"Well, I'm glad we stayed with him as long as we did, then," he said, "And, I'm glad you're alright." He looked like there was more he wanted to say, but he simply climbed up under the covers, got comfortable, and said, "Goodnight, Celestia."

On hearing him say her name, she felt the butterflies start fluttering tenfold. Somehow, it sounded different when he said it. She could barely whisper back, "Goodnight, Bridgot."

It Takes a Village

11

They awoke to Ms. Calvert knocking on the door, "Wake up, dearies! The feasting is about to begin. I've got your clothes waiting for you." They rolled out of bed, and rubbed their sleepy eyes, stretching.

"I'll let you get dressed first," Celestia said.

He looked down at his too-tight ensemble. It appeared as though the pants had been cutting off circulation in the night. "Thank you," he said.

She nodded, too tired to laugh at him, and headed to the bathroom. When she got back, he was happily dressed in his own clothes. She dressed quickly, and they headed out to the town square.

It was decorated with ribbons and balloons, and the villagers were celebrating, singing and dancing. Children were running around, laughing and playing. They all started cheering when they saw them. Someone shouted, "Three cheers for our heroes!"

They gave them three *hurrahs!* and brought them to the center of town to honor them. "We are free, and it's all thanks to you," Colleen said, "We are forever in your debt."

"Really, everyone, please," Bridgot said, "We're just like everybody else. All this isn't necessary."

"Of course it is," Ms. Calvert said, coming out of the house to join them, "You started the uprising. You led us. And she," she pointed at Celestia, "showed us women what we should strive for: to be able to defend ourselves."

"I wish I could fight like you," Colleen said.

"Exactly," a woman in the crowd said, coming forward. She had dark hair and dark eyes, and a large, hooked nose. "And once you all leave—all of you not from this village—we'll be exactly where we were before, because we can't fight like you. Most of our men were killed off. And, as soon as the townspeople come to hunt us down, or the slave traders raid us again, we'll be right back we started."

The cheering quieted, and the villagers looked morose.

"No, you won't," Celestia said, "I won't let that happen."

"And just how do you propose to prevent it?" the woman asked.

"By teaching you," she said, "All of you."

"Margarita," Bridgot whispered sharply.

"How could you teach all of us?" Colleen asked.

"Simple," she said, "We'll host a class for all of you, and show you what to do. After that, it's up to all of you to practice and train on your own."

"How about tomorrow?" Ms. Calvert asked, "In the square."

"It's a date," Celestia said.

Everyone cheered again and began bringing out the food for the feast. They set up several long tables and brought out chairs for them. They ate in the middle of the square, and everyone celebrated—eating, drinking, dancing, and having fun.

After filling their bellies with warm, fresh food, Celestia decided it was time for a dance. She pulled Bridgot onto the dirt-trodden dance floor, despite his protests, and began dancing. She didn't know exactly what she was doing, as she'd only ever been taught ballroom dancing, and the dances of the villagers were far more wild and risqué. However, several of the villagers showed her and Bridgot how to move, and she caught on fairly quickly. It reminded her of playing the piano: she'd get lost in the music and the rhythm, and let passion take over. It guided her movements, rather than the structure and precision of the palace dances. Honestly, this type of dancing felt more natural, and it was a lot more fun.

She and Bridgot danced close, and she could feel his every move, his every breath. His hands went around her waist, and he pulled her into a dip. She snapped back up, her hair flying freely around her. He clasped her hand, and she spun out, and back into him. Each touch electrified her, and she got lost in the dance.

When the music stopped, they locked eyes, frozen for a moment, breathing each other in. His soft, gray eyes made her hazy. As they separated from each other, they realized the villagers were staring at them. Suddenly, they all started cheering and telling them what amazing dancers they were.

"That was incredible! Well done! Bravo!" they shouted.

Celestia fiddled nervously with her hair and shot a sideways glance at Bridgot. He was looking at her in awe, and she could tell he was feeling the way she was. Neither of them was entirely sure what happened, but they knew there was something between them that was entirely new.

As they went to bed that night, neither of them said a word. She was paralyzed, just lying in close proximity. She could barely breathe as she drifted off to sleep.

After lunch, the villagers gathered in the square, and they set up a training space, with an area for dueling, and a line of targets for archery practice. They huddled together, awaiting instruction from Celestia and Bridgot.

"Alright," Celestia said, "Bridgot here will be in charge of the sword training. So, we'll start half of you with him, and he'll teach you how to duel. The other half of you will be with me. I'll be in charge of the archery training, teaching you all how to shoot properly. Once we feel our groups have been sufficiently trained, we will switch. After that, you'll just have to practice what you've learned on your own, for we really must set out. Any questions?"

"Who's with who?" someone asked.

Celestia stepped forward off the stage and walked directly toward the middle of the group. She pointed to which side the people in the middle should go as she walked between them, parting everyone in a clean line. "So," she said, turning toward the group to her left, "All of you will start with Bridgot. Get going." She turned toward the group on her right, as the ones behind her followed Bridgot to the dueling space, "All of you, come with me."

She led them over to the row of targets. "Okay," she said, "We'll start with everyone showing me what you've got, and work from there. There are nine targets, so . . ." she pointed to the people at the front of the group, "The nine of you, line up here."

They lined up at the markers that had been placed a ways from the targets. There was a bow and quiver at each target. "Alright, everyone grab your bow and quiver, and get ready," Celestia said. They did so and waited.

Once they were all ready, she said, "Take aim!" They notched their arrows and took their stances. "Fire!" she shouted.

The first line of people fired their arrows, with only two of them actually hitting the target at all. Both were in an outer ring. She sighed. "Okay, everyone form a line," she beckoned for them all to bring the line closer, "You nine at the back. The next nine, line up."

She went through the entire group of people—a group of about a hundred and fifty—and found only thirty people with any sort of shooting ability.

"Okay, the first nine people, line up again," she said. Once they were lined up, she had them take their stances. She walked down the line and corrected each of their stances individually: "Legs closer together, legs farther apart, try not to bend so much at the waist, lower your bow."

After everyone's stance had been corrected, she had them fire. This time, almost all of them hit the targets. Everyone stared in amazement and excitement. "Next!" she shouted. She kept the line moving and worked on each person's stance.

Once they reached the end of the line, she had them go again, continuing to correct each stance, and help them improve. Some of them learned quickly, starting to hit the target more consistently. She even had a few of them hit bullseyes. When it was time for dinner, they stopped, and the tables were brought into the square again for feasting.

Everyone chattered excitedly about how much they were learning. As Bridgot took his seat next to her, she whispered, "So, how'd it go with your group?"

He smiled, scooping some potatoes onto his plate. "They're terrible," he said through his teeth, "Easy targets. But, they're willing to learn, and that's what's important. Some of the men not native to the village have skill with a blade. But, the rest . . ." he shook his head.

"This might take longer than we thought," she said.

"No," he said, "We'll teach them what we can, and then, it's up to them to practice with each other. We have to get going." He paused, looking at her, "That is . . . if you want to. I'm not going to force you to come with me to my village anymore."

"Thank you," she said, twisting her spoon in her soup and biting her lip. She had forgotten that he'd wanted to take her to his village. Traveling with him had become so natural, she no longer thought about the destination.

She looked at him, "But, I am curious about this prophecy nonsense, and I'd like to see what that's all about, and perhaps clear it up if I can."

He smiled, "Well alright, then. How'd it go with your group?"

"Surprisingly well," she said, "They are terrible, but they learn quickly. I saw vast improvement today."

They continued the next few days to train them. Celestia felt as though her group was quickly becoming skilled archers, so long as they kept practicing. She continued giving them tips to improve, but she didn't have to do much training. She was only waiting for Bridgot to finish training his group, which was taking much longer. It was far more difficult and rigorous to learn sword fighting than archery. There was more to it, and it was harder to give everyone enough one-on-one attention.

He spent a day learning what he was working with, a day helping everyone with their stances and footwork, a day helping with their defensive moves, and a day helping them with their offensive moves, as Farmer Wells had done with Celestia. He spent one more day helping them put it all together and letting them practice with each other.

On the fourth and fifth days, Celestia left her group to practice on their own and came to help Bridgot with his training, so they could give everyone more one-on-one attention. She sparred with several of the villagers and gave them tips to build on what Bridgot had told them. It honestly helped her as well, to get in more practice, and refresh some of her own moves.

The next day, they switched groups, and each of them began again with their training. It felt like déjà vu, as they repeated the previous five days with a different group of villagers. There was still plenty for them to learn, but it would take a lot of practice. Bridgot and Celestia felt they had taught them all they could, without staying too long.

As they dueled with the second group Bridgot had trained, ready for it to be their last day, a young boy came running into the village, shouting, "They're coming! They're coming! The slave traders are coming!"

Everyone started whispering to each other in panic. Some people started running to their houses, some kids started crying, and some people froze.

Bridgot stepped toward the middle of the square. "Everyone!" he shouted, "Please, don't panic!"

"Easy for you to say," the dark-haired woman with the hooked nose said, "You don't live here! You can just leave!"

"This is the perfect opportunity for all of you to practice what you've learned!" he said. "You've all been living in fear! Fear that you can't defend yourselves without your men! The slave traders know this! They prey upon your weakness! They don't believe you can defend yourselves! They see you as easy targets!" he paused, "This is your chance to prove them wrong! This is your chance to make *them* fear *you*! Tonight will not be another raid! Tonight, we will take a stand! Tonight, we will meet them with strength, not fear! And, tonight, we will beat them!"

The village erupted in cheers. Bridgot shot a sideways glance at Celestia. She smiled, giving him a nod to show she fully supported his plan.

"Alright, everyone, gather round!" he said. The whole village huddled around him, and he told them the plan.

They put the children in the bunkers a few of them had in their homes. They were hidden under the houses, covered by rugs and bookcases. The old women joined the children to watch over them, since they weren't strong enough to fight.

Celestia chose the best archers. Since she'd trained them, she knew who they were. They positioned themselves on the rooftops to lie in wait, with Celestia at the helm. The rest of the villagers armed themselves with swords, and hid in the shadows, waiting for Bridgot's command.

The whole village was dark when the slave traders rode up. There were about fifty of them. *The arrogance!* Celestia thought, *They come with only fifty men to kidnap people in a village of around six hundred.* They were almost all burly and brawny, armed with their swords. Though, none of them actually had their swords drawn. *They assume this will be an easy fight,* she thought.

As they neared, Celestia motioned for the archers to take aim. *Hold,* she thought, keeping her hand up to let them know. They hopped off their horses, trying to sneak up silently on the sleeping villagers.

"Fire!" Celestia yelled, breaking the silence. The slave traders were caught completely off guard as the archers shot their arrows, taking down nearly a quarter of them.

"Attack!" came Bridgot's yell, and the remaining villagers jumped out, swinging their swords. The men finally found their bearings, and drew their swords, fighting back.

Celestia had the archers take aim again, "Fire at will!" she shouted, jumping down from the rooftop, and drawing her sword. She wasn't about to miss the chance to practice on a real opponent. She swung and twirled and cut down several of them with ease. It didn't take long for the remaining men to retreat toward their horses and ride away. They stumbled and tripped over each other, some of them missing the horses, and running blindly after the rest of them.

The villagers shouted and cheered, some throwing rocks at the slave traders and yelling after them, some hugging each other and dancing. In the midst of the celebration going on around them, Bridgot and Celestia locked eyes and smiled. Their skills had improved greatly, and they felt ready to take on the world. Not only that, but they had liberated this village. No one would mess with them anymore. It was a moment of pure elation.

The villagers lifted the two of them into the air, cheering for their heroes. They laughed, accepting the praise this time around for sake of the moment. As they surfed across the sea of villagers, they passed by each other, smiling and laughing, and their hands brushed against each other. For a moment, they were the only two people, floating.

As their feet touched the ground, they met up with each other and headed for the widow's house to grab their supplies and their horses. It was time for them to leave. As they got there, she was waiting for them, horses ready.

"This was the best way for me to thank you," she said, "I know you've been trying to leave, and you care not for a hero's send-off. So, I readied your horses for you. The saddlebags are filled. I've put in some food, clothes that fit, and weapons for you, as well as a few odds and ends, like a pot and a fire starter."

They paused for a moment, unsure of what to say. "Thank you," Celestia said finally, "You're right. This is the best thanks we could ask for."

"I figured you two would sneak off after the fight, while everyone was celebrating."

"Apparently, you were right," Bridgot said, smiling.

"There's a clearing not too far from here," Ms. Calvert said, "Stick to the left side of the river. It's through a tangled web of vines most wouldn't attempt to go through. If you can find it, you'll be safe there tonight."

"Thank you," Bridgot said.

"We really appreciate this," Celestia said, hugging her.

She shrugged off the hug, looking as though she was trying not to cry, "Off you go then, dearies."

They led their horses right past the villagers, who were too caught up in their celebration to notice. Once they were outside the village, they mounted their steeds and rode off into the night, pausing to look back for only a moment.

They kept to the left side of the river as Ms. Calvert had suggested. When they found a tangled wall of vines, Bridgot slid off Samson's back to check it out. The vines, which appeared impassible, peeled back like a curtain, revealing a small, but secure little clearing. Celestia dismounted, and the clearing turned out to be just the right size for them and their horses. The vines offered some protection against the nighttime chill, which helped since they couldn't risk a fire. They nestled against their horses' sides for warmth and fell fast asleep.

Bridgot's Village

12

As the soft glow of the sunrise peeked in overhead, glistening through the nest of vines, Celestia felt Bridgot nudging her to wake up. They got their horses ready, and let them graze and get a drink from the river while they scrounged up a breakfast of leftover stew from Ms. Calvert.

They set out toward Bridgot's village once more, getting lost in their thoughts as they were waking up.

When they stopped again for lunch, Celestia asked, "You do know how to get there from here, right? I mean, where are we, anyway?"

Bridgot laughed, "I always know my way home." When she looked at him skeptically, he said, "I've passed through this area before. It's a little off-course, but not terribly far from where we were. It puts us back a few days, but we'll get there."

She nodded, filling up a canteen in the river.

"The only problem is the money's running low," he said, "My village granted me enough for the journey there and back, but since the slave traders took it, the supply Ms. Calvert provided us is a bit more sparse." He pulled out some jerky and greens for their lunch, and they ate quickly, looking out across the water. The forest was beautiful, green and golden, thriving with life. She thought about how different her life had become, and how she might never have seen anything this beautiful if she hadn't left home.

They got back into the routine of the road, traveling by day, taking sleep in shifts at night, stopping in the occasional village to rest and recover.

They kept their stops to a minimum, conserving their funds as much as possible. Just over a week went by, and Celestia was beginning to wonder just how big of a set-back getting captured had caused.

As they were trotting along one day, Celestia said, "Why don't we stop for lunch?"

"I don't think we should stop just yet," Bridgot said.

"Why not? Aren't you getting hungry?"

He turned to smile at her.

She shot him a confused look, "Why are you smiling?"

"Welcome to my village," he said.

She paused as the realization slowly hit her, "We made it?"

"We made it," he said, "It's just over that hill."

Elation shot through her. After all this time, all their travels, they were finally here! It had been over two months since she'd left home, and they had reached his village at last. They galloped over the hill, and she could see a large village ahead. The homes were circular and appeared almost like huts. There were dirt roads going every which way, and people milling about. They paused to take it in.

"Home," Bridgot said.

"We finally made it," Celestia said.

They looked at each other, nodded, and rode into town. As they neared, the villagers gathered in the square, staring at them. A few of the elders came forward to greet them, and as they reached the square, a woman came running up to them, screaming, "Bridgot!"

She looked to be in her fifties, with brown hair that was graying, and gray eyes that looked very familiar. She wore a peasant's dress and a bonnet. When she reached them, Bridgot hopped off Samson's back, and they embraced. Behind her, a man of about the same age, two women who appeared in their late twenties, one holding a baby, two men of about the same, a teenage girl, a preteen girl, and a young boy all came running up.

Celestia climbed down from Razel's back as Bridgot was enveloped in hugs. "Bridgot's back!" they cheered.

"Princess Celestia!" a village elder silenced the crowd, stepping forward. He wore a long, colorful robe, and a large hat.

Celestia froze.

"Welcome," he said, "Your presence is a blessing."

She felt the stares of the villagers boring through her, but was unable to respond.

"We have journeyed a long way," Bridgot said, "and faced many trials along the road. I'm sure she could use some rest."

She looked at him, full of relief.

"Of course!" the elder said, "We shall celebrate your arrival with a feast!"

"She's welcome to stay with us," the woman who'd first hugged Bridgot said.

The elder nodded. "Very well," he continued, "Set out the tables!"

The villagers hurried to fulfill the elder's orders, pulling out tables, chairs, and food.

"Come on," the woman said, "We'll get your horses in the stable and show you to your room before the feast begins."

The older man began leading Samson, as the others ushered Bridgot away excitedly. Celestia followed, leading Razel behind her.

"I've never met a princess before," the woman said, lingering back to walk with her, "I hope you don't find it improprietous, but rather than try to figure out how to act, I should like to simply treat you as any other guest."

Celestia breathed a sigh of relief, "I'd prefer it. Being a princess is truly exhausting sometimes."

She smiled, "Wonderful."

When they arrived at their house, a beautiful, quaint little cottage with a large stable, rolling fields of crops, and a second, smaller house nearby on the property, they went straight to the stable and got Samson and Razel situated.

They all filed inside the main house, which reminded her vaguely of Farmer Wells' house, just darker colors, and a circular shape. The older woman grouped everyone together. "So," she said, "Celestia, I believe formal introductions are in order."

Celestia looked over the group once more, anxious to learn who they all were. She spotted Bridgot in the back, rolling his eyes.

"Well, Bridgot you know, of course. I'm his mother, Katherine. You can call me Mrs. Brown."

When she said the last name, Celestia's eyes widened, and she had to hide her reaction. That was the name Bridgot had given at the inns they'd stayed at, which she'd assumed was just a cover name. *That was his real name?* she thought in surprise. She quickly quelched her thoughts as his mother continued.

"This is my husband, his father, George," she gestured to the man who appeared close to her same age. They both had wrinkles, but not too many.

Their skin looked rough, like they'd worked hard all their lives, and weathered their share of tough times. They both had graying brown hair. His father had brown eyes, and his mother's eyes were gray, just like Bridgot's. His father was tall and burly, with a full beard. His mother was plump, but not overly so, and just slightly shorter than Celestia.

"This is our oldest daughter, Margaret, and her husband, James," she gestured to the woman holding the baby, and one of the men of the same age. The woman looked like a younger clone of her mother, and the man had black hair, green eyes, and a short, scruffy beard. He was muscular, but not burly. He was actually close to Bridgot's size.

"Their daughter, Anne Marie," she motioned to the baby in her arms, "and their son, Phillip," she waved to the young boy. He had to be no more than four. He had black hair like his father and gray eyes like his mother. "They live in our guest cottage. You may have seen it on the way in," she pointed out the window toward the smaller house.

"This is our oldest son, Bryan, and his wife, Brianne," she pointed to the other man and woman close to the age of their daughter and son-in-law. He looked just like his father, but with a shorter beard. His wife had black hair and brown eyes, and she was thin and petite. "They're newlyweds," she said, "So, we haven't figured out where they're going to live, yet. Our Bryan is going to take over the farm in his father's stead." She beamed with pride.

"Bridgot is our middle child," she continued, "This is our daughter, Kyja," she waved to the teenage girl. She was thin—even thinner than Celestia and Brianne. She had brown hair and gray eyes, like most of her family.

"And, last but not least," she said, "This is our youngest daughter, Luanne." She nodded to the preteen girl. She had brown hair and brown eyes, like her father. She was plump and pudgy, but still cute.

"And that's all of us," she concluded, "I'll show you to the guest room, and then we can join everyone for the feast."

As his mother led her upstairs, she felt some relief. She had thought perhaps one of the women was with Bridgot. So, it pleased her to know they were his mother and sisters. For such a small cottage, it had a surplus of rooms upstairs. There was one for his parents, one for his older brother and his wife, and the guest room on the second level. Then, up a ladder, Bridgot's room and each of his younger sisters' rooms on the third level.

The guest room was average size, with a full bed, a nightstand, a dresser, and a small closet. It was faded blue and gray, and light wood. It had a small window over the bed, which she could see the village through. She realized this would be the first time since they set out traveling together, besides their time as slaves, that they wouldn't be sleeping in the same room. It seemed unnatural somehow.

They all headed out of the house for the feast, and she was offered a seat at the elders' table, at the right hand of the head elder. She searched for Bridgot, but he was being pushed along to another table with his family.

"We apologize for the inconvenience, pulling you away from your kingdom. We wouldn't dream of such a thing if not for the prophecy," the elder said.

"Elder Gunther," another of the elders said, "We should not discuss such things lightly."

"And you, Elder Lukehart," Elder Gunther said, "should remember your place."

Elder Lukehart sucked in a breath, biting his lip. He turned to his plate and said nothing further.

"Yes," Celestia said, "Well, my curiosity has gotten the better of me. What exactly is this prophecy?"

"It states that a princess from a great merged kingdom, born at the turn of the century—"

"No, I know what it says," she said, cutting him off, "Bridgot told me. But, what exactly is this 'terrible evil,' and how am I supposed to 'save the land' from it?"

Elder Gunther looked around at the other elders. After a long pause, he said, "I think now is not the time to discuss such things. Tomorrow, we shall invite you and Bridgot to a private meeting, and tell you what you need to know. Tonight, let us simply celebrate and rest up."

Celestia opened her mouth to say something more, but Elder Gunther waved his hand, cutting her off.

"Please, relax, and enjoy the feast. Your arrival in our village is an occasion for great joy!"

She sighed but said nothing further. After all the time she'd waited, she supposed she could wait one more day for answers. The villagers feasted and danced, and it reminded her of the village they'd liberated from the slave traders.

As they cleared away the tables and made a bonfire, she searched for Bridgot. She caught sight of his family, but he wasn't with them. Suddenly, she felt a tap on her shoulder. Bridgot set down a large log near the fire and invited her to sit beside him.

They didn't have a chance to talk, however, as the elders began telling stories to the assembled villagers. They passed around sticks and marshmallows, and everyone toasted them up to eat as they listened.

After several tales had been woven, the villagers began dancing. Celestia thought of the dance she and Bridgot had shared, and wasn't sure if she dared dance with him in front of his village. Luckily, Bridgot clasped her arm and whispered, "Come with me."

They slowly backed away from the fire into the shadows, and she followed him away from the celebration. He led her to his stable and sat on a stool beside Samson. She pulled up a stool next to him.

"What did the elders say?" he asked, stroking Samson's mane.

"They want to meet with us tomorrow to discuss the prophecy," she said.

He nodded contemplatively, "Us . . . or you?"

"They said both of us. You are the warrior of the prophecy, are you not? This affects you, too."

"I think this is where my part in the tale comes to an end. Beyond bringing you here, I don't think they need me anymore," he looked away, pressing his face against his horse's.

"Of course they do," she said, "You told me the prophecy says, and I quote, 'With the help of a great warrior, solver of the unsolvable riddle, born in the village of Chance.' You're supposed to help me fulfill the prophecy. I can't do it without you."

He turned to look at her, a strange expression on his face. After a pause, he said, "You can do anything. You're a princess. You're a warrior. You're a genuine person, and you have a pure heart. You don't need the help of a farm boy from Kataran to do incredible things."

"You're wrong," she said, "I do. I do need your help. I need *you*."

He looked her dead in the eye then, an expression of amazement and yearning on his face. She felt a chill run all through her. There was a tangible feeling of closeness between them, and it made her weak and strong at the same time. She wanted to lunge forward and press her lips to his, even though she knew she shouldn't.

"Your family seems nice," she said, opting to break the tension before she did something she'd regret, "It was very sweet of them to let me stay."

Bridgot shook his head, snapping out of his trance, "Well, where else would you have stayed?"

"Good point," she chuckled, "But, still, they seem nice."

He stretched his arm to scratch his back, "Yeah, I guess."

Celestia eyed him questioningly, "You guess?"

He sighed, "I guess I just . . . don't really feel like I belong." He looked at her, smiling ironically, "You wouldn't know anything about that."

She shot him a wry grin. After a moment, she said, "So, why don't you belong?"

"Well," he said, "Everyone prefers my brother to me. He's the strong one, the manly one, the one taking over the farm. He's always been the favorite. Nothing I've ever done has compared to him. Even after solving the riddle, no one believed I was warrior material; I was scrawny and weak. I relished the chance to prove them wrong. But, now that we're back, despite everything we've been through, and how strong I've grown, it's like . . . nothing's changed." He looked at her with an expression of pure disappointment.

She looked down.

"My older sister has always been like a second mother. She's helped our mother take care of us kids her whole life. Now, she has a family of her own, but she still takes care of us. Her husband is an orphan, so he has no land to inherit for them. That's why they live here. Mother loves it. As for my younger sisters, Kyja and I have always been close. She's the only one who understands me around here. She's the odd one out of the girls, just like I am of the boys. Luanne is the youngest. She's my father's little princess; she gets anything she wants by batting an eye." He looked up apologetically, "I'm sorry. I didn't mean anything by that."

It took Celestia a moment to realize why he was apologizing. When she did, she said, "No offense taken. I haven't really thought about being a princess for a while now. I know it wasn't a jab directed at me."

"Good," he said, "because it wasn't."

"So, did you know your brother was married?"

He looked at her in questioning surprise.

"Your mother said they were newlyweds."

He leaned back as he realized what she was saying, "They got married the day before I left," he said, "So I could be there to witness another moment of my brother being better than me. And my niece, Anne Marie, was born shortly before I solved the riddle, so I haven't missed a thing."

She nodded.

"Now, my parents are petitioning the village council to grant them more land, so they can build a second guest house for my brother. When my sisters get married, their husbands' families will have to provide their homes. One day, after we've moved out, my brother will get the main house, since he's taking over the farm, and my parents will move to one of the guest houses. As for me, I'll have to petition the village council to receive my own plot of land."

She looked down again, "I know what it's like to be the black sheep of the family."

"I know," he said, "You've told me. But," he leaned forward, "You haven't told me why."

"Well, I don't want to be queen. I never have. But, I'm an only child and sole heir to the throne. I've been training my whole life. My mother is very strict about my training," she paused, looking away. She hadn't thought of her mother for a while. It was a strange thought, almost foreign to her now.

"What about your father?" he asked.

She turned back around, coming back to their conversation, "He died in a war when I was a baby. I never knew him."

"I'm sorry," he said, grabbing her hand.

"It's alright. The only thing that bothered me was knowing nothing about him my whole life. His death tore my mother apart. She refused to speak of him, ever. I never even knew what he looked like."

He squeezed her hand empathetically.

"Farmer Wells knew him, you know."

He dropped her hand, looking at her curiously, "Really?"

She nodded, "He fought beside him in the war. He was his right-hand man. That's how he figured out who I was. Apparently, I have my father's eyes."

"He knew?"

Celestia nodded again, "I didn't know if I could trust you right away. It was safer not to say anything. Farmer Wells promised to keep my secret. That's why he trained me, because of my father."

Bridgot looked down silently. After a pause, he nodded. "So . . . why did you run away?" he asked.

"I was four months away from my coronation. I didn't want to be queen. All I've ever known was life inside the palace walls. I felt like a prisoner in my own home. I just wanted to be free. I wanted adventure, excitement, and maybe, to find out who I am. I've gone so long only knowing half of myself. Since my mother refused to tell me anything, I thought maybe I could just find it out here, in the world."

He nodded, giving her a half smile.

"Farmer Wells told me about my father. It was like filling in something that had been missing. That's why I wanted to stay—it was sort of like he was becoming a father to me. He was giving me something I'd never had, that I yearned for," she paused, "I suppose it sounds silly."

"No," he said, "It doesn't." He took her hand again, looking in her eyes, and the tension returned. She felt even closer to him, after sharing things so personal to each of them.

"Come on," he said suddenly, "I want to show you something."

He led her by the hand, half running into the house. They went up the stairs, and he pulled her up the ladder to the third-story, and into his room. It was a beautiful little room. It looked like an attic, and it had a mattress on the floor, a rug, and a few shelves. He pulled her to the window, and she looked out.

She could see the whole town. The lights in the houses twinkled, accompanied by the stars. The bonfire was still raging, like a burning beacon, and the villagers were dancing around it. Celestia was taken by its beauty.

"Beautiful, isn't it?" he said.

She nodded.

"Come on. We'd better sneak back to the fire before someone gets the wrong idea."

A Quest Assigned

13

The next day, Elder Lukehart appeared at the door with a summons for Princess Celestia and Bridgot.

"Of course, right away, Elder Lukehart," Bridgot's mother said. She turned inside, where everyone was seated at the breakfast table, eating, "Bridgot, you and our honored guest are requested. The elders would like to speak with you."

Bridgot nodded, looking at Celestia, and wiping his mouth. He rose and headed to the door.

"Excuse me," Celestia said, rising, "Thank you for the breakfast." She headed over to Bridgot, and they followed Elder Lukehart.

He led them to the largest hut, right in the center of town, at the head of the square.

"Town Hall," Bridgot whispered, "This is where the council of elders assembles." They went inside, and the other elders were assembled around a huge table at the back of the room. It sat upon a large platform. The rest of the room was full of chairs facing the platform, which she guessed were for village meetings.

"Ah," Elder Gunther said, rising, and opening his arms in greeting, "Welcome." He sat at the head of the table, the other elders seated all around, save for three vacant chairs. They rose after he did, and waited for the three of them to circle around to the seats beside Elder Gunther. When they reached them, everyone sat in unison.

After a brief pause, Elder Gunther began, "We have called this meeting to discuss the matter of The Great Prophecy. Bring it forth."

A couple of elders at the end of the table got up, pulled a large scroll off the wall, and unfurled it along the table.

"It states, 'A princess from a great merged kingdom, born at the turn of the century, will be the one to save the land from a terrible evil, with the help of a great warrior, solver of the unsolvable riddle, born in the village of Chance.' Chance is spelled with a capital 'C,' which means it is a name—the name of our own village of Kataran. The warrior of the prophecy is our Bridgot," he gestured toward Bridgot then, who waved awkwardly. "He solved the unsolvable riddle. He brought us the princess. This is Princess Celestia of Ivétoiless," he gestured to Celestia now, "The princess of the prophecy."

Several of the elders began whispering excitedly.

Elder Gunther motioned for them to quiet down, "Everyone, please. We have known of the prophecy all our lives. We waited for the turn of the century to discover who the princess was. We then waited for the one who would solve the riddle. Then, we awaited their arrival in our village. And now, here we sit."

After a long pause, in which everyone began looking at each other, uncertain, Bridgot spoke up, "So, what now?"

"Now," Elder Gunther said, "the real mission begins for the two of you."

"What do you mean?" Celestia asked.

"Well, you must fulfill the prophecy and save us all."

"And how exactly do we do that?" she asked.

He paused, seeming flustered, "Well . . ." he cleared his throat, "We don't know."

"What do you mean, you don't know?" she said.

"We can't be expected to have *all* the answers."

"What?" she practically yelled, rising, "After sending him to fetch me, after all we endured to return here, after all that talk, that big opening speech, the recital of the prophecy, and you don't even know what we're supposed to do?" Her voice rose as she spoke, growing angrier with each word.

"Elder Gunther," Bridgot said, "What *do* you know?"

He cleared his throat again, looking like he'd rather be anywhere but there, evoking the wrath of a princess. He attempted to compose himself as he said, "Only The Oracle knows. You must journey to see her. She can tell you what you're supposed to do. She's the one who prophesied everything."

"And where can we find her?" he asked.

"In the land of Abyumo, on the border between the territories of the wizards and the dragon riders."

"Abyumo?" it was Bridgot's turn to yell, rising, as Celestia marveled at the thought of wizards and dragon riders, "That's just north of the land of Duwazo, where the kingdom of Ivétoiless is, where we just came from!"

"What?" Celestia shrieked, "Are you kidding me?"

"Why didn't you tell me before I left?" he said, "We could have gone straight there, instead of coming back here for nothing!"

"Now, see here!" Elder Gunther stood up as well, "Have some respect for your elders!"

"Respect? After this?" Bridgot said, "We have a mission to save the world from darkness, we could already be finding out what we're supposed to do, *you* caused this huge delay, and you demand respect?" He practically spat.

Elder Gunther looked like he wasn't sure whether to blow up or sit down and stop talking.

"Look," Celestia said, trying to calm herself, "We can't get back the time you've cost us, but I want to know everything you know that we don't. I want to avoid any future *mistakes*." She emphasized the word, eyeing Elder Gunther meaningfully.

He swallowed, "The prophecy goes on to say, 'In order to ensure success, a warrior from each of the races of elf and dwarf must also aid our victors.' So, you must journey north from here, through the land of the elves, and the land of the dwarves, to acquire a warrior from each to help you. You must do this on your way to The Oracle."

"Is that all?" she snarled.

"Yes," Elder Gunther said, "That's all I know."

"Bridgot," she said, "Let's go."

Bridgot shot one last glare at Elder Gunther before following Celestia out of Town Hall. She couldn't help but notice Elder Lukehart chuckling to himself on their way past. She imagined he was quite delighted to see Elder Gunther put in his place.

Once they got outside, she said, "When shall we set out?"

"How about dawn?" Bridgot said, "I think we'll be able to reach Gliken, the land of the elves, by the following afternoon."

"Perfect," Celestia said, walking off.

"Where are you going?" he called.

"For a walk."

"Hey," Bridgot said, walking up to where Celestia was sitting on a boulder just inside the forest.

"Hey," she said, giving him a half smile.

"Is this where you've been all day?"

She nodded, "Yeah."

He stopped as he reached her, and looked in the same direction as her, off into the trees.

"I just needed to calm down and clear my head for a while," she said, watching the bright green leaves rustle in the breeze against a background of softly glowing green-tinted gold.

He nodded, resting his hands on his belt, "Today's meeting did not go well."

"You can say that again," she said, rolling her eyes.

He paused, "Everyone's been wondering where you were—my family, I mean."

Celestia looked at him, "I'm sure a lot of people are wondering where I am."

Bridgot pursed his lips, considering, "That's probably true." He scratched his back uncomfortably.

"But, it seems, I'm somehow destined to 'save the world,'" she sighed.

"It's a big burden to dump on anyone's shoulders," he said, seeming like he wanted to reach out and comfort her, but he stopped himself.

"Tell me about it," she said, curling her knees to her chest, "Everyone's counting on me. And, I don't even know what I'm supposed to do."

He placed his strong, coarse hand gently on her shoulder, "You're not alone. You weren't destined to save anyone by yourself. You'll have help from the elves, the dwarves, and . . . from me."

She looked up.

"I may not be anyone's idea of a warrior, but I'll do my best to help you, and to protect you," he said, looking at her humbly and earnestly.

She smiled, lowering her knees, "Thank you." She did her best to convey her gratitude in a look.

He leaned closer, looking very much like he wanted to kiss her.

Her eyes grew wide, and she couldn't decide if she should jump up and change the subject, or follow her impulse and let those soft, sweet lips caress her own.

"Bridgot!" Bryan called, entering the forest.

They both jumped a little, quickly moving apart.

His brother eyed them suspiciously as he neared. After a pause, he said, "Mother sent me to see what's taking so long. We should be back at the house before nightfall." He shot them both another meaningful look, lingering on Bridgot.

"Yes, I just found her," Bridgot said, "We're on our way back."

As his brother turned to head back to the house, Bridgot said, "Shall we?" and offered her his hand.

Celestia nodded, taking it and rising from the boulder she'd been perched on.

They headed straight for the house, and when they went inside, his mother was waiting. "Bridgot, good, you found her," she said, sandwiching his face between her hands and kissing him, "Celestia, dear, we were worried about you. Are you hungry?"

"Yes, thank you," she said.

As his mom began serving up a plate, Celestia took a seat, adding, "I didn't intend to make anyone worry about me. The meeting with the elders earlier was immensely upsetting. I just needed some time alone."

"Oh, no," she said, "What happened?"

Celestia shot her a confused look, "Bridgot didn't tell you?"

"No," Mrs. Brown said, looking at him.

He slunk to the back door, "I think I'll go check on the horses," and hurried out.

As Celestia watched him hurry to the barn through the window, she noticed that Kyja, who had been in the field, followed him.

His mother shook her head, "That boy, I swear. Here you go, dear," she set the plate on the table in front of her.

"Thank you," she said.

"So, what happened at the meeting? I mean, if you don't mind my asking," she sat catty-corner to Celestia. Her eyes had that twinkle in them she often noticed in Bridgot's eyes, and, for a moment, she was mesmerized, seeing the same eyes in two different people. The corners of her eyes wrinkled when she smiled, and tendrils of her brown hair fell in her face. She noticed they were curly; he had her hair as well.

"Not at all," she said, starting to eat, "The elders weren't very helpful. They didn't have the information we need to fulfill the prophecy, so they're sending us to see The Oracle. We leave at dawn."

"So soon?" Mrs. Brown asked sadly, her eyes losing their twinkle and turning foggy, "I had hoped to have an extended visit with you."

"You're very hospitable," she said, "and it's greatly appreciated. But, unfortunately, we really must set out. The fate of the world rests in our hands."

His mother nodded, "Very well. I shall have Kyja pack your saddlebags tonight, so you have supplies for the road."

"That's very generous of you."

"Think nothing of it," she said, smiling, "Whatever we can do to help."

After everyone got situated to go to sleep, Celestia lied awake, and she heard faint whispers coming from above her. She tiptoed out of the guest room and positioned herself under the ladder.

"Are you really leaving in the morning?" she heard Kyja ask.

"I have to," Bridgot said, "but don't worry, it isn't forever. I'll bring you something from our travels. What would you like?"

She was silent for a moment, "I want you to do me a favor."

"What is it?"

"I want you to ask The Oracle if she sees anything in my future," Kyja said.

"Why would you want me to ask something like that?" Bridgot said.

She was silent again, "Because, I need to know if I'll be stuck this way forever, or if I have a chance at greatness, too."

"Kyja," he said, "Of course you do. You don't need advice from some oracle to tell you what to do, or who to be. *Your* future is what *you* make it."

She didn't say anything.

"I know how you feel," he said, "Margaret and Luanne for you are like how Bryan is for me. But, I think being the family oddballs is a good thing; it means we're different. And, a different mindset is all you need to *do* something different."

Kyja remained silent.

"Promise me something," Bridgot said.

"What?"

"No matter what happens with anyone else, you'll do what *you want* to do."

"Okay," she said, "Then, *you* promise *me* something."

"Okay?"

"Don't forget about me after you save the world."

He laughed, "How could I? I'm saving the world *for you*." Celestia heard the sound of a quick kiss. "Now, get to bed," he said.

"Okay," Kyja said, "You, too."

Celestia hurriedly tiptoed back into the guest room before she could get caught, a million thoughts running through her mind.

The Land of the Elves

14

As sunlight began to stream through the window, Celestia awoke. She crept out of the room at the same time that Bridgot was coming down the ladder.

"Oh, good, you're up," he whispered, "Ready?"

She nodded, and they headed to the stable. As promised, the saddle-bags were full, and they were set for the road.

They got Samson and Razel quickly saddled and set out toward Gliken. As they left the village behind, they looked back at the round houses, and the sun coming up, spreading orange and gold light all around. They journeyed through the day, lost in their own thoughts.

They made camp in a small clearing, and as they were drifting off to sleep, Celestia thought, *Are there really such creatures as elves, dwarves, wizards, and dragons? I guess we'll find out . . .*

As it approached the hour in which they would normally stop for lunch, they noticed a shift—a change in the air around them. The trees seemed different—taller, more gnarled, not quite brown and green, but more silvery and bluish. The light streaming in wasn't the greenish-gold they were used to, but a misty blue with silvery light. A profound silence penetrated the forest, and the air felt ancient and heavy. Celestia wanted to talk to Bridgot and figure out what was happening, but she couldn't summon the words. Their horses bristled, growing nervous and snorting. Their hair stood on end. *Gliken*, Celestia thought, *We made it.*

As they ventured further, a line of strange men on white horses appeared from out of the mist in front of them. They had angled features, and pointed ears, which protruded from their hair. They all wore their hair long; it was smooth, shiny, and flowing. They wore velvety robes that matched the mist and bands around their heads made from precious metals. She saw men of pale skin with silver hair, and men of dark skin with ebony hair.

Bridgot reached uncertainly for his sword.

One of the men came forward—the center-most of the line, "Welcome. We've been expecting you." As the two of them continued to stare at the strange men, he continued, "Right this way." They all turned, and the horses began to vanish into the mist.

Bridgot and Celestia followed, unsure. As they caught up, they began seeing life in the forest around them. But, it wasn't birds and squirrels, deer and fish.

In the water, she saw large creatures, gliding through the silvery waves. A woman appeared at the edge of the river. She was pale and beautiful. Her hair was blue, and her eyes matched. She wore only a bra of blue shells. When she saw them, she hurried to swim away. It was only then that Celestia saw she had a scaly tail where her legs should be.

In the air above them, she saw giant blue and white birds of a species unknown to her. The white birds seemed to generate great gusts of wind with their wings, soaring higher than she could see, up into the clouds. The blue birds appeared to be covered with morning dew, and they flew close to the water, plucking up silvery fish from its surface, and diving even to its depths to retrieve their prey.

On land, she saw silver and white stags, and tiny creatures which fluttered about, giving off glowing lights of various colors. She also saw what looked like people, dressed in clothes made of leaves, with soft, curious faces, and cloud-like hair. Even the trees seemed alive in this forest. She could've sworn she saw the shrubs moving, and she heard whispers all around.

Soon enough, they started seeing structures in the trees: homes, buildings, even staircases and bridges. There were people milling about, but they didn't seem in a hurry like most villages she'd seen. They meandered slowly, with graceful movements.

They followed the line of men on horses to a palace, nestled high in the trees. It was towering and majestic, reaching up into the forest canopy.

A drawbridge was lowered, almost magically, for them to enter by. It unfurled from the very trees, with a railing made of leafy vines. Some of the men waited outside, and they followed the rest up the drawbridge and into the palace.

Inside, it was awe-inspiring. The walls seemed to be made from the trees, but there were no wooden boards; they looked as though they'd grown that way naturally. The paintings weren't hung, but etched into the walls. They were incredibly intricate and detailed. The floors matched the walls, and there were natural windows along the corridors.

They were led down a long corridor to a huge throne room—far larger than her own. It was covered with precious metals and stones, which made the whole room glitter. A dark man with long, black hair, dressed in a velvet robe which appeared to change colors before her eyes, going from purple to white to blue, and a golden, bejeweled crown upon his head, sat upon a throne taller than she could have imagined.

"My lord," the man on horseback who had welcomed them said, addressing the man on the throne, "The princess and her warrior, as you requested."

"Thank you, Thaddeus," he said.

The man bowed to him, and the men on horses left the room. Bridgot and Celestia dismounted, standing before the throne.

"Princess Celestia," he said, "Welcome to the kingdom of Garellis. I am Boreas, its king."

"My great grandfather's name was Boreas," she said, "It's a pleasure."

"Yes," he said, "I knew him—wonderful man."

"You *knew* him, sir?" she asked in bewilderment.

He laughed, "You know nothing of elves, do you, child?"

She shook her head, cheeks flushing in embarrassment.

"Our lifespans are far longer than that of humans," he said, "Four of your years equal one of ours. Your lifespans average eighty years. Ours average four hundred of your years."

Her eyes widened, "So, you were alive when my great grandfather was king?"

He nodded, "Yes. In human years, I am one hundred and eighty-two. In elf years, I am only middle-aged."

One-hundred and eighty-two, she mouthed in amazement.

"Please," he said, "you are most welcome here. Allow my assistant, Marcos, to show you to your rooms. You will, of course, stay here at the palace. There will be a great feast tonight, and tomorrow, the warrior who shall accompany you will be chosen." With that, he waved to Marcos, a dark-skinned elf who was standing near the throne. He nodded, gesturing for Bridgot and Celestia to follow him.

They followed Marcos down another long corridor, and arrived at two huge suites situated across the hall from each other. "Your rooms," he said, gesturing to either side. Bridgot and Celestia each ventured into a room. There was a bed larger than any she'd ever seen, made from plant life. There was a huge window through which she could see the incredible elven city in all its glory. The soft glow of lanterns and small flying creatures lit the spiraling staircases and incredible tree structures. She marveled at this place. She never could have imagined anything like it.

"Are they to your satisfaction?" Marcos asked.

Celestia composed herself, coming back to the main hall, and gave him a deep nod. Bridgot rejoined them as well, his face expressing his amazement, "This place is incredible."

Marcos smirked and nodded, "I take my leave. You may freshen up just down the hall. Thaddeus will come later to show you the way to the feast." He glided off down the corridor.

"Did you know things like this existed?" Celestia asked when he was out of earshot.

"I'd heard stories, and seen pictures, but I've never been here in person before," he answered. "Humans aren't readily welcome in the land of the elves without an invitation," his eyes darkened, looking off down the corridor.

She nodded. After a pause, "Do you know what those creatures were we saw when we got here?"

He looked at her, eyes clearing, "Which ones?"

"All of them," she said, "I've never seen any of them before. There was a woman, when we first got here, in the river. She swam away, but she had no legs. She had scales and fins, like a fish!"

"That's a mermaid," he said, "You know, half human, half fish."

"A mermaid?" her eyes widened.

He laughed, "You've really never heard of anything besides humans?" he asked.

"Well, that, and horses, and deer, and squirrels, and birds," she said, "Speaking of birds, what were those large blue and white birds?"

He shook his head, "Well, the white birds are auristras. They have an affinity for air. Not just like normal birds, but I mean for the element. They can create gusts with their wings—far stronger than any other average bird.

They can fly higher, even into the outer reaches of the atmosphere. They're cousins to their more commonly known counterpart—the phoenix. You've at least heard of those, right?"

She shook her head.

"They have an affinity for fire, they can carry things ten times their weight, their tears can heal you from flesh wounds, and they can go for weeks with no food or water. They'd be perfect for war, but, of course, they're mystical, untamable creatures, and could never be used for such. Auristras are the same, but their affinity is for air instead of fire. The blue birds are dwervas—their affinity is for water."

"What of the people dressed in leaves, dancing between the trees?"

"Nymphs," he said, "They're forest-dwellers—caretakers of the forest. They look after all the plants and animals. They can even speak to the trees."

"Speak to the trees?" she whispered in disbelief.

"Well, supposedly," he said, "That's what the stories say, anyway."

"You don't believe them?"

He shrugged, "I guess it's hard to tell what's true and what's myth when you've never seen them for yourself."

She looked off, through the room, out the window, "And, what are those?" she asked, pointing out the window, "The tiny creatures which give off the different colors of light."

"Oh, you mean the pixies?" he asked, moving forward toward the room so he could see what she was pointing at. "They're tiny, winged people. They glow like lightning bugs, but in various colors. They're generally kind, and they help plants, animals, and beings like elves and humans. They help the plants to grow and blossom, and they help animals find food and escape harm, and sometimes help people with their problems."

"Really?" she asked, "How?"

"I'm not sure," he said, "That part was always fuzzy. I think they have magic powers or something . . ." They stood in the hallway for a moment, before Bridgot said, "We'd better wash up, so we're ready for the feast when Thaddeus comes to get us." He rolled his eyes, smirking.

Celestia nodded, "You go ahead and go first."

It wasn't long after they'd washed up that Thaddeus appeared, summoning them to the feast. Celestia had been watching through her window, seeing the elves below preparing the meal, and setting the tables. The tall, dark, guardian of the elven kingdom led them up the corridor, and out to the feast. The entire grassy plain, the center of this great kingdom in the trees, was filled with tables of food, and elves seated all around them.

Thaddeus led them to the king's table, where King Boreas was seated at the head. There were two vacant places to his left and one to his right. He gestured to the chairs on his left, and Bridgot and Celestia were seated. Thaddeus took the seat to his right. The food was mounds of different kinds of bread, and all sorts of fruits and vegetables, the likes of which Celestia had never seen.

She turned to Bridgot, whispering, "What are these things?"

He looked uncertain as he opened his mouth to answer, but before he could respond, King Boreas spoke. "We have heard much talk of you two," he said, "Everyone is anxious to know the meaning of this prophecy. You most of all, I'm sure."

"Yes," Celestia said, "It's all a great mystery to me now."

"Indeed," the king said. After a pause, "I think you will rather enjoy watching the tournament tomorrow."

"Tournament?" she looked at him in confusion.

"Yes, of course," King Boreas said, "How did you think we would select who would accompany you?"

"They're going to fight each other?" she asked in horror.

"Relax, young princess," he said, "None shall be gravely injured. We are not so barbaric a race. We simply wish to find the greatest one, who is best equipped to aid your quest. Tournaments here are not a fight to the death."

She gave a slight nod, "My apologies. I have seen tournaments of our knights for sport, but, when such a dangerous mission is the prize, I assumed it would be . . ."

"Elven warriors-in-training can only become full-fledged elven warriors by proving themselves. Well, as elves rarely go to war, there is a shortage of ways they can do that. Many of our warriors-in-training have retained that title for decades of our time," he said, "They have a thirst to prove themselves. This quest is their chance."

They sat for a moment, as Celestia was unsure how to respond. Bridgot, to her left, was busily loading himself up on the strange elven foods.

"Please," King Boreas said, "Enjoy the feast. Tomorrow, we shall see who shall accompany you forward."

That night, as Celestia lied awake, sinking into the soft bed of moss and ferns, and watching the colorful, twinkling lights of the pixies, she began to understand the gravity of this quest. Whatever happened, the prophecy was real, and Bridgot's village weren't the only ones who thought it was about her. Tomorrow, an elven warrior would be chosen to accompany them. Though her thoughts threatened to consume her, the smells of lavender and lilies helped her fade off to a restless sleep.

Aurano

15

When she awoke, Marcos was bringing them elven robes to wear during the tournament. They got dressed and joined together in the corridor. He led them out of the palace, and to a row of steps made from the trees, where everyone was gathering for the tournament. They joined King Boreas to watch. She felt strange in these velvety, blue robes, and it was even stranger to see Bridgot in them.

The tournament began as an elderly elf with pale skin and silver hair stepped to the center, announcing, "The Tournament of The Prophecy has now commenced. There will be six rounds. In the first three, the contestants will be on teams. Teams will be eliminated at the conclusion of each round. Performance will be judged by our esteemed panel," he gestured to where King Boreas was sitting.

Celestia realized she and Bridgot were in the row of judges alongside him. Thaddeus was there as well, along with several elven warriors. "Here are your scorecards," King Boreas whispered, handing two cards written in human dialect to each of them.

The announcer continued, "Teams will be scored in five areas: de-livery—meaning whether they win or lose—speed, skill, resourcefulness, and teamwork. For rounds four through six, the remaining teams will be dispersed, and we will have individual duels, which will be scored the same, except for teamwork. Rounds four and five will see warriors eliminated, and round six will be the two with the highest overall scores from rounds one through five going head to head. No scorecards, just one winner and one loser. Round 1! We have on the left, blue team vs. red team, on the right, green team vs. yellow team, and center, pink team vs. orange team."

"Which one first?" Celestia whispered to Boreas.

He chuckled.

"Begin!" the old man leaped out of the way as the warriors-in-training began fighting. Celestia could barely keep up watching any one of the battles, let alone all of them at the same time, as fast as the elves could move. She guessed Bridgot was sharing her struggle. The king and his warriors seemed perfectly able to keep up, as they filled out their scorecards for each team in round 1.

She gave them all high marks for speed and skill, and tried to observe any examples of resourcefulness and teamwork. By the time she had a couple of examples down, the round was over, and there were victors from each fight, based on the number of hits and ejections (which meant anyone who stepped out-of-bounds). She recorded the scores for delivery, and they all handed in their scorecards, to see who was eliminated in round 1, receiving their new scorecards for the next round simultaneously.

"Round 2! The pink, green, and red teams have been eliminated! We have on the left, purple team vs. black team, on the right, silver team vs. gold team, and center, two of our round 1 victors, yellow team vs. orange team. Begin!"

She couldn't believe how fast this tournament was. They moved at incredible speeds. It was quite the change of pace from their usually slow movements, yet somehow, they were no less graceful. She was also amazed that a team could emerge victorious, and still be eliminated if their overall score was lower. This was quite unlike any tournament she'd ever attended before.

Their armor for the tournament matched the colors assigned to their teams. She marveled at how they were able to accomplish some of the colors so seamlessly. The craftsmanship of the elves was as unmatched as their skill in battle. She scribbled down her scores for round 2 as it came to a close, and they switched out the scorecards again.

"Round 3! The purple, gold, and orange teams have been eliminated! On the left, we have black team vs. yellow team, and on the right, silver team vs. blue team. Begin!"

It was no less difficult to keep up with only two battles than it was with three. She did her best, and the round came to a close just as quickly. Her new scorecard for round 4 looked much less complicated, as they would now be judging individual performance.

"The blue and black teams have been eliminated! As we have reached the halfway point in the tournament, we will take an hour-long break to enjoy lunch. When we return, the yellow and silver teams will disperse for individual dueling."

They followed King Boreas back inside the palace, and to the great dining hall for lunch. As the food was placed before them, Celestia said, "If I may ask, why are Bridgot and I part of the judging panel for this tournament? I don't know about him, but I can hardly keep up with their movements."

Bridgot nodded in agreement.

"Well," Boreas said, "The winner is being chosen to accompany you," he gestured to each of them, "So, your input is of value."

"We appreciate that," Bridgot said, "But, I must agree with Celestia, they move far too quickly for human eyes to accurately observe and assess."

The elf-king chuckled, "Don't worry, your scores do not weigh the results as heavily as the warriors'. But, your input is included nonetheless."

After lunch, they went back out to their seats, as everyone else gathered back around for the conclusion of the tournament. The elder elf once again appeared in the center, "Round 4! Warriors numbers 1 through 5 from each of our winning teams will now duel. Begin!" he dove out of the way as five duels began at once in different points of the field.

Each competitor had a number painted on their armor now. On the scorecard, they were labeled yellow 1, silver 2, and so on. It was even harder to keep up with, even though each duel was between two individuals rather than teams. With five going at once, the movements were near impossible to follow. Before she could even assess all of them, she was being handed a new scorecard.

The competitors switched places with the remaining victors, who'd been sitting on a bench at the edge of the field. The announcer walked back out quickly, "Round 5! Warriors numbers 6 through 10 from each of our winning teams will now duel. At the conclusion of this round, our two top scorers from the tournament will duel with no scorecards, for one true victor. Begin!"

As she tried to keep up with five more duels, she was glad to know this was the last round she'd have to judge. It was over as quickly as it began, and once the scorecards were handed in, she breathed a sigh of relief, ready to watch the final duel. One would be a lot easier for her to see.

"Our two final competitors are Warrior 1 from the Silver Team and Warrior 8 from the Yellow Team. One of you will stand at the conclusion of this round. One of you will be chosen for this chance—this chance to prove yourself. The other will go home and maintain your in-training status. Ready?" he looked back and forth between the two warriors, "Begin!"

She watched in wonder as these two incredible elven warriors-in-training displayed their impressive skill. They whirled and parried and leaped with the speed of ten men. There was no timer on this round. They would go until one of them surrendered, stepped out-of-bounds, or were disarmed. The yellow warrior pushed the silver one back, and she was sure he would be knocked out-of-bounds, but, at the last second, he dodged, and slipped around the yellow warrior, pushing him forward. He was millimeters from going out, but he caught his balance and spun on the silver warrior. They fought and fought, pushing each other's limits, and dancing with the edge of the field. As the yellow warrior leapt on top of the silver warrior, bringing his sword down upon his helmet, the silver warrior kicked him off, and he flew out-of-bounds. And, with that, the tournament was over, and the victor emerged, removing his helmet.

"Our winner is . . . Aurano!" the announcer said, holding up the arm of the silver-haired elf. The crowd cheered, and the yellow warrior angrily removed his helmet, revealing his dark hair, beads of sweat trailing down his face. He stormed away from the field as everyone began to celebrate the winner.

"Congratulations, Aurano," King Boreas said, "You fought bravely. You will accompany the princess and her warrior. Remember, you represent all of elf-kind on this quest. If you do well, you shall receive the title of Elven Warrior. Rest and recover your strength; you leave at dawn."

As the morning rays gently began to caress her cheek, Celestia awoke. She got dressed in her own clothes, which had been washed by the elves. She met with Bridgot in the hall, and they headed to the corral next to the palace, where their horses were waiting. The elves had cared for them, cleaned them, groomed them, and fed them. They'd reloaded the saddlebags with food, and added some elven weapons to replace theirs.

"Good morning," Aurano said, walking up with his white stallion in tow. He was garbed in elven robes, his silver hair and pale skin glowing in the waking rays of the sun.

"Good morning," Bridgot and Celestia said in unison. "Your skill in combat is most impressive," Celestia added.

"Thank you," he said, bowing his head slightly.

"Shall we be off?" Bridgot asked, climbing upon Samson's back.

Aurano answered by leaping upon his steed.

Celestia followed suit, and the three of them rode off toward Korga, the land of the dwarves.

They journeyed through the morning, deeper into the land of the elves. The amazing creatures she'd noticed upon arrival were wandering the forest, peering at them in cautious curiosity. A certain feeling of majesty hung about the trees. It lulled them into a profound silence. She could see why the elves were so slow-moving and quiet.

Aurano himself looked ancient and majestic, with his silvery hair, pointed ears, and piercing blue eyes. His movements were graceful and lithe. The mannerisms of the elves were so formal and solemn. Even she, a princess, brought up with the manners of the royal court, wasn't sure how to act around them. Bridgot seemed equally uncertain. He was a lot quieter than normal, he stood straighter, and he spoke quite properly, with muted confidence.

They continued for a couple of very quiet days, falling under the spell of the forest, and feeling all sorts of strange eyes on them. During the day, she felt the wings of the auristras stirring the breeze, she watched the dwervas dive for fish, and soar to their nests with them, wings dripping with water, and she caught glimpses of the nymphs and mermaids, watching them curiously, just as uncertain of her as she was of them. At night, she saw the white stags with their silver horns, almost glowing in the darkness, and watched the pixies flutter all around, illuminating the river and the trees in shades of pink, blue, orange, and purple.

Soon enough, the misty blue and silver tones of the forest turned back to green and gold, and the magic in the air faded. Sound returned, as birds began chirping, and small forest creatures rustled in the brush. She felt as though she could breathe again, after days of silent travel.

"Korga," Bridgot said, pulling up alongside her, "The land of the dwarves."

His voice sounded strange to her, after days of not talking. It almost felt unnatural, opening her mouth, "Do you think they'll be expecting us, too?"

Bridgot pulled his horse to a stop, saying, "I think so."

She turned to look in front of them, and nearly let Razel run into the end of a spear. She quickly pulled her to a stop, looking down at the line of small men in front of them. They were riding shaggy horses, as short as they were. They had long, rough beards of every color. Unlike the elves, who were either extremely pale or extremely dark in their complexions, the dwarves were all shades. She'd never seen so much variety. In her kingdom, her mother was the only person of a darker skin tone. Her grandmother, Queen Dia, was from the far-off land of Tomainda, whose people are very darkly complected. Her grandfather, King Jon, was light-skinned, like everyone else in the land of Duwazo. So, her mother was a mixture of the two. By the time it trickled down to Celestia, she was pale, and fit right in. So, seeing the various skin tones of the dwarves was amazing to her.

"Follow us," the black-bearded dwarf in the middle of the line said in a gruff voice.

Kgansten

16

They followed the little men, venturing further into the land of the dwarves. The forest ended, and they saw several huge entrances to a cave system. A few birds that resembled dwervas and auristras, only they were shades of brown and green, flew past overhead, and burrowed into the ground near the caves.

"What are those?" she whispered to Bridgot, pointing.

"Dirthens," Bridgot said, "Cousins to the dwervas and auristras. Their affinity is for earth."

Celestia marveled at the animals, and their ability to take to the earth as well as the sky. The dwarves led the three of them to the center-most entrance, and they dismounted their horses.

"We'll take care of them for you," a red-bearded dwarf said, and a few other dwarves cautiously led the three horses away, looking petrified of their great size.

Bridgot, Aurano, and Celestia followed the black-bearded dwarf through the huge doors.

It was unlike anything she'd ever seen. She was amazed at how such small creatures could create such a large, intricate structure. The ceilings were at least fifty feet high, if not more. The walls, ceiling, and beams were all covered in beautiful carvings. Within those detailed designs, jewels were embedded to add color. The entire place was a dazzling masterpiece. They were led through the enormous hallways, to the largest throne room she'd yet seen. It was twenty times the size of even the elf king's. It was filled all the way around with jewels and gold.

"Welcome!" a booming voice resounded as they entered. She looked up at the towering throne and saw a dwarf, garbed in gold, with a crown too tall for his head, and a cape lined with fur and jewels, that trailed behind him three times the length of his body. He had ruddy skin and a blonde beard that reached the floor.

"The visitors, your highness," the black-bearded dwarf said, bowing.

"Yes, the princess of the prophecy, and her human and elven warriors. This is the dwarf kingdom of Dirthix, and I am its king, Thanghor," he said, descending the staircase that led up to his throne.

"Your kingdom is impressive," Celestia said.

"You like it?" he asked excitedly.

"The attention to detail is incredible," she said, "It obviously took a lot of time, effort, and skill."

"Indeed," he said, "The craftsmanship of the dwarves is unmatched. As is our hospitality." He snapped his fingers, and two brown-bearded dwarves appeared. "You will, of course, stay here tonight," he continued, "Felix and Seamus will show you to your rooms. Tonight, you will enjoy the feasting of the dwarves, and tomorrow, you will set out for The Oracle, along with the dwarven warrior we have appointed to accompany you."

Felix and Seamus led them from the throne room, through the huge passageways, and to a large room that reminded Celestia of the rooms of her palace back home.

"For the princess," Felix said. They led Bridgot and Aurano further down the hall, to two other rooms, leaving her there. It was spacious and had a bed that took up half the room, along with several pieces of art and furniture. *For such small creatures, they sure do craft everything big,* she thought.

Seamus came knocking on her door later that night. When she answered, he said, "Right this way to the feast, milady."

She followed him down the hall, "Where are Bridgot and Aurano?"

"Felix went to fetch them. Don't worry; we'll all meet together," he said.

They reached The Great Hall, where the feast was taking place. It was at a cross-section of corridors, which covered a massive expanse. It was full of feasting dwarves. Seamus led Celestia to the head table. There was an empty seat to King Thanghor's left. As she sat, she saw Bridgot and Aurano were seated right next to her.

"Princess Celestia," King Thanghor said, "I'd like to introduce you to your warrior." He paused, gesturing to the red-bearded dwarf on his right, "This is Kgansten."

"Pleasure to meet you," Celestia said, nodding.

"No, the pleasure is mine," Kgansten said, "I am naught but a humble dwarven warrior, aspiring to be a Dwarf Lord."

"And this quest will make that happen?" she asked.

"Indeed," King Thanghor said, "A noble quest is merit enough for a warrior's promotion to Dwarf Lord."

Kgansten beamed with pride. Celestia noticed his brown eyes, large cheeks, and hard skin. Hard, as though it had endured years of intense labor, and war. Almost all the dwarves' skin was that way. Kgansten's red, scraggly beard was braided down the middle, to reign in the loose hair.

Everyone enjoyed the feast before them. The tables were filled to the brim with all manner of meats, cheeses, fruits, and mead. Celestia couldn't help but notice that Aurano was only eating the fruit. He sat calmly, politely, and with pride. As the dwarves became rambunctious and rowdy, he sat, unwavering, waiting patiently. She was amazed by how he maintained such constant composure. But, the dwarves were having too much fun for her to ignore. They got drunk, and they began singing and dancing. She and Bridgot joined in, trying their hardest to learn the vigorously complex dwarven party dances. They jumped and swung around, laughed and drank. The feasts of the dwarves were no doubt the liveliest of any race. She'd never enjoyed herself so much in her life. She'd never felt so free, and so alive.

Celestia awoke in the huge dwarven suite, with no memory of how she got there. She wasn't sure what time it was, as there were no windows in the caves. She got up quickly and scurried down to the rooms she'd seen Bridgot and Aurano enter. She wasn't one-hundred percent sure which one was which, but she knocked on the first one and hoped it was Bridgot.

He answered the door, looking completely disoriented. It took him a minute to focus on her, and let the glaze clear from his eyes. After a moment, he looked as though he'd just realized where he was, "What is it?"

"Sorry to wake you," she said, "Do you know what time it is?"

He wiped the exhaustion from his face, and shook his head, "No. I don't know."

She turned and knocked on Aurano's door.

When he opened it, he looked as though he'd already been awake, perfectly calm and composed, as always, "Yes, Princess Celestia?"

"Aurano, do you know what time it is?"

"It is nearly dawn," he answered.

"How can you tell? There are no windows here."

"I am very in tune with the earth, as all elves are."

"Good enough for me," she said, "Come on, Bridgot, we need to set out for Abyumo."

He went back inside his room to get ready, and Aurano said, "I shall meet you both in The Great Hall."

Celestia went back to her room to grab her things, as Aurano strode off to the main hallway. Once she had her belongings ready, she went to meet Aurano. As they stood there in silence, she said, "Can I ask you something?"

He looked at her in surprise. His surprise turned to suspicious curiosity, and he gave a slight nod.

"Why did you not celebrate at the feast? You ate only fruit and drank only water. You did not dance. Why?"

"I am a warrior, milady, and we are on a quest. I must stay alert at all times, and ne'er cloud my judgment with alcohol. We elves are vegetarian," he said, "We only eat what can be made from plant life. We never harm or kill animals, so we don't eat meat. As an elf, we are natural enemies with the dwarves. It would be a crime against nature for an elf to join in a dwarven dance."

"Ain't that the truth," Kgansten said, walking up, "It's bad enough embarking on a quest together."

"Good, we're all here," Bridgot said, finally catching up, "Where are the horses?"

"The royal stable, of course," Kgansten said, "We dwarves would offer no less to the great princess and her warriors. Right this way." He began walking up one of the corridors, and they all followed.

Once they'd gotten their horses saddled and ready, the four of them set out. To get through Korga, they'd have to travel through the caves. Kgansten rode his dwarf horse, which was much smaller than Celestia, Bridgot, and Aurano's horses. It had a long, shaggy mane and tail, and was off-white with gray spots.

They rode all day through the dwarven tunnels, with Kgansten leading the way. Each corridor was impressive, and Celestia spent her time marveling at the dwarves' craftsmanship. The intricate designs glistened with gems all around her. The ceilings went up for miles.

It was a pretty quiet journey, as no one was sure what to make of each other yet. Aurano and Kgansten eyed each other suspiciously as they traveled. Bridgot stuck close to Celestia, watching the other two with uncertainty. Celestia ignored them all and chose to focus her attention on the incredible structure around her instead.

When it got late, according to Kgansten, since Bridgot and Celestia were lost without the sun, they stopped to make camp.

"If we're still in the dwarven tunnels, wouldn't there be rooms available for us, instead of sleeping in the hall?" Bridgot asked.

"Not in this part of the caves," Kgansten whispered, "This is the territory of the Dwarf Lord Dingus. He disagrees with King Thanghor's argument that you're the princess of the prophecy," he looked at Celestia, "He didn't want us to help you, and he'd certainly refuse us room and board. Even though he's obligated to follow the king's orders, he plots to overthrow him, and I wouldn't trust him to provide us anything."

Aurano faltered, looking around suspiciously. They quietly pulled their blankets out of the saddlebags and tied the horses to the short poles protruding from the walls, which the dwarves cleverly placed along the big corridors for their steeds.

"I'll take the first watch," Aurano said, looking apprehensive. He sat straight, with his superior elven posture, and crossed his legs.

"I don't think so," Kgansten said, taking a knee.

"To save argument, why don't I just take the first watch?" Bridgot interjected, looking back and forth between them.

"With all due respect," Aurano said, "This place makes me uneasy. I couldn't possibly sleep, anyway. You all may as well get your rest."

"I'll not have it," Kgansten said, "To trust an elf with the first watch, and in the dwarven tunnels, no less."

"Yes, and in unfriendly dwarf territory. You said so yourself," Aurano smirked.

Kgansten turned red and seemed ready to explode.

"Listen," Celestia said, "I'm the princess. I get to assign watches. If it makes you uneasy, and you feel better staying awake, you take the first watch, Aurano. Kgansten, with all due respect, we all must take a watch. It makes no difference who goes first. You are all honorable warriors, assigned the same task. Get some rest, and you may take the second shift."

Kgansten grumbled, but he did as she said and lied down to get some sleep. Bridgot lied down as well, closing his eyes. Celestia got as comfortable as she could on the marble floor of the dwarven tunnels, wrapping herself up in her blankets, and drifting off.

She awoke to Bridgot, saying it was time to get up. "Is it my shift?" she asked.

"No," he said, "It's time to set out again."

"What?" she asked, wiping the sleep from her eyes and sitting up. Kgansten and Aurano were already saddling their horses. She shot Bridgot a groggy and confused look.

"I didn't get a shift, either," he said, "Kgansten barely got one. Aurano was up half the night."

"Can you saddle Razel for me?" she asked.

Bridgot nodded, starting to get Samson ready.

Celestia got up, walking over to Aurano, "Bridgot tells me you were up half the night."

He remained silent.

"Is everything alright?"

"It will be, once we're out of these dwarven tunnels," he said.

"Look, we're all a little uneasy passing an unfriendly area," she said, "But, it would be better if you got some sleep. You're supposed to protect me. How can you do that efficiently if you're not well-rested?"

Aurano looked down.

"The three of us will take shifts tonight so you can catch up on sleep," Celestia said, "This isn't about some rivalry of dwarves and elves. This is bigger than that." With that, she turned to help Bridgot finish saddling Razel, and they all mounted their horses and continued their journey through Korga.

That night, as they were making camp, Kgansten said, "We should be able to make it through Dirthix tomorrow. Then, it's only a fortnight's journey out of Korga."

A fortnight? Celestia thought. She hadn't realized the dwarven cave system spanned the entirety of Korga. *This place is massive.*

As Aurano bristled, Celestia eyed him meaningfully. He looked down, but finally lied down to get comfortable.

"Kgansten," she said, "You get the first watch tonight. Wake Bridgot when you're done, and then I'll take my turn after him."

"Aye, milady," Kgansten said, nodding. He took his post, standing straight and looking around.

The rest of them got comfortable to get some sleep.

This time, when Bridgot woke her, it was her watch. She noticed Aurano seemed restless, tossing and turning. Kgansten was snoring away, looking completely in his element. Bridgot nestled in, drifting off slowly. The horses were softly snorting in their sleep, and the tunnel was dark and cold. She could see why Aurano was uneasy in this place. It made the hairs on the back of her neck stand up. At least she had no problem waking up fully for her shift.

Time passed slowly, but she occupied herself trying to count the torches on the walls, though she could barely see them, as they were dimmed for nighttime. She noticed further down the corridor that the tunnels went up high enough to let in the outside light. The sun began peeking in, causing little spots on the floor ahead to glow. Finally, she would be able to tell what time it was.

She went to wake Aurano, but he was already up. His elven biological clock was accurate, and it had already told him the sun was rising. She woke Kgansten and Bridgot, and they set out again, out of Dirthix.

The Land of the Dwarves

17

They journeyed a few more days through Korga before they reached a dwarven village. It looked like any other quaint little town, with huts for houses and shops. It was quite the change of scenery from the rooms built into the tunnels in the kingdom of King Thanghor.

"Greetings, friends!" Kgansten called out as they neared, "Frug o Feinedo?"

"Frug!" A dark-skinned dwarf called out, "Ie gyo?"

"Frug," Kgansten said, "We're weary travelers, seeking a place to stay."

"Well, welcome!" he responded, "Our inn is most accommodating." He pointed the way to a large hut with a horse corral.

Kgansten led them over to it, and the innkeeper, a brown-skinned dwarf with dusty brown hair, greeted them and had his horse boy lead their horses to the corral.

It was the first time Celestia had seen a dwarf child. He was so small, and looked like a miniature human child. He had no beard, and only his size gave away his species. She saw dwarven women milling about as well. They had similar builds to the men, but a little more feminine. They had feminine faces, and long hair, some silky, some frizzy, some rough like the men.

The innkeeper led them inside, and all but he and Kgansten had to duck to get through the low doorway. Inside, it looked like a miniature human inn. The ceiling was just barely high enough for Celestia's head, but Bridgot and Aurano had to scrunch down a bit.

"I'll show you upstairs," the innkeeper said, heading toward a staircase.

They followed him, and it was a bit of a struggle for Bridgot, Aurano, and Celestia to get up the small stairs.

"I only have two vacant rooms," he said, "so I hope you don't mind sharing."

They looked at each other. Celestia wanted to room with Bridgot, but she didn't know how to say so without letting Kgansten and Aurano know her feelings. She also knew the two of them would kill each other if they had to share a room.

"Is one larger than the other?" Aurano asked.

The innkeeper looked up at the elf, "They're the same size. I'm afraid they're built for dwarves, not for men and elves."

"Thank you, sir," Celestia said, "We'll figure it out."

He nodded, "I'll leave you to it, then."

Once he was out of earshot, Bridgot said, "I'll stay with the princess. I've been traveling with her longer, and I'd feel safer if I were in the same room than worrying next door."

"And leave a dwarf and an elf to share a room?" Kgansten said, "Sorry lad, I don't think so."

"I'm afraid I must agree with the dwarf," Aurano asserted, "We simply can't share a room. I'll room with the princess. As an elf, I have quicker reflexes. She'll be safest with me."

"Hah!" Kgansten scoffed, "I think not. Elves are so arrogant. She'd be safest with a dwarf. We are in dwarven territory, after all. *I'll* room with the princess."

"Safest with a dwarf?" Aurano sneered, "She'd be dead before we even woke if anything were to happen."

"The two of you can never agree," Bridgot said, "and she doesn't need a couple of quarreling children. Why don't the two of you duke it out, and I'll stay with her so she can actually get some sleep?"

"My axe would fall upon an elven neck before the morn," Kgansten declared.

"Your axe would hardly be lifted from the ground before my arrow pierced your armor," Aurano said.

"Enough!" Celestia said, "I'm sick of your squabbling. You are all great warriors, worthy of protecting me on this quest. If you insist on fighting each other, how will you ever work together?" she sighed, "Kgansten and Aurano, you must learn to put aside your differences if we are to be successful. You will share a room tonight, and every night, until you can learn to get along."

Their jaws dropped as they tried to come up with an argument, but couldn't.

"Go on," she said, "Bridgot will stay with me."

Bridgot grinned from ear to ear as Kgansten and Aurano slowly entered their room like scolded children. Once they were inside, Bridgot and Celestia entered the adjoining room.

"Finally," Bridgot said, "Those two are going to drive me crazy with their fighting."

"You need to stop fighting with them as well," she said, "It's giving them encouragement and fuel."

He rubbed his arm awkwardly, looking down.

"At least we'll be able to get some sleep," she said.

"Yeah," he said, climbing into the bed.

"Goodnight, Bridgot," she said, climbing into bed next to him.

"I hope this doesn't sound strange," Bridgot said, "but, sleeping next to you is oddly comforting."

"I think it's just because we've gotten so used to it, traveling together for so long."

"Maybe," he said, "But, I think it's more than that."

"What do you mean?" she asked.

"Goodnight, Celestia," he said, turning over.

"What do you mean?" she asked again, but he was already drifting off. *What do you mean?* she thought.

When morning came, they set out from the quaint little village. They journeyed through the day and came to a stop that evening for dinner.

"I want to try something," Celestia said.

Everyone looked at her in confusion as they were getting the food ready.

"How did everything go last night?" she asked, "I see you didn't kill each other."

"We decided just to sleep," Aurano said.

"Not talking was for the best," Kgansten agreed.

"Well, that's no way for us to bond," she said, "I want us to get to know each other. Perhaps the two of you will see you have something in common, after all."

They looked at each other and looked back at her doubtfully.

"If it makes you feel any better, I'll start," Celestia said, "I am the daughter of King Ladon of Tristétoiless, and Queen Eva of Ivonneveilles. Their marriage merged their kingdoms, forming our kingdom of Ivétoiless. My father died in a war when I was a baby. I'm an only child, and sole heir to the throne," she looked at them, winding a strand of white-blonde hair around her fingers, blue eyes shining earnestly, "I grew up how many royals do: being raised by the servants, and trained by my mother to one day become queen. In my spare time, I'd practice my archery, even though my mother said it wasn't lady-like. I'd stroll the palace gardens, taking in the beautiful, sweet-smelling flowers, reading amongst them, and enjoying the solitude. And, I'd spend a lot of time with my horse, Razel. I cared for her, feeding her, grooming her, talking to her, and riding her. Being an only child, my sole friend was my lady-in-waiting, Garrita. We grew up together, and spent every waking moment with each other."

She looked away sadly, as she thought of Garrita for the first time since she'd run away, "I never knew anything of life outside the palace walls. The only time I ever left them was for balls and royal parties in neighboring kingdoms. I never knew anything of dwarves, elves, or any other creatures. I was a prisoner in my own home until I ran away, and met Bridgot," she smiled at him, and turned back to her elven and dwarven warriors, "I've seen so much, learned so much, and experienced so much since I left home. I never thought I'd ever have an adventure this incredible."

Everyone sat quietly, not sure how to react to hearing her life story. After what seemed like an eternity, she said, "Bridgot, why don't you go next?"

He shook his head as if waking from a trance, "Uh, sure, okay," he said, "I'm the son of George and Katherine Brown, a couple of farmers from the village of Kataran in the land of Katangalo. I have four siblings: my older sister, Margaret, my older brother, Bryan, my younger sister, Kyja, and my younger sister, Luanne. Margaret is married, with two kids; my nephew, Phillip, and my niece, Anne Marie. Bryan is also newly married, but with no kids, yet," he looked at everyone, not sure how much he should share, "I grew up helping my parents on the farm. I liked to read, which was frowned upon by everyone in my village. They believed scholarly achievement a waste of time, and valued physical labor instead. Our village is responsible for a lot of the land's farming activity, so they thought being a good farmer was the greatest thing you could do."

He paused, looking at everyone's faces before he continued, "I read anyway, whenever I got the chance. I cared for my horse, Samson, and I became my village's errand boy, traveling to markets in neighboring lands. It was my way of escaping the monotony. I was trained in sword combat, as was every man in my village. I lived in the shadow of my brother, who was the pride of the village. He was big and strong, and excelled in all things physical, farming and sword fighting alike. I was skinny and scrawny, and the village book nerd," he grimaced, as if sharing this was too embarrassing for him to go on. But he continued, "When word of the prophecy and the unsolvable riddle reached my ears, I hoped that it could be me, but I knew there was no way I was some mythical warrior. Still, an unsolvable riddle intrigued the scholar in me, and I knew I had to try. After I solved it, and I was pronounced the warrior of the prophecy, and assigned the task of bringing the princess back to the village, I thought things would finally turn around for me—that maybe I would outshine my brother for once. But, despite the incredible challenges Princess Celestia and I faced on the road, when we got back to my village, nothing had really changed. I don't think it ever will, no matter what I do."

Everyone was quiet again, looking away from each other, processing. It took a few moments before Celestia could speak again. "Thank you, Bridgot," she looked at him with understanding, and they both tried to muster a weak smile for one another. After another pause, she said, "Aurano?"

He cleared his throat nervously. It was the least elf-like and the most human she'd ever seen him look. "Well," he began, "I am the son of the great elven warrior, Irvenix, and Irena, the elven beauty of her day. My father, too, died when I was young. I wasn't an infant, but still a child."

Celestia shared an empathetic look with him.

"I had a younger sister, by the name of Arenelle, but she was killed by a dark elven wizard who went rogue. My father tracked him down and killed him, with the help of several elven wizards and warriors. In the process, a dark human wizard, by the name of Nazirdok, killed him. I have trained my whole life to become an elven warrior, in hopes of avenging my father."

Celestia understood now, why he fought so hard to accompany her on this quest. If he became a full-fledged elven warrior, he could gain the status and resources necessary to avenge his father.

"It's just been my mother and I, for years, and I've been dedicated to my training, knowing I'd have to best the other warriors-in-training to get my opportunity. In my free time, I was still training. Hardly a moment went by when I wasn't learning and practicing. All my friends were warriors and warriors-in-training. While many of them focused on caring for plants and creatures, learning about things other than combat, and enjoying elven gatherings, I was focused on maneuvers and techniques. The only thing I did to take a break was care for my horse, Seina, and watch the sun rise each day over the misty kingdom of Garellis."

And I thought my life was a prison, she thought, *His was self-inflicted.* "Well, I hope this quest proves worth it for you," she said, "Kgansten?"

"I am the son of the dwarf knight, Kgandor, and his wife, Ghirthena," he began with pride, "My father spent his whole life trying to become a Dwarf Lord, but he never did it. He was killed on the quest that would have given him the title. As for me, I vowed that I would do what he couldn't. King Thanghor appointed me as the warrior for this quest, in hopes of helping me reach that goal. He is my uncle. I have seven siblings: Kganzeth, Ghitta, Kgandabar, Ghloria, Kganlor, Ghabrie, and Thanghor, named for my uncle. I spend most of my spare time with them. We have dwarven parties, the likes of which you wouldn't believe. We dwarves are very family-oriented. My pony, Gjabreel, was given to me by my brother, Kgandabar, as a gift for this quest," he looked at his steed with pride, beaming.

"You see?" Celestia said, "You both joined this quest for your fathers. There's something big you have in common."

"We have nothing in common," Aurano spat, "I worked my whole life, and battled in a tournament with a hundred warriors-in-training, to *earn* the opportunity to embark on this quest. *He* simply got his uncle to appoint him. He took a hand-out, instead of earning his position."

Kgansten turned beet red, "Why, you!" he yelled, trying to summon words, "You arrogant, pompous, self-righteous, good-for-nothing elf scum!"

"You dare to address me as such?" Aurano retorted, "You entitled, lazy, pampered, dwarf wretch!"

Kgansten lifted his axe, and let out a war cry.

Aurano spun his arrow into his bow at the speed of light.

"Stop!" Celestia yelled, "Both of you!"

"No one tells a dwarf they aren't hard-working!" Kgansten cried, "Least of all an elf! We dwarves are known for being hard workers!"

"You dwarves are known for not being able to reach the table without a high chair," Aurano countered.

Kgansten lunged forward, swinging his axe. Aurano sidestepped, and it hit the marble floor instead.

"I said stop!" Celestia said, "If you kill each other, neither of you get what you want. This quest will fail, and neither of you will reach your goals. Kgansten, calm down. Go sit next to Bridgot. Aurano, you should be ashamed of yourself, provoking a fight like that. Go sit with your horse."

They eyed each other angrily, each of them trying to send a message. But, they did as she said, and separated to calm themselves.

She separated their watches so they wouldn't be awake at the same time, and everyone got some rest.

They traveled the next few days in silence, Aurano and Kgansten eyeing each other, and Celestia and Bridgot not wanting to say anything that might provoke another fight.

Celestia lied awake at night, trying to figure out how to bridge the gap between them and unify their quest. One night, as she was lying awake, searching for similarities between elves and dwarves, Kgansten came to wake her for her shift.

She hadn't gotten enough sleep lately, and she wondered if she could stay awake through her whole shift. She wished she'd taken an earlier one since she'd been awake the whole night anyway. The tunnels were growing darker again, as they'd strayed farther from the areas which let in the sun. With the light, the heat diminished as well, making it colder. The coldness of the floor made it acutely more uncomfortable than it had been already.

As Kgansten began to snore, she started counting torches—her usual tactic for staying awake. Just then, she heard a shuffling noise along the edge of the corridor. She strained her eyes in the darkness, but couldn't see anything but shadow.

"Wake up," she whispered, shaking Bridgot.

"Is it time to set out?" he asked.

She woke Aurano, and Bridgot gained consciousness enough to realize something was off, and wake Kgansten. As he was doing so, they heard a battle cry, and a horde of dwarves ambushed them. They all jumped up, scrambling to arm themselves. Kgansten lifted his axe just as one came down on him. He yelled, fighting off his attacker, and cutting him down. Aurano shot off arrows in the dark. Celestia wasn't sure how he could see well enough to hit his mark. She and Bridgot got their swords and began swinging, somewhat blindly, at the onslaught of dwarves.

Bridgot and Celestia fought back to back, thrusting and parrying in all directions. Kgansten bravely charged into the midst of the ambush, swinging his axe. Aurano managed to pick off many of them with his arrows, but there were too many, and he had to pull out his sword to fight.

Celestia noticed a knob on the wall and realized it was the one that would turn up the torches. She began moving toward it, Bridgot walking backward with her. As she reached it, she hurriedly turned it, and the torches lit the dark corridor.

"Lord Dingus!" Kgansten shouted.

Once they were able to see their attackers, they fought them off much more easily. Aurano sliced his sword through the entire group surrounding him and returned to firing arrows. Bridgot and Celestia separated, going after different groups of them. Kgansten went straight for Lord Dingus, axe raised.

Lord Dingus moved out of the way, and Kgansten's blow fell to the floor. They engaged, fighting each other back and forth. As Bridgot and Celestia wore down the groups they were fighting, and Aurano thinned out the horde with his arrows, Kgansten pinned down Lord Dingus and raised his axe. A dwarf came up behind him as he did so, and raised his axe to strike him before he could land his blow.

"No!" Celestia shouted. Suddenly, an arrow pierced the dwarf's armor, and he fell as Kgansten struck Lord Dingus down. Everyone looked to see who'd fired the arrow, and there stood Aurano, bow still in hand. Kgansten looked behind him, saw the dwarf, and looked over at Aurano. Kgansten nodded, and Aurano smiled.

Celestia breathed a sigh of relief as the rest of the dwarves retreated after their leader had been struck down.

The next week was smooth sailing, as they rode their horses through the rest of Korga. When they stopped one night to make camp, Kgansten said, "We should reach Gachichken by tomorrow. From there, it's a three-week journey west to The Oracle."

"Three weeks?" Celestia asked.

"Yes," Bridgot said, "And if we had headed there straight from Ivétoi-less, it would have only been a matter of days."

Celestia opened her mouth to complain, but Aurano cut her off, "Yes, but if you had gone straight there, you would have had to come all the way back, since part of the prophecy is that an elven and dwarven warrior are to help you if you are to succeed."

Everyone was quiet after that, and they settled in for the night to get some sleep.

Celestia awoke to a growling sound. Kgansten, who was awake for his shift, looked at her as she sat up. Aurano awoke as well, and Kgansten quickly woke Bridgot. They heard the sound again and scrambled to arm themselves. Celestia turned up the torches, and they looked around as the corridor was lit. All they saw were the intricate, bejeweled carvings in the walls, the torches, the marble floors, the mess of blankets where they'd been sleeping, and their horses.

They backed slowly toward each other, so they would be prepared to fight whatever it was together. As they did so, a large creature, covered in black scales, with a sharp, pointed head, a long tail, and stout legs with claws, came around the corner.

"What is that?" Celestia whispered.

"A siladine: a cave-dwelling creature. It uses its sharp head to burrow into the earth, and also to attack its prey," Kgansten said.

"Its prey?" Celestia asked nervously, "What does it eat?"

"Mostly animals that live underground, but occasionally larger things as well," he paused, "You'd better arm yourself, princess. This one looks hungry."

"Its head is impenetrable," Aurano said, "and its scales are tough. Aim for the neck, and, if you can, the underbelly."

"Aye," Kgansten agreed.

Celestia swallowed. As it slowly drew nearer, she felt lines of sweat make their way down her face. As many amazing creatures as she'd seen thus far, she wasn't entirely prepared for the more heinous ones. It looked like a giant black lizard with scales. Its tongue slithered in and out of its mouth; she could see it was forked. On the sides of its great, pointed head, two beady eyes were visible.

They all tried to back away from the creature, in hopes it would go on past them, but as they moved, so did it. It paused and then turned toward the horses.

Aurano quickly lunged forward, swinging his sword down toward the creature's neck. Though he was abnormally fast, the creature saw him coming and moved out of the way in the nick of time. His blade fell upon the creature's head, not even putting a notch in it.

It turned its attention to Aurano, lunging at him. Celestia could see it had no teeth, but sharp, powerful jaws. Aurano leaped out of the way gracefully, trying to get his sword around to its neck. Kgansten rushed over, swinging his axe toward the creature's neck, but his reflexes were too slow, and the creature nipped his armor. Bridgot and Celestia ran over, swinging their swords as well, and trying to help.

The siladine had quick reflexes itself, and it snapped at Bridgot, as Celestia tried to sever its neck. It turned on her, then, and lunged forward, jaws open. Bridgot quickly stabbed it on the inside of its arm, to which the creature responded in pain and anger. Celestia stumbled back, and it went after Bridgot again. Kgansten sideswiped it with his axe, as it nipped Bridgot's leg.

Celestia crawled over to Bridgot hurriedly and looked at his leg. It had a long laceration from just under his left knee to a few inches above his ankle. It was bleeding pretty badly. She tore one of the blankets closest to her and wrapped it around his leg quickly.

As she was doing so, the creature was focusing its attention on Kgansten. He tried to swing his axe down upon it, but it moved faster than him, and it knocked him to the ground. He tried to lift his axe toward the underbelly, but it stepped on his arm, grasping it with its claw. As it opened its jaws to bite him, Aurano swung his sword down, cutting the creature's head off.

Kgansten lied in a pool of purple blood, under the weight of the siladine's body, its severed head a few inches from his own. Aurano lifted the creature off of him, casting it to the side.

Kgansten looked up at him and said, "Now, I owe you *two* life debts."

Aurano smiled, offering his hand.

As he helped him up, Kgansten said, "But, *you* owe *me* for this bloody mess!"

They both chuckled, and Aurano pat him on the back as he reached his feet.

Once they'd gotten in a good laugh, they looked over at Celestia and Bridgot. His leg was wrapped up, but Celestia was sitting by his side worriedly.

"Can you walk?" Celestia asked.

"I'm not sure," Bridgot said, "I think so."

"You saved my life," she said.

"We saved each other," he replied, touching her hand.

She took his hand in hers, holding it tightly, and looking into his eyes earnestly.

"Ahem!" Kgansten said, clearing his throat.

They looked up, Celestia quickly dropping his hand.

Aurano strode over and helped Bridgot up. He groaned as he stood, trying not to place his full weight on his injured leg.

"Try to walk," Aurano instructed.

Bridgot limped forward, with obvious difficulty, holding his breath in pain. After a few steps, he let out a cry and fell. Aurano caught him, and helped him over to the blankets, assisting him to sit.

"Let me look at it," he said.

Bridgot lifted his pant leg, and Aurano undid the makeshift bandage Celestia had made. As he did so, she and Kgansten could see the gash was deep.

"I'm skilled in elven medicine," Aurano said, "It was part of my training. I need my saddlebag."

"I'll get it," Celestia said. She quickly pulled the saddlebags off of Seina, Aurano's white stallion, and brought them over to him.

He opened one of them up, pulling out a small vial. Inside was a glowing, purple liquid.

"This may sting a bit," he said, tapping out a few drops onto the wound.

They all watched in amazement as the flesh on either side of the gash slowly began to merge together, sticking to itself. It moved all the way up to the skin, leaving a line where the cut had been.

"Your body will still need to heal itself," Aurano said, "but this will keep the wound together, and help the healing process to accelerate. You will have a scar, but your leg will go back to normal."

"Thank you, Aurano," Bridgot said.

"That was amazing!" Celestia exclaimed.

"Do you have any elf magic that can get me clean?" Kgansten asked.

"It's not magic," Aurano said, "It's medicine, extracted from a plant."

"Oh," Kgansten sighed, "I suppose I'll have to wait for the next village, then."

"Let's try to get some rest," Celestia said, "We still have a long way to go."

Wanted

18

As Kgansten woke her to tell her it was time to set out again, they all began gathering their things and saddling their horses.

They rode into the afternoon, and finally, Celestia saw a giant doorway.

"We've reached it," Kgansten said, "Through those doors is the end of Korga."

She felt a wave of excitement and relief run through her.

As a couple of dwarves opened the doors for them, they rode outside. The sunlight was blinding after over two weeks in the caves. Her eyes slowly adjusted to the brightness, and she saw a thriving forest, with a little meadow full of blooming flowers. Fresh air filled her lungs, and she'd never been happier to see the sky. Birds chirped overhead, and the scent of the flowers wafted over to her. *Gachichken,* she thought.

The four of them rode their steeds forward into the trees. Back in a human realm, there were no more magical creatures to behold. Bridgot was taking in large breaths of air as well, and Aurano was visibly relieved. He seemed much more at ease than he had in the dwarven caves. Kgansten seemed a little uncertain, leaving familiar territory, but they continued on.

After about a week of travel, they finally came across a village. Their saddlebags were depleted of food, and they were all starting to stink.

Especially Kgansten, who hadn't been able to wash the blood of the siladine off, yet. Their hair was growing out, and getting knotted.

They found an inn and went inside. The innkeeper greeted them—an old woman with white hair, who appeared ravaged by time.

"What can I do for you?" she asked.

"We seek accommodations," Celestia said, "for us and our horses."

She eyed Kgansten and Aurano suspiciously. After a pause, she waved her stable boy over, "Take their horses to the stable." Once he'd vanished through the door, she said, "Right this way." She led them up the stairs, and to two open rooms, "Washroom is just down the hall. Will there be anything else?"

"Our clothes could use cleaning," Celestia said, "and we are rather hungry."

She faltered a moment before responding, "Of course. Lay your clothes on the floor outside your doors, and I'll have the maid wash them for you. The kitchen is closed for the night, but I can make you a few sandwiches, and there will be breakfast available in the morning."

"Thank you," Celestia said.

The woman nodded, heading off down the hall.

"Kgansten," Celestia said, "Why don't you wash up first?"

"Thank you, milady," he said, scurrying off to the washroom.

"So, who's rooming with who?" Bridgot asked.

"Well, it seems as though Aurano and Kgansten are finally getting along," Celestia said.

"Well, we can just stick to our original arrangement," Bridgot said, "I think that'd be easiest."

"I don't think that's such a good idea," Aurano said, eyeing the two of them suspiciously.

Bridgot hesitated, looking at Aurano guiltily.

"*I'll* room with the princess," Aurano said, "Bridgot, you and Kgansten can share a room tonight."

"Fine," Celestia said, "It doesn't matter, so long as we all get some rest."

"Are you sure you mind sleeping on the floor instead of in a bed?" Bridgot asked.

"I'm a gentleman," Aurano said, "It's no matter."

"Come on, Aurano," Celestia said, walking into one of the rooms.

He followed, and Bridgot went into the neighboring room.

When Kgansten returned, Bridgot went to wash up and trim his hair, and the two of them set their clothes outside the door, settling in to get some sleep. The innkeeper brought them some sandwiches, and they all scarfed them down quickly before getting their rest. Celestia went next to wash up, which felt amazing after not bathing for over a fortnight. She attempted to trim and brush out her long, blonde hair, trying not to take too long. And finally, Aurano washed up, setting up on the floor, and giving Celestia the bed.

"Are you sure you wouldn't be more comfortable up here?" she asked, "We could put up a wall of pillows. I know sleeping in a bed feels much better than the floor after so long on the ground."

"No, thank you," Aurano said, "It would feel too improprietous. I must preserve your honor."

"Very well," she said, "Goodnight, Aurano."

They slept in late the next morning, enjoying sleeping in beds for a change. Once they awoke and got dressed, they headed down the stairs, and the innkeeper served them a large breakfast of eggs, bacon, toast, and hash browns. They hungrily devoured it, as she watched in slight horror. It felt so good getting a hot meal in. Celestia had been worried they might not come across a village anytime soon, and their saddlebags were completely empty.

They got their horses from the stable and set out through the town, stopping in the market to refill their food supplies. As Celestia strolled through the stands of wares with Razel—her first time in a marketplace—she marveled at the variety of items for sale. There were clothes, paintings, pots, weapons, food, and jewelry. She paused at a booth full of flowers, taking in the sweet smells, which reminded her of being in the palace gardens. As she did, she noticed a few WANTED posters nearby. And, on one of them, was her face. It said MISSING: PRINCESS CELESTIA OF IVETOILESS. REWARD: 12,000 pounds. Her eyes widened, and she slowly walked away, trying not to bring attention to herself.

As she caught up with Bridgot, she said, "We need to get out of here. Now."

He looked at her questioningly.

"I'll explain later. Let's just get the food, find Kgansten and Aurano, and set out, right away."

"Okay," he said, "I'll finish up getting the food here; you go find them."

She nodded, turning her face toward Razel as she walked, covering it slightly with her hair, and looking for her elven and dwarven warriors. She found them, checking out weapons and armor at one of the booths. She shook her head, "You two don't need any more weapons; you have plenty. Come on; it's time to go."

They set down the pieces they'd been examining, thanked the seller for his time, and followed her back over to Bridgot. He was just checking out with full saddlebags. The gold coins they'd received from the elves and the dwarves came in handy when buying supplies.

"Ready?" she asked.

"Yep, we're good to set out," he said, handing saddlebags to everyone and attaching Samson's.

They strolled out of town, back into the forest, and hopped on their horses, riding away.

"So, why did we have to leave in such a hurry?" Bridgot asked, riding up alongside her.

"My face was on a MISSING poster in town. It seems there's a 12,000-pound reward for anyone who finds me and returns me to my kingdom."

"Well, that complicates things," Aurano said.

"Indeed," Celestia affirmed.

"We must use extreme caution the rest of the way through Gachichken," Aurano stated, "We can't afford to delay this quest."

It was just over a week before they came across another village.

"There aren't many towns in Gachichken, are there?" Celestia asked.

"Most of them are in the south," Bridgot said, "The soil in the north is dry and barren, so they can't produce crops up here."

"I see," Celestia said, "Well, that's good and bad for us."

"How's that?" Kgansten asked.

"Good, because there aren't many people around to recognize me, and we can get through unnoticed more easily," she said, "Bad, because we don't have many places to wash up, rest, and refill supplies."

"Aye," Kgansten said, "That's true."

They ventured into the town and found an inn.

"Kgansten," Aurano said, "You room with the princess tonight. You're the only one who hasn't taken a shift with her, yet."

Kgansten nodded. Bridgot and Celestia couldn't say anything as they separated into the two rooms the inn provided them. It felt good to wash up again, and she couldn't wait 'til morning, when they'd get a hot meal and refill their food supply.

Sinking into the soft, comfortable bed, it was easy for her to fall asleep. Poor Kgansten took the floor, and Bridgot and Aurano shared the other room.

Celestia woke up in the middle of the night with a cold chill. She looked around the dark room, but couldn't explain the sense of dread she felt. She looked down at Kgansten, who was sound asleep beside the bed.

She slid down to the floor, tightening her skirt and putting on her shoes and corset quietly. She peered out into the hallway, but there was nothing there. No one and nothing stirred in the darkened inn. She tiptoed over to the other room, peeking inside. Bridgot was sound asleep, but Aurano was awake, fully clothed, sword drawn, watching the door.

"Princess?" he said, "What is it?"

"You sensed it, too, didn't you?" she asked.

His eyes darkened, and he strode over to the door, pulling her inside and looking out into the hall.

"What did you sense?" he asked.

"I don't know," she said, "It's hard to explain. Just, something felt . . . wrong."

He nodded, scratching his chin in thought. After a pause, "I think we need to leave."

"Now?" she said, "It's the middle of the night!"

"I know," he said, "Just trust me."

She paused, contemplating, then nodded.

He woke Bridgot, and she went back to the other room to wake Kgansten. As she was shaking him, she heard a faint noise. It sounded like people yelling outside. Kgansten shot up, dressing and arming himself quickly.

Bridgot and Aurano burst into the room, Aurano saying, "Let's go. Now!"

Celestia and Kgansten rushed over, and they ventured into the hallway. Bridgot wrapped an arm around Celestia, pulling her close as they snuck down the stairs. The yelling outside grew louder, closer.

"What is it?" Celestia asked, clinging to Bridgot, "What's going on?"

"Angry mob," Aurano said, "I'm not sure why they're coming, but I don't want to stick around to find out."

They stopped as they heard banging on the door. A light turned on across the inn, and the innkeeper headed for the door. As she was doing so, the four of them ducked into the kitchen.

They listened as she answered, "What's all this, then?"

There was a rustling of paper, and someone asked, "Have you seen this woman?"

A pause, and then, "What business is it of yours if I've seen her?"

"She's a missing princess. We caught wind of her being sighted here. There's a fair reward being offered for whoever turns her in."

"Well, I want a piece of this reward," the innkeeper said.

They heard faint whispers from the assembled crowd. Finally, the voice said, "Very well. You shall have an equal cut for turning her over . . . if you can produce her."

"She's upstairs, accompanied by a man, a dwarf, and an elf," she said.

They heard footsteps as the mob followed the innkeeper up the stairs. As soon as the front door swung shut, they hurried out of the kitchen and out the back door.

"Bridgot, Kgansten, get her out of here," Aurano said, "I'm the quickest and the quietest. I'll get the horses and meet you in the forest. Go!"

Aurano silently ran off toward the stables, and Bridgot began pulling Celestia toward the forest behind the inn. The three of them took off running, ducking into the cover of the trees as quickly as they could. They moved deeper into the forest, catching a glimpse of the mob in front of the inn—torches, pitchforks, and all. It was just like the stories she'd heard of the dangers of peasants.

Kgansten struggled to keep up, with his short, dwarf legs. They kept running, trying to put distance between them and the village as quickly as possible, and hoping Aurano would soon catch up with the horses.

They heard shouts erupt behind them, as the mob realized they weren't there. They ran hard, branches hitting their faces and scratching them. Celestia's heart raced as she ran, looking over at Bridgot and Kgansten. Soon, the town, and the torches, became a faint dot in the distance, and they slowed down a bit, trying to catch their breath.

"Where's Aurano?" Kgansten gasped, coughing and wheezing, "What's taking him so long? I can't hardly keep up." He placed his hands on his knees, breathing heavily.

Bridgot and Celestia looked at each other uncertainly. Kgansten sat on a nearby rock, letting the air flow freely.

"I'm not sure," Bridgot said, "Is everybody alright?" He looked at Celestia with concern, inching closer to her.

Celestia sucked in a breath, looking back at him. She could see how protective he was toward her, and it surprised her. "I'm alright," she said.

"I will be, once I catch my breath," Kgansten said.

"I knew you'd have difficulty keeping up, dwarf," Aurano said, riding up, with the horses in tow.

Kgansten stood quickly, "What difficulty? I'm fit as a fiddle."

Aurano smirked.

"Are you alright?" Celestia asked, "How did you get away with the horses without being seen?"

"I didn't," he said, "They're coming after us. Let's go, get on your horses!"

As the three of them mounted their horses, they could see he wasn't kidding. The entire mob was galloping toward them, flaming torches in hand. They rode their horses forward, hurrying to get away before they were spotted. It was too late, and the mob behind them rode harder, trying to catch up.

"I thought you said leave it to you!" Bridgot yelled, "You're so quick and quiet, they won't notice you!"

"They didn't see me enter the barn," Aurano said, "But, when I was leaving with four giant horses, it caught their attention!"

Suddenly, Kgansten rode over to Aurano, raising his axe. As Celestia opened her mouth to stop him, he knocked an arrow out of the air, and she realized it would have hit Aurano.

He turned from his conversation with Bridgot, and nodded to Kgansten, "It seems you have repaid one of your life debts, dwarf," he said.

"Make that both," Kgansten said, as he positioned himself behind Aurano, and an arrow struck his armor.

Aurano grabbed his bow and quiver and began firing back at the mob. Celestia did the same, and Bridgot tried to help as much as he could. While his archery had greatly improved, it was far more difficult to fire from horseback than on foot. Kgansten rode to the front of the line since he had no skill with a bow.

As Aurano and Celestia's arrows thinned them out, the mob started to retreat, unable to combat their skill level. The four of them rode hard through the night, and into the wee hours of the morning, to ensure they weren't followed. They slowed down toward lunchtime, and let their horses rest, grazing on the grass, and drinking from the nearby river.

"We should reach Abyumo in just a few days' time," Bridgot said, "It should be safer for us there than here in Gachichken."

"The royal army is probably already riding out to intercept us," Celestia said, "as soon as they get word I've been sighted in the area."

"The magic of the wizards shall shield us from discovery," Aurano said, "as soon as we reach Abyumo."

"Sad to say, we're safer *outside* the human realm," Celestia said, looking at Bridgot.

"Indeed," he agreed, nodding.

"Well," Kgansten said, "We'll have to find somewhere secluded when we stop to make camp. Then, hopefully, with a bit of luck, we'll make it there before we're discovered."

They rode carefully over the next three days, sticking to areas with the most coverage from the main road. They made camp in secluded parts of the forest, as Kgansten had suggested, and set their watches in pairs.

As Celestia was drifting in and out of consciousness one night, she overheard Bridgot and Aurano talking.

"You like the princess, don't you?" Aurano asked. After a pause, "She's asleep, I'm sure. We're all tired. She needs her rest."

Bridgot was silent.

"It's most imprioetous, you know," Aurano said, "You're a peasant. A princess and a peasant simply cannot be together. I'm not sure what you hope will happen, but you should focus on the quest, and let it be."

"It's not so easy," Bridgot said, "I'm not sure I *can* let it be." He sighed, "You wouldn't understand."

"What do you think will happen when this quest is over?" Aurano asked, "Whether I understand your feelings or not is of little consequence. You will both return home, and you will never be allowed to marry. There is no ending in which you end up together, happily, forever."

Bridgot was silent again.

"I'm sorry," Aurano said, "I know this isn't what you want to hear. But it's what you *need* to hear. You humans always think with your feelings, but hardly ever with your heads. You should never have let yourself fall for her. I apologize if I sound cold and uncaring, but I'm saying this *because* I care. I don't want to see you get hurt, and I know you will unless you let your feelings go now."

"You think I don't know that?" Bridgot said, "I've known from the beginning that I *shouldn't* fall for her. I've known from the beginning that it will never work. But, I couldn't stop myself. You telling me now doesn't change anything. I guess, when this quest is over, I'll just have to live with the heartbreak."

Aurano sighed, "Well, as long as you know that. If that's what you must do, then that's what you must do."

Celestia held back her tears, so they wouldn't know she was awake. She hadn't truly thought about what her plans were beyond this quest. Aurano was right. If she did return home when this was over, her mother would never allow her to marry a peasant. She clutched her hand to her heart, and her final thought before she drifted off was, *Maybe I won't go back . . .*

The Oracle

19

"We should reach Abyumo by lunchtime," Bridgot said the next morning, as they set out.

"Maybe we actually will make it before they find us," Celestia said.

"Speak of the devil," Aurano said, "and the devil shall appear."

Celestia shot him a questioning look. Just then, she heard the horns. The royal guards had found them. "Ride!" she yelled, "Hurry!"

They took off, riding their horses hard. Making it to Abyumo was their only hope now. The trees disappeared, as they entered a clearing. The guards rode forward, trying to intercept them. Celestia took the lead, riding Razel faster than she ever had. *There's no way I'm going back,* she thought, *Not now. I've come too far.*

Aurano nearly kept pace with her, with Bridgot just a little ways behind. Kgansten's poor pony tried its best to keep up, but it was left in the dust. Luckily, the guards weren't interested in him. They wanted only the princess.

As the wind whipped through her hair, and the land became a blur, she laughed. After everything she'd faced since she'd run away, the guards were nothing now. She had found freedom. She had found herself. And, she had found her part in this quest.

Celestia crossed the border into Abyumo, followed by Aurano and Bridgot. Kgansten followed up the rear, narrowly making it over before the guards. When they reached the border, they ran into an invisible barrier and were unable to cross.

"I guess you were right, Aurano," Celestia laughed, easing Razel to a stop, "The magic of the wizards *is* shielding us."

Everyone slowed to a stop, and Kgansten caught up, patting his steed, and telling him, "Good job."

"What's this?" a booming voice asked.

They all turned to see a tall old man with a beard that reached his ankles, and a long, pointed hat, walking up, staff in hand.

"Who wants to know?" Aurano asked, eyeing him uncertainly.

"I am Thaandor," he said, "Protector of the border, and keeper of The Oracle. You must be the princess and her warriors, am I right?" He smiled, winking at Aurano.

"Keeper of The Oracle?" Celestia asked, "We finally made it?"

"Indeed," Thaandor said, "And, she is most anxious to speak with you. Follow me." He turned around and began walking.

They followed him slowly, looking at each other. He led them to a tall, elliptical building, the likes of which Celestia had never seen. It glowed from within, and the curved walls seemed to form the doorway organically.

"She has requested to first speak with the princess alone," Thaandor said, blocking their path with his staff.

Her warriors looked as though they were about to object, but Celestia dismounted her horse, saying, "Very well. You three wait here."

She slowly inched toward the door, looking up at the magnificent, ivory structure. As she neared, the glow intensified, and she had to squint. The door blew open, shining light outward, and all but blinding her. She lifted her arm to shield her eyes and ventured inside.

Once the door was closed behind her, the wind and the light died down, and she could see. She was in a room made entirely of ivory, and, in the center, a young woman sat, cross-legged. She was glowing—the cause of the light. Her hair was floating up around her, glowing gold and amber. She wore a turquoise top that hit above her navel, with sheer sleeves, and matching pants, with sheer legs.

When she opened her eyes, they were glowing white, with no pupil or iris. "Welcome, Princess Celestia," she said in a haunting voice.

Celestia thought she should feel afraid, but she didn't, "Are you The Oracle?"

She smiled, "Why have you come?"

The question took her by surprise. "For answers," she said.

"What is it you seek to know so badly?"

"Is this prophecy really about me?" Celestia asked.

"What does your heart tell you?" she responded.

"Everyone else seems to think so, but I'm not convinced," she said.

The Oracle smiled, "You are indeed the princess I prophesied about. You are the only one who can save the land."

"And how exactly do I do that? What is this 'terrible evil?'"

"In the land of Kogatsa, in the kingdom of Khanjgi, a dark wizard lives, by the name of Nazirdok," she said.

Upon hearing the name, Celestia faltered, "Nazirdok?"

The Oracle gave a nod, "He is preparing to perform an ancient ritual— a ritual which will solidify his rule, and plunge the land into darkness for the next hundred years, under his reign."

Celestia's eyes widened.

"To fulfill the prophecy, you must stop him."

"But how?" she asked, "How can I stop him? Why me?"

"Whatever it takes, you must prevent the ritual from being performed. If you are successful, all lands of this world will live in peace for the next hundred years. But, if you fail to stop this ritual from happening before the stars align in a fortnight, I see nothing but death, destruction, and devastation in all of our futures."

Celestia stared at The Oracle, processing what she was telling her. "But, why me?" she asked again.

"Send in your warriors," she said, "I have some things to tell them as well. I cannot tell you why it is you. Only *that* it is you. Go now. Time is becoming even more precious by the second."

Celestia headed back out as the doors reopened. Once she was outside, she said, "The Oracle would like to talk to the three of you now."

Bridgot, Aurano, and Kgansten ventured up to the door, going inside.

"What she told you was for your ears alone," Thaandor said, "And, what she tells them isn't meant for you."

"How long have you served The Oracle?" Celestia asked.

He smiled, "Long enough."

"Are the two of you always so cryptic?"

He laughed, "I suppose she is, and it's kind of rubbed off."

"I see," she said. After a pause, she asked, "Are you a wizard?"

Thaandor smiled again, slyly. He raised his staff, and a light shone out of its top. As it did, droplets of water fell from the sky, plopping against her cheek. She laughed, looking up into the sudden rain, raising her arms and twirling.

When she looked back at Thaandor, she saw that the door had re-opened, and Bridgot was staring at her, smiling. She felt warm, seeing his smile. As Kgansten and Aurano caught up, Thaandor raised his staff again, and when the light cleared, the rain was gone, and everyone was dry again.

"What was that all about?" Kgansten asked.

"I was just asking Thaandor here if he was a wizard," Celestia said, "And the answer is yes, he is."

Just then, she saw a bird fly overhead. It was red and orange, and she knew right away that it had to be a phoenix. It glowed, as though it were covered in flame, and it resembled the auristras, dwervas, and dirthens she'd seen.

"What must we do?" Aurano asked.

Celestia looked back at her warriors.

"To fulfill the prophecy," Bridgot said.

"Oh," Celestia said, "We must get to the kingdom of Khanjgi, in the land of Kogatsa, in a fortnight, and stop a dark wizard from performing a ritual."

All three of her warriors' eyes widened.

"What?" she asked.

"We can't get to Khanjgi in a fortnight," Bridgot said, "It's a five-week journey at a minimum."

Celestia gasped, "What do we do?"

Everyone stood in silence for a moment, before Thaandor said, "I know what you need. Come with me."

He whistled, and a gray, speckled stallion galloped over from around the corner. He leaped upon it, and the four of them rode along behind him.

As it grew dark, Thaandor said, "We shall stop here to make camp. Tomorrow, we shall cross the threshold of wizard territory, and into the territory of the dragon riders."

"Dragon riders?" Celestia asked nervously.

Thaandor nodded.

"Why are we going there?" Bridgot asked, "It's in the opposite direc-tion of Khanjgi."

"Sir," Aurano said, "I, too, do not understand. I thought perhaps you were taking us to a wizard capable of transporting us by magic."

"I'm afraid there are no wizards capable of such a feat; it would take too great a toll. It would be the equivalent of lifting all four of you, and your horses, and carrying you all the way there on foot. No single wizard could accomplish it."

Everyone was silent as they set up for the night.

"So, where *are* we going?" Celestia asked.

"You shall see, soon enough," Thaandor said, "Get some rest."

When morning came, Thaandor continued to lead the way. They stopped for lunch, which was sparse, as their supplies had been drained once again. Celestia hoped they'd find somewhere to refill soon, else they'd be starving, or have to spend time and energy hunting. A short while after they'd started out again, Thaandor said, "Here it is."

Seeing nothing around but empty land, Celestia asked, "Here what is?"

"The border between the wizard realm and the dragon rider realm."

They moved forward, and Celestia noticed a shimmering wall. As they crossed it, everything changed. The grassy plain of the wizard realm was gone, and they were standing in a barren wasteland. She no longer saw phoenixes in the air, but bat-like creatures, off in the distance. Up ahead was a huge, dark structure. It spanned a great distance, but she couldn't yet see its full size.

Her warriors were marveling as much as she was at the change of scenery, and they continued to follow Thaandor across the desert plain. As they moved across it, the structure grew. Beyond it, she could see mountains. And, as the structure grew nearer and larger, so did the creatures that had at first resembled bats.

Celestia's eyes widened as she realized the massive size of these creatures. Even the smallest of them was four times the size of her horse. They had shining scales of various colors, huge, membranous wings, sharp teeth and claws, long tails, and breath of fire.

"What are those things?" she asked Bridgot in terror.

"Dragons," he said warily.

Dragons and Riders

20

The structure she'd seen was far more massive than she had anticipated, spanning a few miles in every direction, and high up into
the clouds. They followed Thaandor up to the drawbridge, where a
group of men and elves in armor stood.

"Who goes there?" they demanded.

"It is I, Thaandor, keeper of The Oracle. I have brought a few friends.
We wish to speak with Kirstiana."

They looked at each other and nodded, lowering the drawbridge to
let them in. Once the five of them were inside, they closed it behind them,
saying, "Right this way."

One of them led them through the gigantic city, and Celestia saw
humans, elves, and dragons everywhere. Up close, the dragons were even
more terrifying. Some were the size of buildings, and bigger. She had never
seen creatures this large before. They passed a blue-scaled dragon as they
walked, and she watched as it breathed fire into a pit for cooking. Each
tooth was the size of her entire body. It took a long while to get past it,
covering ground equal to its length. Razel bristled nervously.

"Shh," Celestia said, "It's okay, girl."

"Who's Kirstiana?" Aurano asked.

"An old friend," Thaandor said, "And, queen of the dragon riders."

Celestia only vaguely heard them as she stared, speechless, at the incredible creatures called dragons. The guard led them to the palace at the
top of the city. It was illuminated in green and gold; it looked as though it

were made entirely from jewels and gems. She looked up in amazement. A few servants led their horses away as they entered the palace.

They followed the guard through the glittering palace to the throne room. It was three times the size of King Thanghor's. Inside was a giant, glittering, amber dragon. And, on a tall throne beside it, a woman with auburn hair, sun-kissed skin, and golden armor, sat. Upon her head was a shining crown, and upon her shoulders, a fluid cape trailed behind her. Large, spiky earrings dangled on either side of her head, and her hair was pulled back and tucked to hold her crown.

"Thaandor," she said, giving a slight nod.

"Milady," he said, bowing.

"What brings you here?"

"I seek your help," he said.

She paused, deliberating, "With what?"

"As you know, The Oracle has prophesied that a princess from a great merged kingdom would be accompanied by three warriors, from each the races of man, dwarf, and elf, to save the land from darkness."

"Yes," she said, "Everyone knows of this prophecy. What of it?"

Thaandor gestured behind him, "This is Princess Celestia and her warriors—the princess of the prophecy."

Kirstiana looked over at them, "Greetings, friends. I trust you have spoken with The Oracle and learned what you must do."

"That's why we have come," Thaandor said.

She turned her attention back to him.

"We need your help," he said, "The Oracle said that in order to fulfill the prophecy and save the land from darkness, they need to get to the king-dom of Khanjgi, in the land of Kogatsa, in less than a fortnight. It cannot be done by horseback."

Kirstiana bristled. After a pause, she leaned back in her throne.

"Please," Thaandor said, "They can't do this without you."

"What you ask," she said, "is impossible."

"Without you, yes," he said, "But, with you, no."

She placed her hand against her chin, contemplating.

"Please," Celestia said, "If there's a way . . . a way we can fulfill this prophecy before the stars align, we'll do anything. If we fail, the world will be plunged into a hundred years of darkness, with only death and destruc-tion for all the lands of this world, including yours."

Kirstiana looked at her, then, first with surprise, then with a flash of anger, and then with a half smile. Everyone waited in silence to hear what her answer would be. She rose from her throne, descending the steps beside it, and walked up to them. As she neared, Celestia could see her amber eyes gleaming.

Her dragon stirred, but she said, "Rest, Solstra. Everything's alright." After a pause, she said, "Follow me."

They followed her out of the throne room, and she whispered something to her servants on the way out. They went down the hall and entered a room near the size of the throne room. There were large archways all the way around it, and a table in the center, surrounded by chairs.

"Have a seat," she instructed, sitting at the head of the table. The five of them sat to her left and right, as several men and women in different colors of armor entered the room, taking the remainder of the seats. Celestia froze as she saw the reason for the great number of arches. Several dragons of various colors stuck their heads into the room.

"Ladies and gentlemen," Kirstiana said, once everyone was seated, "I have called this meeting to discuss a pressing and serious matter."

Several of those assembled stirred, whispering to each other.

"Relax," she said, waving her hands. Once everyone quieted down, she continued. "These individuals," she gestured to Celestia and her warriors, "are the princess of The Great Prophecy and her warriors. According to The Oracle, they must get to Kogatsa in less than a fortnight. By horseback, 'tis impossible. But, by dragonback . . ."

Dragonback? Celestia thought in disbelief. This was Thaandor's great plan? To have them *fly* there? On a *dragon*?

"Absolutely not," One of the seated women said.

"This is an outrage!" One of the men shouted, rising, "An abomination!"

"These are not dragon riders!" Another man said, "They have no business *near* a dragon, let alone riding one!"

"Everyone, please," Kirstiana said, gesturing for them to take a seat. They reluctantly obliged. "Now," she said, turning toward Celestia, "I believe you have something to say?"

Celestia's eyes widened, and she swallowed.

Kirstiana nodded, looking at her expectantly.

"Yes," Celestia said, clearing her throat, "The Oracle has spoken. You know that she foresees all. And, she has seen the two possible outcomes of this quest. If we fail to get to Khanjgi before the stars align, the world will plummet into darkness for the next hundred years," her voice grew stronger as she spoke, "There will be nothing but death and destruction dealt to people of all lands."

The people at the table shifted uncomfortably, exchanging glances with one another.

"But," she continued, "if we succeed, the world will live in peace, and all peoples within. We can't possibly hope to get there in time on our own. We need your help. The fate of the world for the next hundred years rests with you."

After a pause, where everyone seemed to be processing the information they'd been given, Kirstiana rose and said, "You all understand the situation. It's time to make a decision. Those in favor?"

The majority of them raised their hands.

"Those opposed?"

A few of them raised their hands.

"Arguments?" she asked.

A man with dark skin, garbed in silver armor, rose, saying, "We cannot be called upon to help the world with its problems. Dragons are mystical, ancient creatures, deserving of our respect and understanding. Only dragon riders can bond with them and truly appreciate them. These outsiders can't hope to come into our midst at the word of an oracle, and borrow some dragons! It's a disgrace that you would consider it, my queen."

"Anyone else?" Kirstiana asked.

They were silent.

"Does anyone wish to change their vote?" she asked.

No one raised their hand.

"Very well," she said, "The vote carries. Tomorrow, we shall have a tournament, and the day following, you all shall set out on dragonback for Kogatsa. Meeting adjourned."

The people seated at the table got up and left, and the dragons pulled their heads out of the archways.

"Tournament?" Celestia asked after they'd all gone.

"You don't really think we'd allow you to just take our dragons with no one to keep an eye on you, do you?" Kirstiana said, "We'll be sending a dragon rider to accompany you, as well as a dragon caretaker."

"Forgive my impatience," Celestia said, "But, each day we waste is a day of travel lost. With time already so pressed, I'm not sure it's the best idea to delay. Couldn't we have the tournament today, and set out at dawn?"

She smirked, "Trust me, you'll get there in time. You all are welcome here tonight. Please enjoy the feast this evening. Loretta will show you to your rooms."

She snapped her fingers, and a young woman in a servant's dress appeared, "Right this way." She led them down the glittering hallway of the palace, and to four suites, with enough room in each one for a dragon. The bed frames were made of the same jewels the whole palace was made from, but with soft, cushioned bedding.

"I'll come and get you all a bit later for the feast," Loretta said, "Please feel free to relax and wash up. There's a washroom just there," she pointed to the left of the suites.

"Thank you," Celestia said.

Loretta nodded, bowing, and scurrying off down the hall.

When Loretta came to get them for the feast, they were cleaned, groomed, and refreshed. She led them to a room even larger than the throne room, full of tables in the center, with dragon riders seated at them, and dragons around the edges, waiting to be fed. Celestia gulped as they entered. Being in a room with massive, hungry creatures was not her idea of a good time.

"I hope they don't run out of food," Celestia said.

Bridgot laughed.

"Me, too," Kgansten said.

"I'm sure they're well-prepared," Aurano stated.

They were seated beside the queen as the food was brought out. There were human and elven delicacies all around, as well as several foods Celestia had never seen. It was impossible to go hungry with all of the things they had to offer. After so long on the road with depleting saddlebags, it felt wonderful to truly get full. Everyone enjoyed themselves, even Aurano.

Celestia watched in amazement as the dragons were fed. Whole animals were brought before them, and they tore through them with their huge, sharp teeth, and swallowed them with ease, belching flames. She turned back to her plate, trying not to make eye contact with any of them.

Bridgot and Aurano seemed as fascinated as she was, watching the immense creatures. Kgansten looked as though he had gone in his pants. He was petrified; his eyes were glued open in terror. The dragon riders seemed perfectly at ease, eating, chatting, and having a good time.

When the feast was over, they returned to their rooms, clean, with full bellies, and went straight to sleep, sinking into the soft, welcoming beds. Even Celestia, with her mind full of worry about the quest ahead, found it easy to drift off.

Loretta showed up at their doors in the morning, and they followed her through the glittering palace hallways to a colossal arena, where they were seated beside Kirstiana. In the center, there were several dragons and their riders, waiting.

"Our finest riders have gathered," Kirstiana said excitedly, "You're in for a real treat. You may have been to tournaments before, but you've never seen one quite like a tournament of dragon riders!"

An announcer appeared in the ring—a mere spec amongst the dragons, "Contestants will be disqualified for the use of any illegal moves, as previously discussed. Contestants will be eliminated for going out of bounds. Contestants will attempt to collect the flags from the tail of each competing dragon. If your flag is taken, you will be eliminated. Last one flying wins!"

He scurried out of the ring as the tournament began. The dragons took to the sky, riders upon their backs. There were dragons of every color, turning the arena into a blurry rainbow as they flew about. They each went after another, attempting to take the nearest opponent's flag. Celestia marveled at how the dragons soared through the air, and at the riders' skill upon their backs. They were able to stand, jump, and swing around, trying to grab the other flags and defend their own.

Several of them were eliminated quickly, some for flying out of bounds, which terrified Celestia, as she watched them fly into the stands, praying they wouldn't crash into her and her warriors, and some for having their flags taken.

The sound of wings beating permeated the arena like thunder. It smelled like a campfire, and Celestia leaped into Bridgot's arms as a turquoise dragon flew past, breathing fire, close enough to warm their faces. He blushed, and they exchanged intimate, yet terrified glances.

"Isn't this wonderful?" Kirstiana asked.

"Hell no!" Kgansten yelled, ducking down, and covering his head.

"It is a bit frightening," Celestia said, still clinging to Bridgot.

"Well, you'd better get used to it," she said, "since you'll be riding them soon!"

As the group thinned out, there were fewer dragons tumbling into the audience, and it was easier to see the individual dragons and riders who were competing. They surfed along their dragons' saddles and tails, some even leaping through the air to collect opponents' flags. They'd grab the flag, and then let themselves fall. Their dragons would always manage to catch them somehow.

Celestia was amazed and terrified at the same time. She had to close her eyes whenever anyone fell, but, when she peeked through her fingers, their dragon was right there, waiting. She was thoroughly impressed with their skill, and even when she had to look away, she couldn't do so for long—she had to see what was happening.

Soon, there were only a handful of riders left. One, in particular, caught Celestia's attention: a dark-skinned human woman on a green dragon. She glided around the other riders with ease, swooping out of the way when they went for her flag, and strategically leaping onto the other dragons when their riders were distracted. She was graceful and focused, and it seemed none of the other riders could touch her.

As more and more of them were eliminated, she waited on the outskirts, circling. A black and a red dragon clashed in the center of the arena, the riders of each locked on, struggling to reach the other's flag first. The green dragon circled, as its rider leapt from its back, landing on the tail of the only other remaining dragon—a pink dragon. She snatched the flag as the rider jumped up to stop her, and she stood on the tail, smiling, holding the flag triumphantly, and let herself slide off. Her green dragon swooped beneath her, and she landed upon its saddle. As the red and black dragons and their riders were still fighting, distracted, she dove below them, snatching the flags from their tails in one clean, graceful movement.

As the three dragons and their riders were eliminated, she was the only one left. The announcer returned to the arena, saying, "And our winner is . . . Ezmyra, and her rider, Nastazya!"

The crowd cheered, and Kirstiana leaned over, saying, "Nastazya is one of our most promising riders! You should be honored to have her accompany you on your quest!"

Once the tournament was over, Kirstiana led them to another section of the palace. They went through a pair of tall doors, and into a room with two dragons. Celestia and her warriors entered cautiously, behind Kirstiana.

"These," she said, making a grand gesture, "are your dragons." After a slight pause, she added, "Well, temporarily."

One was glittering purple, and the other was shining black. Celestia stared at the colossal dragons in awe, unsure. Bridgot stayed a step behind her, staring as well. Kgansten remained near the door in sheer terror. Only Thaandor and Aurano ventured a bit closer.

"The black one is Diamante, and the purple one is Tourmethyst," Kirstiana said, "They both lost their riders some years ago, tragically. We weren't sure if they'd come around again. But, without a sense of purpose, they volunteered for this quest."

Everyone was silent for a minute, looking down sorrowfully.

After a pause, Celestia piped up, "There are five of us. How will we all fit on two dragons?"

"There are four of you," Thaandor said.

"You're not coming with us?" Bridgot asked.

"This quest is not meant for me," he said, "I am needed by The Oracle."

"*We* need you," Celestia said, "None of us know magic. We're going up against a dark wizard. We need someone who can help us fight against his powers."

"I'm afraid I wouldn't be very useful to you, then," he said, "He is too powerful; I'm no match for him."

"So, how are we supposed to fight a wizard?" Celestia asked.

"Trust your heart," Thaandor said, "The prophecy says *you* are the only one who can stop him, not me."

"But, I can't do magic," she replied.

"I know," he said, "But, I trust The Oracle. She's never been wrong before." With that, he turned around and walked out.

"I'll let you get to know your dragons a bit," Kirstiana said, "You leave at dawn. And, don't worry about your horses; they'll be in good hands here. I take my leave." She headed out of the room, leaving the four of them alone with two dragons.

Nastazya

21

urano eased forward slowly, bowing to the ancient creatures. Bridgot and Celestia stood together a ways back, watching. Kgansten hadn't moved from the doorway. Aurano reached a hand forward, gently touching the snout of the black dragon. Diamante leaned his head against Aurano's hand, encouraging him to give him a good scratch. Aurano smiled, petting the great dragon.

"I'm impressed," Nastazya said, coming around from the other side of the room.

Celestia got a closer look at her. She had ebony skin and hair, and emerald eyes. Her hair was in a tight, twisted bun, and she wore a black bodysuit, with accent lines of green, which accentuated her curves. She had black gloves and boots, and a green belt along her natural waist.

Aurano paused, staring at her.

"Most beings, other than dragon riders, are too frightened to get close to a dragon, let alone touch one," Nastazya said.

"Well," Aurano said, clearing his throat, and taking his hand from Diamante's snout, "I was told they volunteered for this quest. If they wish to help us, why would they harm us?"

She smiled, "Indeed."

"I was most impressed by your performance in the tournament," Celestia chimed in.

"Thank you," Nastazya said, looking at her.

"Yes," Aurano said, "It was evident your skill was unmatched."

She smiled at him, "Well, you've gotten to know Diamante. Why don't you say hello to Tourmethyst?"

Aurano gave a slight nod and reached for Tourmethyst's snout. He backed away, snorting smoke from his nostrils. Aurano showed no fear, saying, "My apologies, Tourmethyst. I only wish to extend you my gratitude." He stood still, waiting, until Tourmethyst slowly settled back into place, nudging his hand in acceptance. Aurano patted his snout and gave him a bow.

"Well done," Nastazya said, "You're a natural. Perhaps they should see if an egg hatches for you. You could be a rider—you never know."

Aurano smiled, "It would be a dream come true to be a rider. I'm not sure if that's my destiny, though."

"I'll see to it you get a shot," she said. She turned to the rest of them, "Come on. You all need to get to know these two if you're going to be riding them tomorrow."

Bridgot and Celestia looked at each other. With hesitation, they inched forward together. Celestia reached for Tourmethyst as Bridgot reached for Diamante. The two dragons accepted their snout pats willingly, nuzzling their hands.

"Good," Nastazya said, "See? Dragons aren't so bad."

Celestia smiled, "No. They're not as frightening as I thought."

It was Nastazya's turn to smile. Then, she turned toward Kgansten, who still hadn't budged, "Come on, dwarf. Don't be shy."

"My name's Kgansten," he said gruffly, unmoving.

"Very well," she said, "Come on, Kgansten."

He slowly shuffled forward, and Celestia could see the beads of sweat all over his face. He looked as white as Seina's mane. He crept past the four of them and stood before the two dragons, panicked. He stood paralyzed, not daring to lift his arm. The dragons looked at each other, and then Diamante nudged him with his snout, and his massive tongue flicked out of his mouth, licking Kgansten's face.

Kgansten fell backward, passing out. He woke up quickly though, flailing about, and scrambling back.

"It's alright, Kgansten," Celestia said, "They won't hurt you."

Nastazya laughed.

"I thought you feared nothing this quest could throw at you," Aurano said.

Celestia watched the internal struggle Kgansten was having between his pride and his fear. Finally, pride won out, and he said, "I don't. I just . . . didn't want to overwhelm the poor beasts with too much attention."

They all laughed.

"I'll see you all in the morning," Nastazya said, heading back out of the room.

"Let's get some rest," Celestia said, "We're going to need it for the journey ahead."

As sunlight began to trickle into the suite Celestia was sleeping in, the light filtered by the bejeweled structure, she awoke. Her stomach was in knots as she dressed and gathered her things. She had no idea what to expect, riding a dragon. And, truth be told, she was anxious about the concept of flying.

She met up with Bridgot, Aurano, and Kgansten, and they headed to the room where Diamante and Tourmethyst waited. Nastazya was there with her dragon, Ezmyra, and a pale man with black hair in a peasant's outfit.

"Good morning," she said, "Are you all ready to go?"

"Definitely," Aurano said.

"Who's he?" Bridgot asked suspiciously.

"This is Forx," Nastazya said, "He's one of our dragon caretakers. He'll be accompanying us."

Forx nodded to them, shuffling around the dragons, and making sure their saddles were tight.

"Well, let's get going," Celestia said, "There's no time to waste."

"I like your enthusiasm," Nastazya said, "Let's go."

"Who's riding with who?" Kgansten asked shakily.

"Well, Diamante is more easy-going than Tourmethyst," Nastazya said, "so you should probably ride upon him if you're nervous. Aurano, why don't you go with him? As calm as you are, I think it would help. Bridgot, Princess Celestia, why don't you two ride Tourmethyst? Forx will ride with me on Ezmyra."

Celestia was relieved to be riding with Bridgot. As nervous as she was to fly, she thought the calming effect he had on her would help. The two of them headed over to the purple dragon, and Bridgot climbed into his saddle. Celestia had to lift her leg quite a ways to reach the stirrup. As she struggled to hoist herself up such a great height, Bridgot extended his hand to help her. He pulled her up, and she squirmed around a bit getting into the saddle behind him.

Nastazya leaped upon her emerald dragon's back with ease, and Forx climbed into the saddle behind her. Aurano had to help Kgansten up into the black dragon's saddle, much to Kgansten's embarrassment. Celestia could see the panic on his face as he sat, frozen in the saddle. Aurano swung himself up, climbing in front of Kgansten.

Once everyone was situated in their respective saddles, Nastazya said, "Just steer the way you would steer a horse! Keep calm, and hold on tight!" With that, Ezmyra took off, flying upward, and out through the open ceiling.

"Hang on, Kgansten!" Aurano yelled, shaking the reins. They weren't connected like horse reins, around the heads of the dragons, but were looped around the underbelly in front of the saddle. Diamante took off, flying up, as Kgansten clung to Aurano for dear life.

"Ready?" Bridgot asked.

Celestia answered by wrapping her arms around him tightly and taking a deep breath.

"Here goes nothing," he said, giving the reins a shake.

Tourmethyst launched himself upward, spiraling toward the sky. As they left the ground, Celestia got butterflies in her stomach, and she wanted to scream, but couldn't open her mouth. They headed up and out of the glistening palace, and the entire massive city below became a little dot. They soared into the clouds, and Celestia stared in amazement as the purple dragon slowed down enough for her to catch her breath, and take in her surroundings.

She had never imagined flying would be this magical. Tourmethyst leveled out, and she could see Diamante and Ezmyra in front of them. Nothing else stirred this high in the air. She felt as though she had reached the heavens. The oranges and pinks of the sunrise illuminated the white, fluffy clouds in a beautiful ring of light.

Celestia slowly released her death grip from Bridgot's waist and splayed her arms out to either side. She let out a laugh, feeling the most incredible rush. As the dragons sped forward, through the sky, she yelled, "Woo!"

Bridgot turned toward her, smiling over his shoulder. Nastazya's voice rang out ahead as she responded with a "Woo!" of her own.

Celestia was amazed at how fast they were able to go, and how much ground they were able to cover. By the end of the day, they had traveled back out of Abyumo and across the land of Cardeas, just north of Gachichken.

When it got dark, they decided to land in the trees and make camp. Celestia watched as Ezmyra dove down, followed by Diamante. Bridgot pulled up on the reins, and Tourmethyst plunged toward the earth. Celestia's stomach dropped to her feet, butterflies returning tenfold, and she let out a scream as they plummeted.

They spiraled into the trees, a few branches clipping them, and landed in a clearing. "Great job," Bridgot said, patting Tourmethyst's side.

He and Celestia slid off of the purple dragon's back. Her legs were killing her. She wasn't used to sitting on such a wide saddle. She had to hike up her skirt just to straddle it. Everyone gathered around to set up camp. Poor Kgansten looked as though he would be sick.

"How's that for a rush?" Nastazya asked.

"It was amazing!" Aurano shouted.

Celestia had never seen him so excited. "It was incredible," she said.

"They barely need any direction," Bridgot added.

"They're not horses," Nastazya said, "They're highly intelligent creatures. They can carry a conversation with the best of them."

"They can talk?" Celestia asked in wonder.

"Well, with riders," she said, "We can communicate with our dragons."

"How?" she asked.

Nastazya smirked, sitting on a boulder, "You become a rider when you're brought before a dragon egg, and it hatches for you. Humans and elves from all over the world come to Abyumo to see if they could be a rider. The dragon rider council decides who is allowed before the eggs. If they find you worthy, you're taken to a room full of dragon eggs. You walk up and down the aisles, touching the eggs, seeing if any will hatch for you. Dragons only hatch when they come into contact with their rider. They can wait hundreds of years for the right person to come along. If one hatches for you, you become a rider. You and your dragon are bound to each other until one of you dies. A dragon can only ever have one rider, so if they die, the dragon remains riderless the rest of their life."

Diamante and Tourmethyst let out groans of sadness, and Celestia and Aurano patted their sides sympathetically.

"A rider, too, can only ever have one dragon, once the bond is formed. So, if their dragon dies, they're no longer a rider," she continued, "When you're bonded, you hear each other's thoughts, feel each other's emotions, and you become one with your dragon. It's unlike anything else in this world."

"So that's why you all treat dragons with such reverence," Celestia said.

"Dragons are ancient, magical creatures," Nastazya went on, "When you become a rider, your lifespan increases tenfold. You also become gifted with magic. That's why wizards and dragon riders live in such close proximity. We're able to work together on certain magical projects."

"Do think it wise to entrust them with so much inside information?" Forx asked.

"I think it would be foolish not to," she said, "They need to know what they're working with just as I do. If they know nothing of dragons and riders, how can they display the proper regard?"

Forx silently turned back to his stew, which they had prepared as they'd been talking, eyeing them with suspicion.

"Well, there's not much to know about us," Celestia said.

"I've already been informed of your skills," Nastazya said, "You, princess, are a gifted archer, and a passable sword fighter. Bridgot, your human warrior, is just the opposite—a skilled swordsman, and a passable archer. Kgansten, your dwarf warrior, is unbeatable with an axe. And Aurano, your elf warrior, is naturally unmatched in both archery and sword fighting."

"How do you know so much about us?" she asked.

"I make it my business to know who I'm traveling and working with," she said.

After a pause, "You said you're gifted with magic?"

Nastazya smiled slyly, reminding her much of the expression Thaandor had had when she'd asked if he was a wizard. She leaned over and grabbed Celestia's bowl of stew. Her green eyes glowed like two shining emeralds as she stared at it intently. When she handed it back, it was hot.

"Whoa!" Celestia said, nearly dropping it. After a pause, she asked, "How powerful are you?"

"Dragon riders are more powerful than wizards if that's what you're wondering. We have greater reserves of strength and energy than they do, since we're able to tap into our dragon's magic."

"You could help us defeat the dark wizard, then," she said.

Nastazya's smile turned to a frown, "Unfortunately, the wizard we're going up against is too powerful. He has access to other sources of energy and power, that make him untouchable by magic such as mine. Only Merlin himself could help you."

Celestia sighed, *So Merlin wasn't just a legend.* Even she knew he was long since dead. "How do you know so much about the dark wizard?" she asked.

"I went to see The Oracle the night before we left," Nastazya said, "and she told me what we were up against."

"She told you?"

"Yes. She said I needed to know the extent of what I could do, and what *he* could do, so I didn't do anything rash and foolish, else I'd jeopardize the success of this quest."

Everyone was quiet for a moment.

"Well, on that note," Bridgot said, "I think we should divide watches into pairs. Why don't Aurano and I take the first shift?"

"Sure," Nastazya said, "Forx and I will go after you."

"Very well," Celestia said, "Kgansten, try to get some sleep. Looks like we'll be sharing a watch."

Once everyone had settled down to get some rest, Celestia heard Nastazya and Forx's breathing slow next to her. She tried to drift off as well, but couldn't seem to. Her head was full of thoughts of dark wizards and magic and prophecies.

"What do you think The Oracle meant?" Bridgot asked, "When she said each of us has a part to play before this quest is over?"

"Only time will tell," Aurano said.

"I'm more concerned with the fact that one of us is going to die," Kgansten said suddenly, "She really inspired confidence, didn't she?"

"He speaks," Aurano said, "I thought you'd be frozen forever."

"Not quite," Kgansten retorted, "Though, I'm still not a fan of large creatures, or leaving the ground. But, for the sake of this quest, I'm afraid I must continue on."

"Shouldn't you be asleep?" Aurano said, "You know it's not your shift, yet."

"I couldn't possibly sleep tonight," he replied, "Not with everything that's going on." After a pause, he added, "So, who do you think it will be?"

They were all silent for a moment, before Aurano said solemnly, "I think we all know. The Oracle said one of us will die to save the princess, and that it must happen, in order to succeed. Which of us is most likely to risk their life for her?"

They were silent again.

"You should get some rest, Kgansten," Bridgot said. His voice was strange.

Die? Celestia thought, heart clenching in her chest, *I don't want anyone to die for me, least of all Bridgot.* She had never thought of the possibility of anyone not coming back from this quest. Perhaps it was too morbid a thought. Knowing The Oracle had told her warriors that one of them would have to die saving her in order for this quest to succeed, she wasn't sure if it was worth it. She cared about all three of them. And, deep down, she knew Aurano was right: it was most likely Bridgot.

Ezmyra

22

The next morning, they woke, ate breakfast, and climbed back upon the three dragons, taking to the sky. Celestia held Bridgot tightly as they flew, appreciating the feeling of his warmth, and his rippling muscles, under her fingers. Now that she knew they didn't have forever, each second with him was precious to her. She rested her head against him, closing her eyes and breathing him in. The sound of his heartbeat against her ear was wonderful.

They flew through the day, across the land of Fluorasti, making it nearly halfway through by sunset. The magic of flying through the air wasn't the least bit depleted the second day. She looked out, over Bridgot's shoulder, past Tourmethyst's head, at the vast expanse of the world below. High over the trees, over the people, over the river, up in the clouds, with nothing but horizon ahead, she felt freer than she ever had. She could see the appeal of being a dragon rider, now.

When they landed that evening, they decided to rotate their shift partners, so everyone would be together at least once. Celestia was paired with Forx, Bridgot with Nastazya, and Kgansten with Aurano.

"So, what's it like, being a dragon caretaker?" Celestia asked once everyone had seemingly drifted off.

Forx turned his dark eyes on her, and then looked away, unanswering.

"Why are you so suspicious of us?" she probed.

He turned back toward her, "I don't trust people until they prove worthy of my trust."

"What must we do to prove worthy?"

"It takes time," he said, "There must be a few examples of trustworthiness. I don't know any of you well enough, or for long enough, to have any examples. I take my job very seriously. Dragons command the utmost respect, care, and effort. I strive for all three."

"I can appreciate that," she said, "But, I think, despite the fact that you claim to reserve judgment until you have examples, you are judging us to be untrustworthy, with no examples of that, either."

Forx looked at her. His eyes widened a moment, and he opened his mouth, as if to say something, but changed his mind. He narrowed his eyes and pursed his lips, crossing his arms.

She could tell she had made an impact with her point, but she could also see she would get no further conversation from him. She focused on the darkened forest around them, and the great, sleeping dragons. Even in the dark, their scales shone. Diamante's jet black color blended right in. Tourmethyst and Ezmyra sparkled like gems, with their bold, beautiful hues. Their bodies gave off such warmth that they didn't need a fire as they slept to ward off the cold, night air.

The next day, as they were flying along, Celestia marveled at Tourmethyst's wings. The membranes formed lines that created the main structure and design, while the rest of the wings looked thin and fragile, like colored paper. To the touch, they felt like skin. They resembled giant bat wings, which made sense since the dragons had looked like bats from a great distance. They were strong and leathery, despite their fragile appearance. Somehow, they were able to carry these immense beasts through the air.

The days were spent entirely in the air, from sunrise to sunset. Celestia spent her time observing the small imperfections of Tourmethyst's wings and scales, marveling at the breathtaking views, and napping against Bridgot's back.

The nights were easier to bear, with a partner for each shift, to offer some conversation. She was glad she'd already partnered with Forx since he wasn't much to talk to. As they landed for the night, with only a small expanse of Fluorasti left to go, she was partnered with Nastazya for her shift, Bridgot with Kgansten, and Aurano with Forx.

When Aurano woke her for her shift, she was eager to chat with Nastazya, and get to know this incredible dragon rider. "So, what was it like?" she asked once they were seated at their post.

Nastazya shot her a questioning look, "What?"

"When Ezmyra hatched for you, and you became a rider," Celestia said.

She smiled, looking as though she were reliving the memory, "Well, I was twelve years old at the time. It's best if you're young when they hatch, so you can really grow together. I grew up in a village in Cardeas. We were poor, and there wasn't much opportunity for a better life there. My mother died when I was ten, and my father didn't know how to care for a young lady. So, he treated me the same as my brothers. Living so close to Abyumo, we all knew of the dragon riders. I desperately wanted to be one, if for nothing else than to get out of there."

Celestia nodded in understanding.

Nastazya continued, "My father sold my horse so I'd have enough money for the journey. There certainly wasn't enough for a return, so it was rider or bust. I prayed every night that I would even get the chance. I walked all the way there. When I got there, I wasn't the only one. I got ushered into a class of around twenty recruits, all fighting to be chosen as worthy of going before the eggs."

"They only choose one?" she asked.

"They choose whomever they deem worthy," she said, "however many that may be. They're taken before the eggs individually, though, so nothing gets confused. Anyway, when I was chosen, they brought me to that room. All my hopes and dreams rested on that moment. I don't know what I would've done if none of them hatched for me. I was terrified of the possibility. I walked carefully through the field of eggs, letting my hands gently glide over each one. As I turned a corner, I heard a crack. I froze, and then turned around to see an egg cracking open. When the shell exploded away, there she was—a little, green beauty. I knelt before her, and she came right up to me, nuzzling my leg. I reached down to pet her tiny head, and when my hand touched her, I felt it."

"Felt what?" Celestia questioned.

"It's hard to explain," Nastazya answered, "It's sort of a jolt, a shock, a tingling feeling all through you, when you become bonded with your dragon for life. You've noticed how my eyes are green, right?"

"Yes," she said.

"Well, they used to be brown. When you're bonded with your dragon, your eyes become the color of their scales. Like I said, the two of you become one. I could hear her thoughts suddenly, and she could hear mine. I scooped her up and carried her with me to the door. The council was waiting, and when they saw that a dragon had hatched for me, they bowed in respect. It was the first time in my life that I felt like *somebody*. I had purpose; my life had meaning. I was no longer a poor, peasant girl. I was a dragon rider."

Celestia sat for a moment, taking it in. "So, what attracted you to this quest?" she asked.

"That's easy," Nastazya said, "I'm still considered a fairly new, young rider. At least, compared to the veterans. So, to gain the respect and favor of the other riders, I need to prove that I can handle something this important."

Celestia nodded, understanding.

"I can't fight this wizard for you," Nastazya said, "But, I can at least help."

"Thank you," Celestia said, "That's more than anyone else can do."

As they woke Kgansten and Bridgot and settled back down to sleep, Celestia wondered for the millionth time, *How in the world am I going to stop a wizard?*

Of Love and Friendship

23

The next day was beautiful weather as they flew along, a warm breeze caressing their faces. Celestia felt in her element, just enjoying the purple hues of the sky, especially as they reflected off Tourmethyst's scales.

When they landed to make camp, everyone got comfortable, as Nastazya and Aurano took their posts for their watch. Celestia had just begun drifting off, when she heard Nastazya say, "I'm impressed with your ease and care around dragons. I think you really could be a rider. It's most unnatural for any others."

"Thank you," Aurano said, "But, I'm perfectly at ease with all creatures of the world until they show a desire to hurt me, or others. I've dedicated so much of my life to training for combat, that I have no desire to generate conflict. We elves are naturally peaceful creatures."

There was a pause before Nastazya said, "You're not like anyone I've ever met, Aurano. No one has ever shown the deep compassion and understanding for all of God's creatures that you possess."

Another pause and Aurano stuttered, "I-I'm nothing special. I'm only an elven warrior-in-training. There are hundreds of us."

"No," Nastazya said, "There's only one like you."

Aurano gulped, "Th-thank you." He cleared his throat, "But, I think you're far more extraordinary."

"Me?" she asked, "Really?"

"Definitely," he said softly, "From the moment I saw you, I could see that you had more spirit, more drive, more dedication, and more skill than anyone I've yet known. You have such a caring heart, a strong disposition, and a thrilling soul."

It was the first time Celestia had seen this side of Aurano. He was nervous and stuttering and speaking so softly and sweetly. Even the talkative Nastazya was at a loss for words. It warmed Celestia's heart, hearing the two of them. She couldn't help but smile as she tried to drift off to give them some privacy.

"Thank you," Nastazya said finally, "Most guys will only offer compliments based on appearance. I've never met a man who could speak to my very soul the way you do." She paused, "You know, I've always considered myself independent. I thought it would just be me and my dragon forever. But, for some reason, when I'm near you, I feel warm, and my stomach does more flip flops than it does when I'm doing a twisting dive with Ezmyra. I've never been one for romance, but when you talk to a girl the way you do, it gets her thinking."

"Thinking about what?" he asked.

"About a life outside of combat," she said, "Settling down someday."

"I would never ask you to settle," he replied, "You have too many amazing gifts to share with the world." He paused, "You know, building a life doesn't have to mean settling."

"If we were together, I don't think it would be," she said softly.

Celestia finally drifted off, dreaming of love.

When Kgansten woke her for her shift, she took her post beside Bridgot. Once Kgansten and Forx had settled in, he said, "We're making great time. It's incredible! I was worried we wouldn't be able to make it, even still. But, we're already in Mashang. A three-week journey by horseback, in just four days!"

"Really?" Celestia asked excitedly.

Bridgot nodded, "When we crossed Cardeas in a day, I couldn't believe it. Then, through Fluorasti. The two combined are about the length of Gachichken. Mashang is north of Korga. At this rate, we'll be through it in only a few more days, and into Kogatsa."

Celestia nodded solemnly, contemplating.

"We have to be careful as we're crossing through Mashang, though."

"What do you mean?" she asked.

"They're allied with Kogatsa. If this dark wizard *has* taken over the kingdom of Khanjgi, then we can assume this is unfriendly territory."

Celestia's eyes widened, and she sat quietly, thinking. This quest got more complicated by the minute.

"But, to be fair," Bridgot said, "Who would dare to attack us in the night with *three dragons* lying around our campsite?"

Celestia laughed, "No one I can think of."

Bridgot smiled.

"Bridgot," Celestia said, turning serious.

"Yes?" he asked.

"I'm scared for this quest."

His smile faded, and his gray eyes twinkled with concern, "What is it?"

She looked at him, "What if something happens to one of us?"

His face darkened a moment and then turned back to concern. "Don't worry," he said, taking her hand, "Everything will be alright."

She looked away, "You're lying."

"What?" he asked in surprise.

She looked back at him, her blue eyes full of sorrow, "I heard you."

He shot her a questioning look.

"I heard you the other night when you were talking with Kgansten and Aurano. The Oracle said one of you is going to die?"

Bridgot sighed, looking down, "I thought you were asleep."

"I know," she said, "I'm sorry. I didn't mean to eavesdrop. My mind was going a million miles a minute, thinking about this quest, and I couldn't sleep."

He looked away.

"I can't lose you," she said.

He turned back toward her, "You would have lost me, anyway. I'd rather it be because I died to save your life than because this quest ended and we weren't allowed to be together."

A tear rolled down her cheek, glistening in the moonlight.

Bridgot wiped it away, holding her face in his hand, as he said softly, "It's an honor, to die saving the world—to die for *you*." He kissed her hand, and then turned and walked away, patrolling the perimeter of their campsite.

She let a few more tears roll away, trying to keep an eye out through her blurred vision.

The next day was hard for her, as she sluggishly went through the motions. Even flying couldn't take her mind off of what was to come. She felt utterly broken and empty. She wanted to turn around and forget this whole quest. She found herself weighing the options, of allowing the world to be plunged into darkness for a hundred years if it meant he would live. But, she knew all the lives that would be lost if this dark wizard was successful would be far greater a loss than the life of one. It was just that, to her, that one was worth the most.

When they landed to make camp, Bridgot and Forx took their post, and everyone else settled in to rest.

When Bridgot woke her, Celestia took her place beside Aurano, staring off into the distance. Once the others had settled down, starting to snore, Aurano said, "You should not lead him on."

Celestia looked at him, puzzled.

Aurano looked back at her, "Bridgot. You know as well as I that you can never be together. Why do you continue to flirt with him?"

"You mean the way you flirt with Nastazya?" she countered.

Aurano cleared his throat, leaning back, "I do no such thing."

Celestia smiled, "I overheard the two of you last night. But, beyond that, I saw the way she flustered you when you met."

Aurano looked away, "That's different. We could actually be together when this is over. But, a princess and a peasant? Never."

Celestia looked down, "Neither of us meant for this to happen. I love him."

Aurano was silent. After a pause, he said, "I'm sorry. This quest isn't easy on anyone, but the two of you most of all."

She looked away, "I think maybe I made a mistake, leaving home."

"No," Aurano said, "You found adventure, you found yourself, you found love. How many people can say that? You've lived more since you left home than you ever would have if you'd stayed. But, beyond that, this quest isn't about only you. It's about the fate of everyone in the world."

"Thank you," she said, "You're a good friend, Aurano."

They sat silently, staring into the darkened trees, lost in their own thoughts until their shift was over, and they woke Nastazya and Kgansten, settling back in to rest.

As they flew closer and closer to Kogatsa, the days grew darker. It was harder to see, and it slowed their progress. The clouds shifted from white to dark gray, and the sun was barely visible. The land below looked dark and desolate, with little sign of life. The quest felt heavier to bear in the bleak surroundings.

They barely found a clearing to make camp in through the darkness. As they were eating dinner, Nastazya said, "If Thaandor can make it happen, my guess is that the army will arrive in Kogatsa shortly after we do."

"Army?" Celestia asked.

"You didn't really think it would only be us against a wizard, did you?" Aurano asked, "The dwarven and elven armies were already moving when we left. They weren't sure where the prophecy would lead us, but they knew where darkness was brewing, and that's Khanjgi."

"Our armies are probably already there," Kgansten said.

"Well, the dragon riders will take a bit longer to persuade," Nastazya said, "Thaandor told me he'd take care of it. He has a way of convincing Kirstiana. Hence, how the four of you were able to borrow dragons."

So, that's why he stayed behind, Celestia thought.

"At least it won't take them as long to get there," Aurano said.

"Dragonback *is* the best way to travel," Nastazya added.

"Are you saying there's to be a war?" Bridgot asked.

"Oh yes," Nastazya replied, "The armies of the dark wizard have been coalescing for a while, as the time for the ritual nears. He is well-prepared for a fight by now."

"Our armies have no idea what they're up against," Aurano said, "They only knew that a dark and deadly force was gathering for a fight."

"Indeed," Kgansten agreed, "They'll need more help if he's managed to amass a sizable force."

"Someone should call on the humans," Bridgot said, "Your armies will need all the help they can get."

"The humans who could and would ally with us will never reach the battlefield in time," Aurano said.

Everyone was silent for a moment, looking at each other.

"I wish I'd known all this before I left," Bridgot said, "We could have recruited forces, and let everyone know what was happening."

"The Oracle didn't do us any favors with such a vague prophecy," Celestia added.

"It does no good to dwell on what could have been," Nastazya said, "We must focus on the task at hand."

"Why did you all wait til now to mention armies, and a war?" Celestia asked.

"We weren't sure of its relevance to the prophecy," Aurano said, "And, rather than worry everyone unnecessarily, we decided to focus on the quest, and what *we* need to do."

"King Boreas said the elves rarely go to war," she said.

"That's true," Aurano affirmed.

"He said warriors-in-training don't get much chance to prove themselves because of this, so everyone was fighting in this tournament for the chance to accompany us on this quest. Why would you go for the slim chance of winning this quest, rather than just go with the elven army?"

Aurano shifted, "A quest of this importance would promote me to a high rank more quickly than simply fighting in a battle. Plus, King Boreas had already chosen his warriors, and *they* were choosing the warriors-in-training who would accompany them. They all had their favorites, and I knew I wasn't on that list."

"And you, Kgansten?"

"King Thanghor knew this quest would make me a shoo-in for Dwarf Lord. He needed to select someone carefully, and so, of course, he chose me. Many fine young warriors were sent to the battlefront."

Celestia nodded, "Very well. Everyone get some sleep. We're going to need our strength in the days ahead."

Bridgot and Aurano took their post, and everyone lied down. Celestia's head was spinning, *A war? Why did The Oracle say nothing of it, at least? We're not just going up against a dark wizard, but one who's prepared, with an entire army at his disposal. Can we really do this?*

As she and Kgansten woke everyone to set out again, a knot was forming in her stomach. When Tourmethyst launched into the air, Celestia could see lightning in the distance. The thunder clapped loudly, up in the clouds. *There's a storm ahead,* she thought, *And, not just the one in the sky.*

As they flew through the day, Celestia noticed a dark mass on the land ahead. It grew larger and larger as they flew until she could make out what it was. *An army!* she thought, *Is this the army of Nazirdok? It's massive!*

They landed not too far from the end of Mashang, and the beginning of Kogatsa. As they heated up their stew, Nastazya said, "We shouldn't enter Kogatsa by dragonback. We'll attract too much attention; he'll see us coming."

"What are you suggesting?" Bridgot asked.

"I'm suggesting we walk the rest of the way," she said.

"Are you crazy?" Bridgot asked, "We don't have enough time for that."

"We do, now," Aurano said, "We set out from Abyumo with only eleven days to get to Khanjgi. We've reached the border of Kogatsa in seven. On foot, it's a two-day journey from here. That leaves us with two days to make a plan and stop the ritual. Nastazya's right—we should walk."

Bridgot sighed.

"I agree," Celestia said, "We don't want to give him any more of an advantage than he already has."

"Then, it's settled," Nastazya said, "We set out on foot tomorrow. Let's get some rest."

Nastazya and Celestia shared a shift that night, followed by Bridgot and Kgansten, and then Aurano and Forx.

"Thank you for siding with me," Nastazya said, as the two girls sat on a boulder, watching over the sleeping guys.

"I wasn't choosing a side," Celestia said, "I was deciding on a plan. And, I agree that I don't want him to see us coming."

Nastazya was quiet a moment, before she said, "Forx will stay here with the dragons. We brought him to care for them; he's not a fighter. Things are about to get tough, and I may have to keep Ezmyra on standby, in case we need help. I don't know what awaits us in Kogatsa, but if you thought anything you've faced so far was a challenge, I'd wager this will top it."

The Land of Darkness

24

When morning came, they loaded up their supplies so they could carry them, and set out, leaving Forx and the dragons in the clearing.

"We'll meet back here when it's over," Nastazya said, waving.

"What are they supposed to do for six days?" Celestia asked.

"The dragons will be able to fly around and go hunting, and Forx will do what he does every day: care for dragons. He has some books to read in the saddlebags when the dragons are satisfied."

"Still, it's a long time to just wait in a clearing."

Nastazya turned serious, "Better than what he would face if he came with us."

Bridgot, Celestia, Kgansten, Aurano, and Nastazya ventured solemnly into the trees, keeping an eye out all around them. They walked through the day, venturing into Kogatsa. No one dared to speak in the dark, cloudy forest, for fear of attracting attention to themselves. Celestia had never seen a forest like this before. Normally, the forest gave her a feeling of peace, adventure, and life. Here, it felt frightening, dangerous, and spooky. Perhaps it was because it was so dark, even in the daytime.

When they stopped to make camp at the end of the day, everyone was on edge. Aurano looked the way he had when they'd been in the dwarven tunnels. His silver hair stood on end, his blue eyes narrowed, and his pointed ears twitched. Kgansten scratched his red beard nervously, brown eyes scanning the trees. Bridgot rubbed his arms as though he were cold. Even the fearless Nastazya looked uncertain.

They set up their sleeping area uneasily, no one really wanting to sleep in a place like this. Celestia's legs were tired from walking all day. She appreciated the horses and dragons all the more, now. Walking all day took a toll. Even so, it would be hard to get any rest here.

"Ezmyra will stay within mental range of me," Nastazya said quietly, "in case we need help. But, far enough away that no wandering eyes will see us traveling with a huge dragon."

"I thought they were all to wait in the clearing," Celestia said.

"Diamante, Tourmethyst, and Forx," Nastazya responded, "but, not Ezmyra. I thought we might all feel safer knowing we have a dragon close enough to come to our aid if needed."

Celestia nodded.

"I'll take the first watch tonight," she said, "Ezmyra will be my partner. You all can pair together for watches."

"Very well," Aurano said.

"Celestia and I will take the next watch," Bridgot chimed in quickly.

"Looks like we're partners," Kgansten said, looking at Aurano.

"Good. Now, I know it's not easy, but you all need to get your rest," Nastazya said.

They all settled in, as best they could, and tried to sleep. It was easier than Celestia had anticipated, since she was so tired. When Nastazya woke her for her shift, she sat beside Bridgot anxiously, looking around.

"It's hard to sleep in this place," Bridgot said.

Celestia nodded in agreement. After a pause, she said, "Why did you request me as your partner?"

Bridgot looked at her, "I would rather have no one else. This place makes me nervous. Your presence is calming."

She smiled, "Yours calms me as well. I was glad we were paired riding dragonback, for I was nervous to fly, at first."

He returned her smile, taking her hand in his.

The next morning, they set out again, trudging slowly through the forest. As they walked, Celestia felt a drop of water on her cheek. When she looked up, the sky opened, and it began to rain. They heard the thunder crashing, and saw flashes in the distance, above the trees. They were soaked quickly, forcing their way through the mud. Celestia felt her blouse sticking to her arms, and sticking to her torso beneath her corset. Her skirt stuck to her legs, and her shoes were getting caked with mud. She looked over at Bridgot and saw his predicament was much the same, his muscles visible through the shirt that was clinging to his chest. The rain *plinked* as it hit Kgansten's armor, and Aurano's silvery hair turned a deep shade of gray as it clung to his face and neck. Nastazya's boots sank into the mud, up to her calves, and Celestia could see the lines of water streaming down her ebony face.

There was nowhere they could take shelter as they plodded along. It rained most of the day, and then stopped, as suddenly as it had started. They all looked up, and the sky partly cleared as they did, revealing a few rays of sun.

"Whew," Nastazya said, looking around, "If that's the worst this forest has to offer, this may be easier than I thought."

"We'll have to take the ferry into Khanjgi," Aurano said, "There's no other way."

Nastazya nodded, "Well, we're already wet. Let's go."

The five of them approached the edge of a great river, where there were a few large, wooden rafts, manned by some ferrymen.

"Ho there!" Nastazya called, "We need transport."

The ferryman, a tall, skinny man, with dark, narrow eyes, nodded. They all climbed aboard the ferry, and Nastazya handed him some money from their supply, "You'll get the rest when we reach the other side."

He took it, nodding again, and glaring at them. He began to push the ferry across the river with his pole. They all sat, happy to take a breather from all the walking. As they rested, Celestia noticed a couple of large creatures in the sky above them. They almost looked like dragons, but were longer and more narrow. They had dark, dull colors, with no shine. "What are those?" she asked Bridgot.

He looked up. "Vekkens!" he yelled.

Everyone looked up, then, and quickly armed themselves.

"What's a vekken?" she asked.

"To say they're similar to dragons would be an insult," Nastazya said, "though they are related. They have no scales, but reptilian hides. They're smaller, slimmer, and longer than dragons, and they can't breathe fire."

"They're bad news," Kgansten added.

"They're like the dragon's evil twin," Aurano assessed.

"So, it's safe to say they're not friendly," Bridgot concluded, looking at her.

Celestia rose, pulling out her bow and notching an arrow. Bridgot already has his sword drawn, and Kgansten had his axe. Aurano had also pulled out his bow, and Nastazya had a crossbow ready. The ferryman seemed unperturbed, focused on pushing the raft along.

One of the vekkens dove at them, jaws open. Aurano shot it in the neck, and Kgansten hit it with his axe. The creature screeched but didn't fall. As it circled again, Nastazya shot it with her crossbow. It narrowed its sights on her, diving again. As it did, Ezmyra shot out from the trees, breathing a jet of flame across the vekken. It struggled to fly away, but Ezmyra caught it in her jaws before it could. She tossed it into the trees and went for the second one. The other vekken was prepared for her attack, and they locked into a fight.

As the five of them were watching the battle between the second vekken and Ezmyra, the first vekken composed itself, and dove at them again, right for Celestia. Bridgot swung his sword, slicing into its leg. It turned on him, and they engaged each other, Bridgot thrusting and parrying for his life. Aurano drew his sword to help, but the vekken swung its tail, knocking him from the ferry.

Aurano clung to the side of the raft, getting dragged through the water. Nastazya hurried to his aid, trying to pull him back up. Kgansten hurried over as well, grabbing his other arm. Celestia drew her own sword to help Bridgot, swinging at the vekken's underbelly. It turned to bite her, but Bridgot reacted quickly, plunging his sword into the creature's heart. It shrieked as he did, and wrapped its claw around him, pulling him into the river as it fell.

"No!" Celestia yelled. *He's not going to die saving me,* she thought, *I don't care what The Oracle said.*

As Nastazya and Kgansten pulled Aurano back onto the ferry, Celestia dove into the water, sword first. The current nearly swept her away, but she clung to the tail of the vekken, and worked her way up, pulling herself along its length. Her grip strength came in handy, and she maintained her hold on her sword. She opened her eyes, barely able to see through the rushing water, and used the momentum of the current to her advantage, swinging her sword and slicing through the vekken's leg that was holding Bridgot in its claw.

Once he was freed, she grabbed the neck of his shirt as his unconscious body rushed past her. She realized she didn't know what to do now, clinging with one hand to Bridgot, and with the other, her sword, and the dead vekken. She had no way to get back to the raft, and they were quickly sinking with the weight of the creature.

Suddenly, a hand clutched her arm, and she released her hold on the vekken, allowing it to tumble away into the abyss. She was hoisted upward, through the water, still clutching Bridgot and her sword. As they were pulled onto the raft, she could see that the hand that had grabbed her was Nastazya's, and she had formed a human chain, with Kgansten in the middle, and Aurano up on the ferry.

She gasped for air, saying, "Thank you."

"You gotta be crazy," Nastazya said.

Celestia turned to Bridgot and started trying to push on his chest, to pump out the water and revive him. Aurano pushed her out of the way, starting to do the compressions himself. Celestia watched, panicked, not focused on anything else. After a few nerve-wracking moments, a little stream of water spilled out of Bridgot's mouth, and he sat up, breathing.

"Bridgot!" Celestia yelled, pushing past Aurano, and wrapping her arms around him.

Awareness slowly came to him, and he looked at her.

She looked up as she felt a gust of wind, and saw the other vekken crashing to the ground, headless, on the side of the river they'd just come from. Ezmyra vanished quickly into the trees, and Nastazya stood proudly, admiring her dragon.

"You-," Bridgot began, "You saved me."

"Of course I did," she said, holding him tight, "I don't care what some oracle said. I'm not going to let you die for me. I love you."

"You love me?" he said, looking at her.

Celestia met his eyes, tears streaming down her already-soaked face. He kissed her, pulling her into him eagerly. She let herself melt into his embrace, enjoying the feeling of his arms around her, and his sweet, gentle lips against her own. She wanted this moment to last forever.

He pulled away slightly and met her eyes. "I love you, too," he whispered.

It was her turn to kiss him, lunging at him and pressing her lips into his with everything she had. They barely noticed as the ferry bumped into the shore, and the ferryman tied it off, accepting the remainder of the money from Nastazya.

"Come on," she said, "We have to go."

She, along with Aurano and Kgansten, got off the raft, heading into the forest ahead. Bridgot and Celestia smiled at each other, and got up, following them. They didn't have far to walk before they could see the main city of the kingdom of Khanjgi in the distance. The sun was just setting, and they decided to make camp there.

"We'll work up a plan tomorrow," Nastazya said, "Let's all get some sleep. Bridgot, why don't you and Aurano take the first shift, then Celestia and Kgansten, and I'll take the last shift with Ezmyra."

"Very well," Bridgot answered. He was grinning ear to ear, despite still trying to fully catch his breath. His curly, brown hair glistened with water droplets, which spilled over every so often, rolling down his face. He took his post beside Aurano, who was still drying as well, his hair appearing splotchy, with different shades of silver and gray. Nastazya, Kgansten, and Celestia settled in to get some rest, all still dripping with water as well, forming small pools where they lied. As she drifted off, Celestia couldn't help but smile. Despite the bleak situation, and the impossible mission ahead, she held onto her piece of happiness; it was her island of hope in this vast sea of despair.

Nazirdok

25

When rays of orange and red pierced through the trees, everyone awoke. They got a meal together for their breakfast and began trying to come up with a plan.

"How can we possibly sneak into the city?" Celestia asked, looking down the hill toward the tall, black stone walls, and the open clearing leading to the only entrance.

"First," Aurano said, "we should assess if there's another way in. It would be best not to use the front gate."

"There doesn't appear to be another way," Celestia said.

"Things are not always how they appear," Nastazya countered, "We should at least exhaust the possibility first."

"Exactly how do we do that?" Bridgot asked.

Just then, they heard muffled sounds a few yards away, through the trees. They all looked at each other. After a pause, they crept quietly, using the trees for cover, over to where it was coming from. There, they saw several workers loading crates of cargo into large, buoyant barrels, and placing them into a narrow stream, which led all the way into the city. They watched as the barrels were carried away by the water, and how the stream led into a small opening at the base of the city wall, just large enough for them to fit through. Celestia exchanged glances with each of them from behind the tree she was stationed at. They all looked as though they had the same idea.

They snuck back to their campsite and looked out into the clearing around the city. Across the way, as the sunlight hit them, they could see the war camps of the dwarves and the elves. They were nothing compared to the army they'd seen flying in.

Nastazya gathered a pool of liquid into one of the bowls they had. She set it on the ground and waited for the ripples to cease. They all watched in wonder, trying to figure out what she was doing. Once the surface cleared, she stared at it intently, her green eyes glowing the way they had when she'd heated Celestia's stew.

"*Balgadeer*," she said. Everyone observed as the water transformed into a picture. It was Thaandor's face.

"Nastazya," he said.

She smiled, "Thaandor."

"How did you do that?" Celestia asked in wonder, as they all gathered 'round.

"Magic," she said, "How do you think I knew so much about Thaandor's progress convincing the dragon rider army to come help? Speaking of which," she turned her attention back to Thaandor, "Please tell me they're almost here."

Thaandor hung his head, "I'm afraid it was of no use. I could not sway the dragon rider council. After using all my chips to get them to let us borrow dragons, they wouldn't hear of sending more riders into battle."

Nastazya looked away, "The armies of the dwarves and the elves will not be enough to fight the army of Nazirdok."

"Nazirdok?" Aurano said, eyes widening, and face turning pale, "*He's* the dark wizard we've come to stop?"

"Fulfill the prophecy," Thaandor said, "and the war will cease." With that, his picture faded away, leaving behind plain water once more.

Nastazya looked at Aurano, "What is it?"

"He's the wizard who killed my father," he said, "I've trained my whole life to become an elven warrior, just so I could return the favor."

Nastazya's eyes widened. "Don't do anything rash," she said, "He's too powerful. You must keep a level head, no matter how hard it is for you. Otherwise, we'll never succeed in stopping him."

Aurano stood frozen, a look in his eyes Celestia had never seen.

"Please," Nastazya said, going over to him and placing her hand against his cheek, "We can do this. We can stop him, and avenge your father at the same time, but only if you follow the plan, and maintain your composure."

Aurano closed his eyes. After a long pause, he nodded. "Very well," he said, "What's the plan?"

Nastazya smiled, turning back to everyone, "Just before dawn, we head to the cargo hold, and climb into the barrels. As the sun rises, and the first workers appear, we shall be sailing down the stream, and into the city. From there, we will have to think on our feet. We must get to the castle, find the wizard, and stop the ritual."

"Why not go tonight, after the workers leave?" Kgansten asked.

"The ritual isn't 'til tomorrow night," she said, "We want to spend as little time in that city as possible, to avoid detection."

Everyone nodded in agreement.

"I say we get some extra rest today, then," Celestia said, "since we finally made it. We're all exhausted from traveling, and we'll need our strength tomorrow."

"A very good idea," Nastazya said.

They spent the rest of the day eating some of their extra food (they hadn't been sure how much to bring since they didn't know how long the journey would take) and napping. They were all focused on the mission ahead, so there wasn't much in the way of conversation. When night came, they continued sleeping, everyone getting plenty of rest. Celestia was relieved to be able to catch up on sleep before attempting to stop a dark wizard's ritual.

A little while before sunrise, they all woke up and headed over to the cargo hold. It was dark, and they could barely see the barrels, but they set five of them in the stream, where they were held in place by a small gate. One of them would have to pull the lever once everyone was in the barrels, and then hurry to jump into their barrel before they all took off down the stream.

"Okay," Aurano said, "Everyone get into the barrels. I'll pull the lever. As an elf, I'm naturally quick, and I can easily make the jump."

Kgansten climbed in first, since he was the shortest, and had the greatest difficulty climbing into something so tall. As he was doing so, they heard a rustling sound in the brush. They all stopped and turned around. As he fell inside the first barrel, several creatures began coming forth from the trees. They looked like nymphs to Celestia, only they were dark, garbed in black, with grayish skin, dark hair, and inky, menacing eyes. They had wings as well, and razor-sharp teeth, which were visible due to their creepy smiles.

"Faeries," Bridgot said, drawing his sword.

Celestia, Aurano, and Nastazya drew their swords as well, readying themselves. The faeries chuckled maliciously, raising their hands, glowing balls of blue light appearing in them.

"Quick, into the barrels!" Nastazya yelled.

They all jumped as the faeries threw the balls of light in their direction. They hit the ground where they'd been standing, and exploded, launching them backward from the blast. Nastazya jumped up, sheathing her sword, and throwing her own ball of green light at the faeries. She lit up the forest as the creatures were hit with the force of her power. Ezmyra appeared, ripping the heads off a few of them as a magical battle ensued.

"I said get into the barrels!" Nastazya shouted again as she fought them off.

Celestia jumped into the second barrel and Bridgot into the third. Aurano lingered, not wanting to leave Nastazya. More and more faeries swarmed out of the forest, overwhelming even Ezmyra. They watched in alarm, unable to help, as it looked like the rider and her dragon wouldn't be able to hold them off.

She looked at Aurano, "Get in! Hurry! I'll be right behind you!"

He leaped into the fourth barrel, and she pulled the lever, opening the gate and releasing the barrels. "Come on!" he shouted, "Quickly!"

She looked at him sorrowfully, and Celestia could see she didn't intend to follow.

"No!" he yelled, trying to scramble out of the barrel. It was too late, and, as the barrels rushed down the stream, they watched in horror as Nastazya and Ezmyra fought to the death against the faeries. "Nastazya!" Aurano screamed, reaching for her helplessly.

Nastazya was struck with a blast from the faeries, and they could hear Ezmyra's cries from the bottom of the hill as her rider fell. The dragon snapped, killing hundreds of the sinister creatures in agonized rage. But, there were too many. They swarmed in like bees, covering Ezmyra, and bringing her down.

"Duck!" Bridgot yelled, and they had no time to mourn as they reached the entrance, and had to dive into the barrels to make it under the wall.

They felt their momentum cease, as the barrels collided with the cargo at the bottom of the stream.

"The boys started early this morning," a gruff voice said.

"Well, bring them ashore before the rest come down," another voice said, "I'm going to get some breakfast before they really load us up."

"Aye," the first voice said, "I'll come, too, once I get these up here."

They felt their barrels being lifted from the stream and set on the ground. They waited until they heard footsteps walking away before they popped out of the barrels, peeking around the corner. They saw a little bed and breakfast, where two burly men, presumably the ones they'd overheard, were eating.

"We must get to the castle," Bridgot said, "But, we can't just waltz right up to it. We'll have to disguise ourselves."

"Would these help?" Kgansten asked, pulling a couple of cloaks off the wall.

They turned toward him.

"Yes," Bridgot said, taking one. He handed it to Celestia, "Put this on."

She did, and then asked, "What about the rest of you? There's only one other cloak."

"I'll blend in," Bridgot said, "No one knows who I am; I'm just a common peasant. Kgansten, if you climb on Aurano's back, the two of you can wear the other cloak, and look like a hunchback. We'll have to separate if we are to succeed. Meet me at the castle." With that, Bridgot casually strolled around the corner, easing into the crowd that was making its way to the market.

"I'm sorry, Aurano," Celestia said, "I cared for Nastazya, too. But, she made a choice. We'll have time to mourn later. Right now, we must focus, and stop this ritual," she touched his shoulder, looking at him sympathetically. Then, she lifted the hood, grabbed one of the hooked poles they used to pull the barrels in, using it as a cane, and made her way around the corner, hobbling along like an old beggar woman.

The people in the crowd avoided her as though she were a leper. She watched as Kgansten and Aurano finally came around the corner. They did, indeed, resemble a hunchback. People avoided them even more than her. *This just might work,* she thought.

They made their way up to the castle, slowly, trying not to be too obvious. No one paid any mind to a hunchback and a beggar. Celestia couldn't even see where Bridgot had gone. He really did blend into a crowd. It took most of the day to make their way to the castle. The sun was already setting as they snuck over the castle wall, into the courtyard.

They gathered in the bushes, trying to figure out how to get inside. Time was running out. They had to act quickly. Bridgot noticed a few guards coming close to the brush. One of them was extremely short. It was almost too perfect. He looked at Aurano and Kgansten, and they nodded.

Once the guards reached the brush, they grabbed them, pulling them in, and knocking them out swiftly. Bridgot, Kgansten, and Aurano dressed themselves in the guards' armor and stepped out of the brush. Bridgot reached in and pulled Celestia out roughly.

"What are you doing?" she asked angrily.

"Shh," he whispered, "Keep the hood up and play along." More loudly, he added, "Let's go. I'm sure the king would love to hear why you were sneaking around his castle."

Bridgot took one arm, and Aurano took the other. Kgansten led the way, carrying a large spear. Celestia realized this was the perfect disguise to take her directly to the dark wizard: three guards and a prisoner. They walked right into the castle, searching the corridors, and trying to find where Nazirdok was conducting the ritual.

None of the other guards questioned them as they made their way through the castle. They walked up and down the corridors, searching. There wasn't anything on the bottom level, so they journeyed up the stairs.

When they reached the top, they heard shouts outside. They looked out the nearest window and saw a sight they couldn't believe. The great army of Khanjgi had reached the city, and they could see the mass of soldiers posted throughout. The armies of the elves and the dwarves were just outside the city wall, banging on the front gate. Sentinels were firing arrows into them. They were running out of time.

They hurried down the hall, hastening their search. As they were exploring a corridor in the west wing, they saw flashes of light coming from one of the rooms. They stopped, and heard a raspy voice coming from within. It sounded as though it were reciting an incantation in another language. They looked at each other. Slowly, they crept closer, until they were just outside the door. Celestia peered inside, and saw a figure in a black, hooded cloak, standing before a table in the center of the room. On it, she saw several strange objects, and, above it, a skylight. Through that, she could see the stars overhead. They were beginning to align, directly above the table.

She looked back at her warriors, nodding. They looked at her, understanding. With a rush of determination and adrenaline, they all charged into the room, going straight for the table. As they did so, the dark wizard turned around, and Celestia could see his face. It was pale and angled, with sharp, crooked teeth, pitch-black eyes, and malicious features. In an instant, he hit them all with a blast of black magic, knocking them into the wall.

As Celestia looked around the upside-down room, noticing the light, rough wood of the floor and bookcases, and the peculiar magical artifacts,

Nazirdok turned back to his ritual chant, ignoring them. She and her warriors collapsed to the floor, struggling to return to their feet. Once they did, they rushed at the table again. He again caught them with his magic, pinning them against the wall.

This time, they couldn't move. He was holding them in place with one hand, and conducting the ritual with the other. Celestia looked over at her struggling warriors in dismay, unsure how they could possibly win against this wizard. Several stars lined up, with only a few left to move into alignment.

She floundered, trying to get free of his spell. Suddenly, she dropped to the ground, breaking free. She ran for the table, ready to flip it. Nazirdok turned at the last second, seeing her, and quickly knocked her back with another curse. As he did so, he released his hold on her warriors, and they rushed him.

They each began charging at the table, and he knocked them back, one at a time, growing more annoyed with each one. None of it broke his concentration, as he maintained his chant, watching the stars overhead. He obviously didn't view them as a threat, but, as they kept trying to reach the table, he began to see them as a nuisance. Aurano shot over to the table, fingers brushing it as Nazirdok launched him across the room. Kgansten swung his axe, charging him, as Bridgot went for the table. He hurled them into the wall, knocking them out.

He created a strong wind, pinning them against the wall as he continued the ritual, with only one star left out of alignment. Celestia began inching her way forward, fighting against the wind. Nazirdok didn't notice until she was right by the table. With purpose, he lifted her against the wall by her throat, looking in her eyes. His were cold and unfeeling.

"Are you the princess of The Great Prophecy?" he asked, smiling, "The only one who can stop me? If this is the best you've got, The Oracle was mistaken. You're weak and pathetic. How could a princess compete with a wizard? What a joke."

With that, he dropped her, pinning them all to the wall once more. Bridgot and Kgansten came to, seeing that they were still in the midst of their defeat. Celestia struggled against the dark wizard's magic again, trying to break his hold. With a sudden burst of light and energy, his spell was broken, and Celestia felt a tingling sensation all through her. As she looked down, she realized she was glowing blue. The blast had knocked Nazirdok back. Seizing her window of opportunity, she charged forward, right for the table.

"No!" Nazirdok yelled in anger, rising and summoning his powers.

As he cast a curse to stop her, Aurano ran forward, jumping between them. The blast knocked him into the wall as Celestia flipped the table over, spilling all of the ritual objects across the room, just as the stars aligned overhead.

"No!" Nazirdok yelled again, falling to his knees as his ritual was ruined. He glared at Celestia, rising to his feet again, and summoning his dark magic to him. As he did so, his body slowly dissolved into ash, blowing across the room.

Celestia stared in disbelief, feeling relief wash over her. Just then, the ashes lifted from the floor, forming a figure made from black magic, staring at her with ashen eyes, smiling. It charged toward her as she stood there, eyes wide.

"Celestia!" Bridgot yelled, struggling to reach his feet.

The form crashed into her, spiraling around her in a twister of dark energy. She screamed, feeling the energy scratching and suffocating her. She swung her arms around wildly, trying to fight. As she realized it was futile, she stopped, trying to focus and recreate the energy blast from before. She thought about what she had to do, and who she had to do it for: Bridgot, her mom, Kgansten, and Aurano.

As she did, she felt it roll through her once more, blasting through the black magic around her. It shrieked, scattering away and regrouping. The starlight above shone brighter, blinding them all, and, with a burst of energy, radiated into the room, obliterating the ashen form, and knocking them all back. The world went black.

The Pain of Loss

26

When Celestia came to, she saw that the dark wizard was gone. The very atmosphere in the room had changed. When they'd entered, it had felt heavy, with an air of dark magic. Now, it felt light and peaceful. It felt like it was just a room. Sunlight was streaming in, highlighting the dust particles in the air. She wondered how long she'd been out. She got up slowly, looking around. Bridgot was just waking as well, and she hurried to his side.

"Are you alright?" she asked.

He nodded, senses returning, "Did we do it?"

"Yeah," she said, "I think we did."

He smiled, rubbing his head, "How long was I out?"

"I don't know," she said, "I only just woke as well. It's daylight out there." She looked up at the skylight.

Kgansten opened his eyes, looking around.

"Kgansten," Celestia said, "Are you alright?"

"I think so," he said, holding his head as he sat up, "Where's Aurano?"

They looked around and saw him knocked out in the corner. Celestia shuffled over to him, shaking him gently. As she did, she gasped.

"What is it?" Bridgot asked, "What's wrong?"

Celestia turned to look at them, "He's dead."

Kgansten's mouth opened and closed, as tears formed in his eyes. He ran over, turning Aurano's body. He was ice cold to the touch, his face was colorless, and, as Kgansten turned him, they could see his eyes were open, rolled to the back of his head. Kgansten let out a wail of mourning, louder than any Celestia had ever heard. If the armies hadn't ceased battling yet, the sounds he uttered would be enough to stop them.

Celestia's eyes welled up with tears, and they spilled down her cheeks freely as she stared at her fallen friend. "It's all my fault," she said, "The Oracle was right: one of you did die to save me, but it wasn't you, Bridgot."

Bridgot slowly neared, his eyes tearing as well. "It's not your fault," he said, "He made a choice." He looked down, "We should close his eyes."

Celestia and Kgansten nodded, and Bridgot came between them. He reached forward, hand trembling, and closed Aurano's eyes. The three of them sat together, weeping, and turning to each other for comfort as they mourned the loss of their friend.

It seemed like an eternity that they sat there, before Bridgot said, "We should bury him." He lifted Aurano's motionless body from beneath the weeping dwarf and princess and headed for the door. They slowly followed, wiping the tears from their eyes.

As they exited the castle, they could see that the war had, indeed, ceased. The army of Nazirdok had vacated the city. The citizens stared as they passed by, unsure what to do. They could see the people had been celebrating, but, on seeing them, they stopped. The elven and dwarven armies watched solemnly as they passed, removing their helmets, and placing them over their hearts.

They headed across the clearing, back to the forest, where Nastazya and Ezmyra had fallen. When they reached the site, they could see the massive green dragon and her incredible rider lying there, lifeless. Bridgot set Aurano down, and he and Kgansten dug a couple of graves, as Celestia gathered flowers from the hillside, placing some around the body of Ezmyra, and braiding the rest into a couple of wreaths.

They laid Aurano and Nastazya in the two graves, covering them with dirt, and placing the floral wreaths on each mound. One of Ezmyra's talons was on the ground a little ways from her, from where she had clawed some of the faeries.

Kgansten lifted it, saying, "We should bring this back to the riders, for their memorial."

Bridgot and Celestia nodded, as she said, "Well, Aurano got both of his wishes."

Her two remaining warriors looked at her questioningly.

"He avenged his father. Nazirdok is dead. And, now he shall be with Nastazya, forever, side by side." She looked down, as more tears streamed from her eyes, "God rest them all, our dear friends: Aurano, Nastazya, and Ezmyra."

The hike back through the forest was hard, as they all mourned their friends. Succeeding in their quest and fulfilling the prophecy was bittersweet in light of the circumstances.

When they reached the clearing where Forx was waiting with Tourmethyst and Diamante, he said, "You're back. Where's Ezmyra? Where's Nastazya?"

They hung their heads solemnly, presenting him with Ezmyra's talon. He stared at it a moment, silent. Finally, he looked up, "What have you done?"

"They were swarmed by faeries," Bridgot said, "Hundreds of them. They died saving our lives."

"We cared for them both," Celestia said, "More than you know." She hung her head, "Our friend Aurano died as well."

Forx looked at them, seeing their tear-stained faces. After a while, he said, "We should get Diamante and Tourmethyst back to the riders."

They all nodded, and Bridgot helped Kgansten onto Diamante's back. Forx leaped in front of him, taking the reins. Bridgot and Celestia climbed into Tourmethyst's saddle once more, and they took flight, heading back across Mashang, toward Abyumo.

The week-long journey by dragonback felt a lot longer this time around. Even the thrill of flying, and the beauty of soaring through the clouds, couldn't relieve their sadness. It was a quiet trip, as they mourned the whole way, each of them dealing with their grief in their own way.

When they arrived in Abyumo, at the home of the dragon riders, Thaandor and Kirstiana were waiting. "Welcome back," she said, "I trust the quest was successful?"

They nodded as they climbed down from the great dragons' backs for the last time.

"Where are Nastazya and Ezmyra?" she asked.

Forx came forward, presenting her with Ezmyra's talon.

Kirstiana gasped, looking at it. Her expression went through many shades of grief, anger, and disbelief. After a long pause, she said, "Take this to the dragon rider council. We shall host a funeral, to honor them properly."

Forx scurried away with the talon.

"How did this happen?" she asked.

"They died saving our lives from hundreds of faeries," Celestia said, "If it weren't for their sacrifice, we would never have succeeded. They're heroes to us, as well as trusted friends."

Kirstiana nodded, "You all shall stay for the funeral, and set out the following morning."

Celestia opened her mouth to object, but Kirstiana waved her hand, "You may stay in the same rooms you had before. I'll have Loretta prepare them." With that, she walked out, golden cape trailing behind her.

"What happened?" Thaandor asked once she'd left, "How did you do it?"

"I'm not sure," Celestia said, "I broke through his spell. Light and energy blasted from me, and I felt tingly. I was glowing blue, and I flipped the table where his ritual pieces sat. He tried to stop me, but Aurano jumped in front of me. He was killed." She looked away sadly, "Then, he just sort of dissolved, and there was a blinding flash of light from the stars. It knocked us out. I don't know what happened."

Thaandor's eyes widened as she spoke. He paused once she'd finished, processing, before he said, "You glowed blue?"

"Yes," she answered.

He nodded, smiling, "So, you can do magic after all. You're a witch."

"What?" she said, looking at him in surprise.

"Sometimes, you don't get your powers 'til later in life," he said, "It's not uncommon."

"I'm not a witch," she said, "I can't be."

Thaandor smirked, "We should test your powers." He grabbed a bowl and led them to the washroom near their suites. He filled it with water and brought it out, setting it on a windowsill. After the ripples cleared, and the water was still, he said, "Come closer."

Celestia moved nearer to the bowl until she could see the water clearly.

"Now, place your hands on the sides of the bowl, softly. Try not to disturb the water."

She did so, staring into the bottom of the bowl.

"Close your eyes," he said, "It makes it easier since it's your first time." Once her eyes were closed, he continued, "Okay, now, concentrate.

Try to picture your home. Remember each detail, and picture it clearly in your mind."

Celestia concentrated hard. She pictured her mother, for the first time in a long time. She pictured the light brown of her skin, her caramel-colored waves, and her chocolate eyes.

"Now, recite the incantation, *Balgadeer*," he said.

She did so, and when she opened her eyes, her mother's face appeared on the water. She looked distraught. As she watched, she sat upon her throne, purple ballgown billowing around her. The servants went to and fro, asking her things and telling her things, and her face remained blank. Her eyes showed her sadness in them. Suddenly, she faded away, leaving nothing but the blank surface of the water.

Everyone was silent for a moment, before Thaandor said, "You have powers you don't yet realize. You'll need training."

"I don't understand," Bridgot said, "How did she best a powerful, practiced wizard with no experience and no training?"

"Well, most of it was luck," Thaandor replied, "But, when a wizard first gets their powers, they're at their most powerful. He probably wouldn't have been able to touch her. As the situation sits, he was merely caught off guard when she got her powers. He wasn't able to defend himself from the blast. When he cast his curse, Aurano intercepted it. And, when he tried to summon his powers again after the ritual was interrupted, they destroyed him, because the ritual he was performing bound him to it."

"Bound him to it?" Celestia asked.

"Yes," he said, "If he succeeded, the forces he was summoning would have granted him nearly limitless power. He would have been able to deal out death and destruction to anyone he pleased, unchecked. But, since he failed, the forces that would have benefited from such devastation claimed him instead. They would not leave empty-handed. He had already completed his chants, it sounds like, and therefore, he was bound to the fate of his ritual. If he succeeded, he would receive the powers it summoned. If he failed, he would die."

They all looked at each other.

"I'll let you get some rest," Thaandor said, "See you all at the funeral tomorrow."

Bridgot, Kgansten, and Celestia followed Loretta when she came to fetch them for the funeral. They were led into the arena that had housed the dragon rider tournament, and were seated beside Thaandor, each of them handed a candle. Celestia could see the arena was full of people, there to mourn the losses.

Kirstiana stood beside her amber dragon, Solstra, in the center. The rest of the dragon rider council was there as well, and they all stood before a shrine. It housed a few candles, a large painting of Nastazya upon Ezmyra's back, several of their belongings, and Ezmyra's talon.

"We are gathered here today," Kirstiana began, "to celebrate the lives of two such heroic and honorable warriors as Ezmyra and Nastazya. They showed such promise, but, were taken too soon. As many of you know, they were chosen after winning our tournament, to accompany the princess of the prophecy and her warriors. During the course of this quest, they were ambushed and killed. Our great dragon, and her rider, sacrificed themselves for the good of all, to prevent the world from being plunged into an age of darkness. They will be profoundly missed."

With that, she stepped up to the shrine, taking a candle and lighting it with magic. Each member of the dragon rider council did so as well, and they began passing the candles around the arena, as each person that was gathered there used them to light their own candle. Once all the candles were lit, the original ones were passed back to Kirstiana and the council, who returned them to the shrine.

"These candles represent the light that these two heroes brought to all our lives," Kirstiana said, "Everyone here has been touched by the both of them. Let us not ever forget this moment or either of them." After a pause, she said, "Now, a few words from friends and family."

Celestia watched as an old man came forward. He was obviously a poor peasant, with a scraggly beard, and ragged clothes. His face looked just like Nastazya's, and she realized this was her father.

"Hello," he said, "I don't know many of you, and many of you don't know me. I am Nastazya's father. My little girl grew up dreaming of nothing else but becoming a rider. She lost her mother young. I couldn't afford to care for her." He looked down, ashamed, "I sold her horse to fund her journey here, to Abyumo, to the city of the riders. She wrote to me often. I was so proud of her." He paused, choking back tears, "I'm still so proud of her. Though I miss her terribly, she fulfilled her calling, and now, look at her—memorialized a hero." His tears welled up, and he could no longer contain them as he went back to his seat beside his sons.

As several of Nastazya's rider friends and their dragons made their way forward to speak, Celestia allowed herself to weep. She looked at Bridgot and Kgansten, who were both in tears as well, and leaned against Bridgot's arm, listening to the stories of Nastazya and Ezmyra's training.

Once the stories had been told, the funeral ended, and the dragon rider council took the painting and the talon, to be placed alongside the shrines of the other fallen dragons and riders. The three of them sat for a while, letting their candles melt down before they left the arena.

As they passed Kirstiana in the hall on their way back to their rooms, Celestia said, "That was a really beautiful service."

Kirstiana nodded, "Thank you. It's been an honor, hosting you in the hall of the dragon riders. I hope you all find purpose and fulfillment in your lives." She touched Celestia's shoulder, nodding, before she continued down the corridor, saying, "Farewell."

A Journey Ends

27

As the morning sun streamed in, spreading green fractals of light over the room, Celestia awoke. She met with Kgansten and Bridgot, and they headed to the stable to get their horses. The riders already had them saddled, ready and waiting. Celestia paused as she saw Seina, whinnying, and waiting for Aurano.

They set out through Abyumo, guiding the riderless horse behind them. The journey across Gachichken seemed unbearably long, though they didn't attract as much attention as they had on the way there. Each night, all Celestia could think about was Nazirdok, as she tossed and turned in her sleep. Each day, all she could think about were her fallen friends, picturing their faces, and wishing they were there.

When they reached the dwarven tunnels at Korga, they entered, fearing not for siladines or unfriendly dwarf armies. After everything that had happened, those things were the least of their concerns. By the time they reached the kingdom of Dirthix, it had been nearly two months since they'd departed from Khanjgi, and they still felt the loss of their friends terribly.

The people of Dirthix rushed out to greet them as they arrived, cheering. They hopped off of their horses as King Thanghor came forward, pulling Kgansten into an embrace. "Welcome back," he said, "Three cheers for Kgansten, hero of the dwarves!"

The crowd *hurrahed*, and then Thanghor had a sash and a medal brought forth. "I now pronounce you . . . Dwarf Lord. Congratulations," he said, putting the sash over Kgansten's head, and attaching the medal to the breastplate of his armor.

Kgansten stared down at it, but not with pride. A strange expression crossed his face, but Celestia understood. He'd finally received everything he'd always wanted, but it no longer mattered to him. In light of the loss of his dear friend, being awarded seemed wrong.

"Tonight, we celebrate with a feast!" King Thanghor proclaimed.

Felix and Seamus came forward, leading them to their rooms. The three of them rested up for a while, and when they were seated for the feast that evening, they sat together, staring at their plates as the dwarves celebrated around them. After everything that had happened, a celebration seemed out of place. Kgansten made an effort, for sake of his kin, but even he couldn't summon his full cheer.

As most of the dwarves began to get drunk and dance, King Thanghor noticed their low spirits. "What is it?" he asked, "What's wrong?"

"It's nothing," Kgansten said.

"Aren't you happy to finally be a Dwarf Lord?" he asked, "You did it!"

"I know," Kgansten said, "I am happy. It's just . . . this quest took its toll. We lost a few dear friends along the way."

"Well, you're home now," King Thanghor said, "Safe and sound, with your own kin. You've done what your father couldn't: you're a Dwarf Lord. The time for mourning is over. Now, it's time to celebrate!"

Kgansten nodded, taking another swig of mead. His fellow dwarves pulled him onto the dance floor, as several of them began dancing on the tables. As much fun as Celestia had had at their first celebration, she couldn't bring herself to join them this time. She and Bridgot went back to their rooms and went to sleep.

When they woke, they went to get their horses from the royal stable, and Kgansten was there, waiting. "You didn't really think you were going without me, did you?" he asked.

"What do you mean, Kgansten?" Celestia said, "You're home."

"There's one more thing we have to do," he replied, "And I wouldn't miss it for the world."

Celestia looked down solemnly, and she and Bridgot nodded.

"Let's go," Bridgot said.

They set out for Gliken, the land of the elves, with Seina in tow. Once they exited the dwarven tunnels, it was only a few days' journey through the elven woods to the kingdom of Garellis. The trance that the forest put on them didn't feel as though it had as great a hold, now. Kgansten marveled at the silvery trees, with their bluish leaves, and the creatures of the forest—stags, pixies, dwervas, auristras, and mermaids. It was his first time seeing such sights.

When they reached Garellis, Thaddeus led them before King Boreas. The dark-skinned elf king rose when they entered, seeing the riderless stallion behind them. "What became of Aurano?" he asked.

"He died saving me," Celestia said, bowing her head, and stepping before the king, "The dark wizard Nazirdok cast a curse at me, and Aurano leapt in front of me. If not for him, the prophecy would never have been fulfilled. If not for him, we would have failed."

King Boreas sat back in his throne, looking at them. After a moment, he said, "We shall host a memorial service for him tomorrow. At its conclusion, you all may set out on your paths, wherever those may lead."

The three of them nodded, and Marcos led them to their rooms. They got some rest, and, a little while before dawn, they were awakened by Marcos, who showed them the way to the funeral. It seemed as though the entire elven city were circling, lanterns in hand, singing a song of mourning. Though none of them knew what it meant, they felt the power and the emotion of the words. They were seated beside King Boreas, as the elves circled, singing their song.

A shrine was up in the center of the circle, and they had placed Aurano's bow and quiver upon it, along with his sword. As they watched, an elven wizard sang to a canvas, and, as he did, a painting appeared upon it, depicting Aurano.

Several individual elves approached the shrine, singing. The rest of them toned their voices to a soft hum as each one sang their piece before Aurano's shrine. Celestia didn't know what the words were, but she understood them nonetheless. She realized each of them were telling stories of him, expressing their experiences and their grief. The sweet, mystical, anguished sounds the elves emitted brought her to tears once more.

As their song wound to a close, the service ended, and King Boreas dismissed them, saying, "The rest of the service is private, for elves only. We appreciate your attendance, and thank you for caring about our beloved elven warrior."

"Elven *warrior*?" Celestia asked.

"Yes," King Boreas said, "He earned the title before his death. Therefore, he shall be honored as such."

Celestia nodded, smiling.

The king noticed Kgansten's tears, and said, "It is most surprising, indeed, that a dwarf and an elf could become friends. I think it's a testament to his character. I thank you, Kgansten, for coming today."

"Don't thank me for such a thing as this," Kgansten said, "I would be nowhere else."

King Boreas bowed his head slightly, looking at him in approval. "It is time you were off," he said, "It's been an honor."

The three of them got their horses, readying to set out.

"Goodbye, Kgansten," Celestia said, hugging him.

"Goodbye, princess," he said, "It's been a privilege."

"Don't be a stranger," Bridgot said, patting him on the back.

He laughed, "You, too. I hope to see both of you again in the future."

They smiled, waving to each other, as Kgansten departed back home, to Korga. Bridgot and Celestia leaped upon Samson and Razel's backs, setting out for Bridgot's village. As they left Gliken, Celestia felt a weight lifted from her. She felt as though she finally had closure on her friends' deaths, and now, she was able to begin to heal. As they journeyed through the forest, she felt lighter, hopeful for life once more.

When the sun came up a day later, the two of them headed over the hill into Kataran. As they approached, the villagers came up to meet them, cheering. The elders came forward, and Elder Gunther said, "You've done it. Thank you." He pat Bridgot on the back as he dismounted Samson, saying, "Welcome home."

Bridgot smiled, nodding to Elder Gunther. Just then, his family caught up. As Bridgot turned to see them, they all rushed over, smothering him in hugs and kisses. Celestia smiled. She could see that this was where he belonged. As the thought crossed her mind, so did another, *I belong in Ivétoiless. That's my home.* She realized she couldn't stay. No matter what she felt, she knew in her heart they couldn't be together. She decided then and there that she would sneak away in the night, and make the return journey. *It would be easier on him if I just disappeared,* she thought.

"And, of course, you're welcome to stay with us," his mother was saying. She hugged Celestia suddenly, and though it took her by surprise, it was nice. She felt welcome, like she was part of their family.

They headed back to the house as the villagers prepared a celebratory feast to honor Bridgot. Once they got there and situated the horses in the barn, Mrs. Brown said, "The council finally granted us extra land, so, as you can see, we've built the second guest house!"

Celestia looked where she was pointing, and saw that, indeed, they had built another guest house, identical to the first one. "Congratulations," she said, "That's wonderful."

They all went into the house, and, once everyone had gathered in the main area, Bridgot's mom said excitedly, "We have another announcement as well." She looked at Bryan, and, after a pause, she said, "Bryan and Brianne are expecting!"

As she made the announcement, Brianne stepped forward, and they could see her belly was beginning to grow. She wasn't very big yet, but she had a little baby bump. She beamed a great smile, and she and Bryan gave each other a quick kiss, as he put his arm around her happily.

"Congratulations again," Celestia said, "It seems a lot has happened in the time we were away."

Bridgot was silent, as the family began hugging and celebrating again.

"Well, you two go get cleaned up," Mrs. Brown finally said, "The feast will be starting soon."

Celestia headed upstairs to wash, and Bridgot headed to his sister, Margaret's house. It felt wonderful, cleaning her hair, her skin, and her teeth. While traveling, she always felt disgusting, not being able to really clean herself.

As she washed, she thought again of what she had to do, and she wasn't sure she could do it. She loved Bridgot, and she knew she could have a life with him in his village. It was the only way they could stay together. But, she missed her mother, she missed Garrita, and she knew it was her duty to be queen. If she didn't go back, she'd regret it forever. *Maybe he could come with me,* she thought, *There must be a way . . .*

Queen Celestia

28

At the feast, Celestia watched as the villagers celebrated. Bridgot sat by the fire, catching up with Kyja. Celestia knew his sister needed him. His family needed him. His village needed him. This was his home. Before she could talk herself out of it, she got up, sneaking off to the stable while everyone was distracted. She got Razel saddled and ready, and began leading her out of the barn.

"Going somewhere?" Bridgot asked.

She looked at him, eyes wide, as she stuttered, "I . . . I was just . . ."

"You were just slipping off during the feast to go back home," he said.

She sighed, nodding.

"Have you learned nothing of the dangers of the road?" he asked, "I'm going with you."

"You can't," she said.

He looked at her.

"Bridgot, you belong here. This is your home. Your family needs you, especially Kyja," she paused, "I don't belong here. It's time I fulfill my duties, and take my place as queen."

After a long pause, he said, "You still should not travel alone. Allow me to escort you back."

She reluctantly nodded, not wanting to make the goodbye any more painful. He got Samson saddled and reined, climbing upon his back. He pinned a note for Kyja on the stall, and they set out for Duwazo. The three-week journey had no detours this time around, as they paid close attention for slave traders, and decided not to stop at Farmer Wells'. They'd had enough of goodbyes, without adding another one to the list.

When they finally reached Ivétoiless, Bridgot followed Celestia up to the front gate of the palace. The guards saw her and scrambled to open the gate, one of them running inside to inform the queen. They dismounted, and a couple of guards took their horses, leading them to the stable.

"I'll be back shortly," Bridgot said, following Celestia inside.

As they entered the throne room, Princess Celestia saw Queen Eva, sitting upon her throne, looking at her as though she'd seen a ghost. "Celestia!" she finally exclaimed, rushing toward her.

She ran forward to meet her mother, and they embraced.

They both began tearing up as Eva said, "I'm so sorry. I should've told you. I should've told you about your father."

"It's okay, mother," Celestia said, "I'm sorry, too."

They hugged again, and she thought it felt good to be home, and that she'd missed her mother more than she'd realized. As they were embracing, Bridgot slowly began to back out of the room, seeing it wasn't his place.

Queen Eva finally noticed him, saying, "And, who's this gentleman?"

Bridgot and Celestia looked at each other, as she said, "This is Bridgot. I have so much to tell you, mother. To make a long story short, after I ran away, I discovered I'm the princess of an ancient prophecy, destined to save the world from darkness, with the help of a human warrior, an elven warrior, and a dwarven warrior. We also had help from a dragon rider. I've seen so many unbelievable things, I don't know if you'd ever believe them, mother. But, Bridgot is my human warrior. He saved my life more than once. I wouldn't be standing here without him." As she spoke, Celestia locked eyes with Bridgot, and she knew it would be harder than she thought to say goodbye.

Queen Eva watched her daughter closely as she spoke, and when she finished, she said, "Well, it seems I owe you a debt of thanks, Bridgot." She offered her hand, and he shook it as she said, "Truly. Thank you for bringing my daughter home safely."

"Think nothing of it," Bridgot said, "It was my duty, my honor, and my privilege." On the last word, he looked back at Celestia, and she could see he was about to leave. "Now that she's home, I really must be going," he said, bowing to the queen and backing out of the room.

"Young man," Queen Eva said, stopping him.

He turned around, "Yes?"

"I must insist on you staying here at the palace, at least for the night. It's the least I can do."

"I'm afraid I really must be off," he said, "But, thank you, anyway."

Celestia felt her heart dropping as he walked away. Once he'd exited the throne room, her mother turned to her, giving her a knowing look.

"What?" Celestia asked, trying to seem oblivious.

"Don't try to act as if you don't know," she said, "I'm your mother. It's written all over your face."

She looked back at her mother guiltily.

"Why are you still standing here?" she asked.

"What do you mean?"

"You love him. Go!"

"But, I'm a princess. He's a peasant. We cannot marry. I don't understand," she said, looking at her mother in confusion.

"He's no peasant," Queen Eva said, "He's a knight. And knights can marry princesses."

Princess Celestia looked at her mother in elation.

"Now, go!" she said, "Get!"

Celestia ran outside, trying to see where Bridgot had gone. He was just riding out from the stable upon Samson's back. "Bridgot!" she called.

He turned to see her and rode over, leaping from his horse, and landing in front of her.

"I know you belong with your family, and I belong here, and it'd be asking a lot to ask you to stay . . . I think I'd be asking too much to ask you to be king. But, if you did want to, I—"

He cut her off, taking her in his arms and kissing her. "I don't know if I'd make a good king," he said, "But, I know you'll make a great queen. And, I know I want to spend the rest of my life with you." He got down on one knee, saying, "I don't have a ring. I wasn't expecting this to happen. All I know is I love you, Celestia. I may be no more than a poor farm boy from Kataran, but, if you'll have me, I'd be the happiest man in the world. Will you marry me?"

"You're wrong," she said.

He looked at her questioningly.

"You're not just some poor farmer. You're a warrior of The Great Prophecy. You're a knight. And, I know you'd make an amazing king. You're strong, brave, and noble. But, beyond that, you have a huge heart, and I know you'll care for the people of this kingdom the way they deserve. I would be honored to marry such a great man."

"Is that a yes?" he asked.

She nodded, "Yes."

They embraced, and he stood, lifting her into the air as they kissed again.

"Come on, milady. We must get you up and ready. Your mother is waiting for you," Garrita said.

"Five more minutes," she said, burying her face in her pillow.

"Do you really want to be late today?" Garrita asked, "It's your wedding day, after all." She helped her up and took her over to the tub she'd filled for her bath. Celestia slipped out of her nightgown, revealing her pale skin, and climbed into the tub. Garrita helped her wash and then dried her off.

"Is everything ready?" Celestia asked as Garrita helped her slip her undergarments on.

She silently lifted her white ballgown around her and started lacing the corset before she answered, "Yes, milady." She pulled the laces tight, adding, "But, are you sure you want to do this?"

"Absolutely," Celestia said.

They smiled at each other, and Garrita helped her slip her shoes on, brushing her hair and putting it up. She added her veil and tiara, and assisted with her makeup and jewelry.

"You look beautiful," she said.

"You need to get ready, too," she said, "You're my maid of honor. Hurry!"

Garrita quickly changed out of her servant's dress, and into the blue gown Celestia had picked for her to wear. Once they were all ready, they hurried to Queen Eva's room, where she was waiting to see her daughter.

"Well, aren't you a sight?" her mother said when they entered. She was wearing a flowing lavender gown, with a gold crown upon her head.

Princess Celestia smiled at her mother, looking down at the billowing skirt of her wedding dress.

"Garrita, would you give us a moment alone, please?" Eva asked, looking at her.

"Of course, your majesty," she said, backing out of the room and closing the door behind her.

"You know," she said when they were alone, "I never told you what your father's last words were. In fact, I never told anyone."

Princess Celestia looked at her mother, afraid to say anything that would make her change her mind.

"He asked me for three favors," she said, "Number one: that I remain queen. He knew I didn't want to. I had wanted to step down and become nobles, to avoid him going to war. I had been an only child, same as you, and I had never wanted to be queen, either. He changed my mind. But, he knew his death would make me want to abandon the throne. So, one of his final requests was that I remain queen."

"You didn't want the throne, either?" Celestia asked.

"No," she said, "You're just like me in that way. But, unlike me, who decided to fulfill my duty because of the love of my life, you were willing to give up the love of your life to fulfill yours."

She gave her mother a half smile, touching her arm.

Queen Eva cleared her throat, continuing, "Number two: that I take care of you." She paused, looking down, "I'm afraid I didn't do a very good job of that. I left your care to the servants and nannies, lost in my grief. For that, I'm sorry."

"It's alright, mother," she said, "I understand now what he meant to you. I know how hard that must've been."

"Still, I made it hard on you, too. And, I shouldn't have."

Princess Celestia looked at her, "Thank you, mother. I forgive you."

Her mother nodded, straightening up, and preventing herself from crying. She cleared her throat, continuing, "And three: that I never forget him. To which I, of course, responded with, 'How could I?' But, I don't think I fully understood what that meant." She paused, "By refusing to speak of him and removing his pictures from the castle, I all but erased his memory. I failed him. And, you know the last thing he said to me after he made these requests?"

Celestia shook her head.

"He said, 'I love you,'" she let a few tears fall, then.

She reached out and hugged her mother. They stood there a moment, before her mother pulled away, wiping her eyes, and saying, "But, you know what? I'm returning his memory to this castle. All of his pictures have been restored, and he will be spoken of by all the land, and honored as a hero. That's what he deserves."

Celestia nodded.

"Alright," she said, clearing her tears away, "Now, let's get you down the aisle."

The three of them headed to the doors where she would make her entrance, and waited until they heard the announcer say, "Now, presenting the bride, Princess Celestia!"

The doors were flung open, and she grasped her bouquet as the butterflies hit her stomach. She smiled, walking forward, up the aisle, her mother beside her, arms linked, and her maid of honor, Garrita, carrying her train. When she reached the top of the aisle, she saw Bridgot, garbed in black royal robes, with Kgansten standing next to him—the best man.

Bridgot's family was there as well, in the audience, waving excitedly. Anne Marie and Phillip were running in circles as Margaret yelled at them and James tried to catch them, and Brianne was holding her new baby as Bryan stood beside her. Bridgot's parents were fussing over Luanne, trying to make her behave like a lady, and there was Kyja, in the middle of it all, smiling at her big brother proudly.

He smiled back at her, but when he caught sight of Celestia, they locked eyes, and they couldn't look away. She reached him, and they grasped hands, as Garrita and Queen Eva took their places. The priest began the ceremony, but they barely followed what he was saying, as they were caught up in each other. They recited their royal vows, exchanged rings, and waited for the priest to say, "You may now kiss the bride."

Once he did, Bridgot pulled her into a kiss, and Celestia found it hard to keep kissing him as she grinned from ear to ear. She threw the bouquet into the crowd, and when she turned to see who had caught it, she couldn't help but laugh. There was Kyja, with the most surprised expression she'd ever seen, frozen, with the bouquet in her arms.

The priest called for everyone's attention as they immediately transitioned into the coronation ceremony. Princess Celestia stood before the throne, reciting her vows to the kingdom, for her queenship. As she concluded her promises, the priest took the crown from her mother's head and placed it upon Celestia's.

Then, Bridgot stepped before the other throne, reciting his vows to be king. The priest took the king's crown from a pillow brought forth by a servant and placed it upon Bridgot's head.

"People of Ivétoiless, may I present King Bridgot and Queen Celestia!"

Epilogue

"Are you ready?" Bridgot asked, smiling at his wife. He was garbed in blue royal robes, with a cape, and a silver crown upon his head. Celestia smiled back at him. She wore a blue empire-waisted dress with a chiffon skirt and a bedazzled top. It had long off-the-shoulder sleeves. Her silver tiara gleamed upon her head as she said, "The question is: is he?"

They looked down at the newborn baby in her arms. Everyone had turned up for the presentation of their heir's birth—the elves, the dwarves, Bridgot's family, and the entire kingdom. Even Farmer Wells made it out.

As Bridgot and Celestia waited behind the door at the top of the stairs, looking down at his tiny face, they heard the announcer, "Presenting the child of King Bridgot and Queen Celestia, heir to the throne of Ivétoiless, Prince Aurano!"

THE END

Pronunciation Guide

Characters

Celestia	(seh-less-tee-uh)
Bridgot	(brī-jut)
Aurano	(or-on-oh)
Kgansten	(gan-sten)
Nastazya	(nuh-stah-zee-uh)
Ezmyra	(ehz-mee-ruh)
Diamante	(dee-uh-mon-tay)
Tourmethyst	(tour-meth-ist)
Forx	(forks)
Thaandor	(thann-door)
Nazirdok	(nuh-zeer-dock)
Kyja	(ky-zha)

Cities/Kingdoms/Villages

Ivétoiless	(eve-ay-twol-ess)
Kataran	(kat-uh-ran)
Garellis	(guh-rell-iss)
Dirthix	(der-thix)
Khanjgi	(con-jee)

Countries/Lands

Duwazo	(dew-way-zo)
Katangalo	(kat-ann-gall-oh)
Gliken	(glī-ken)
Korga	(core-guh)
Gachichken	(guh-cheech-ken)
Abyumo	(ab-bee-you-moh)
Cardeas	(car-dee-yes)
Fluorasti	(floor-ah-stee)
Mashang	(muh-shang)
Kogatsa	(koh-got-suh)

Learn Dwarvish

Frug o feinedo translation: friend or foe?

Ie gyo translation: and you?

The Unsolvable Riddle

Born from ash
To ash return
But, not all of us will burn

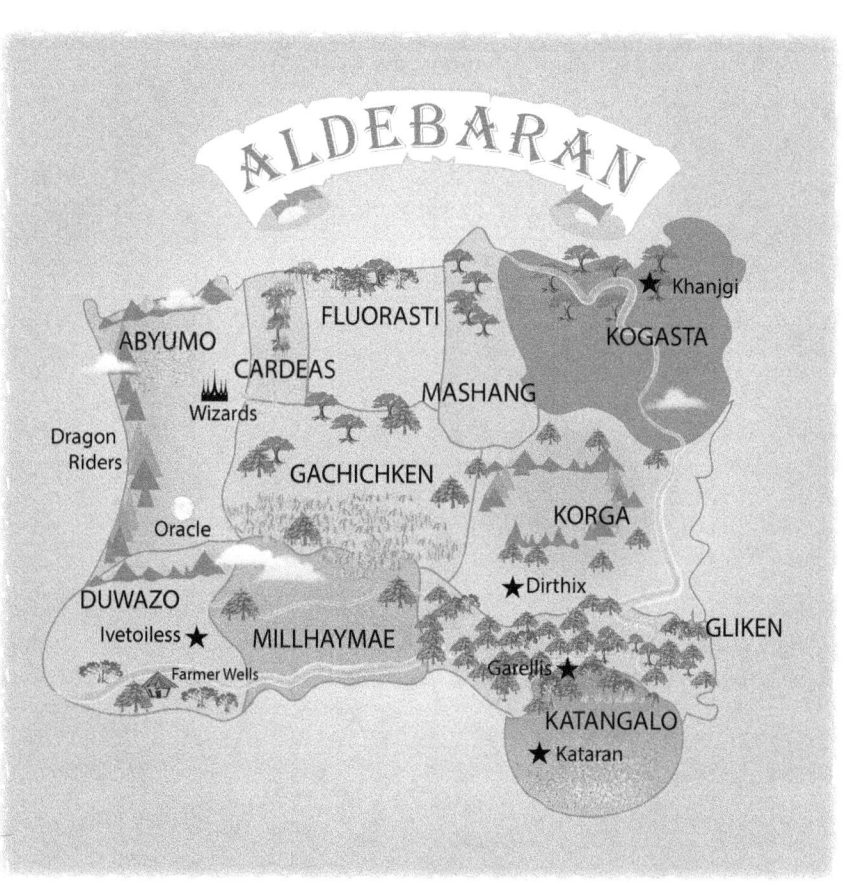

www.ingramcontent.com/pod-product-compliance
Lightning Source LLC
Chambersburg PA
CBHW051821020726
47502CB00005B/1566